dhika Swarup spent a nomadic childhood in India, aly, Qatar, Pakistan, Romania and England, which ive her a keen sense for the dispossessed. She studied Cambridge University and worked in investment inking before turning to writing. She has written inion pieces for Indian broadsheets and the Huffgton Post as well as short stories for publications cluding the Edinburgh Review.

Where the River Parts

Radhika Swarup

SANDSTONEPRESS
HIGHLAND | SCOTLAND

First published in Great Britain and the United States of America
Sandstone Press Ltd
Dochcarty Road
Dingwall
Ross-shire
IV15 9UG
Scotland.

www.sandstonepress.com

Editor: Moira Forsyth

The publisher acknowledges support from
Creative Scotland towards publication of this volume.

ISBN: 978-1-910124-76-5
ISBNe: 978-1-910124-77-2

Cover design by Rose Cooper, Valencia, Spain
Typeset by Iolaire Typesetting, Newtonmore.
Printed and bound by CPI Group (UK) Ltd, Croydon CR0 4YY.

For Papa.

Acknowledgments

A million imperceptible elements have gone into the making of this book. Hazy memories of adults discussing the past when they thought us children asleep. Passing conversations. A throwaway comment. A lament on a changed Delhi. Greater detail slowly emerging from the shadows as I grew older. Acknowledging all those who have contributed to my personal sense of Partition would be impossible. At the very least, though, I owe a debt to the Goswami and Dogra families for being my bridge to Asha's world.

I owe an immense debt of gratitude to my tireless agents, Claire Roberts and Erica Spellman-Silverman. My heartfelt thanks to the team at Sandstone. Especially to Moira Forsyth and Bob Davidson, for loving the book, and to Moira for her gentle (but firm) editing.

I'm immensely thankful to my eagle eyed readers for catching out so many inconsistencies and typos in early drafts: Mike Dalton, Keara Donnachie, Rajiv Dogra, Ben Kay, Amna Boheim, Liz Salter and Divya Shah. To Isabelle Grey for her unstinting kindness and advice. To Susie Harries for generously sharing her marketing wisdom.

Most of all, to my family for tolerating me while I wrote. To my son Maanas for his encouragement, and for suggesting a title for my next book: Where the River Lands. To my daughter Anaia, for being such an easy baby and allowing me to write this book during her infancy. And above all, to my husband Amarendra, for his advice, support and understanding. This book wouldn't have been written without him.

Parting is all we know of heaven,
And all we need of hell.

Emily Dickinson

The *tonga* cart jolted hard and came to a stop. A wave of muted panic rose from the passengers. Some sighed their frustration, some were roused from a restless sleep, others – older, in painful consciousness of what lay in wait – held in a mounting hysteria at the back of their throats. The horse, dark as the night they were travelling in, snorted through steaming nostrils before pacing back. The cart lurched to one side, the crowd jostling along with it.

Asha felt a fresh wave of nausea well up inside her. 'No,' she prayed silently. 'Please no. Not here.'

She needn't have fretted. Someone from further up the packed cart – another young, lost girl perhaps, or maybe a humiliated matriarch – retched and leaned noisily over the side. A new wave of frustration rose, and now people began to voice their irritation. Firoze stood up. He held his hand high, urged restraint. 'Brothers,' he said. 'You don't know where they are lying in wait. We must be silent.'

'Why have we stopped then?' came a rough voice.

The back – filled largely as it was with Asha's family – started complaining about the halt. Someone in the front objected, and the debate looked like turning lively when Firoze jumped off his perch. All fell silent at once,

1

watching anxiously as he bent to the road to inspect the obstacle.

'*Yah Khuda*,' he invoked. 'They've placed a huge boulder on the road. There's another further ahead. They must be nearby.'

They worked quickly. The men in the cart joined Firoze and together they set to moving the rocks to the side of the road. The cart had fallen absolutely still, and now the night seemed to heave with noise. A cricket chirped in the distance, and the crowd shrivelled in their fear. Was that the sound of gunfire? A boy stepped on a twig, and all turned towards the night – was this them, was this the Muslim butchers? The wind appeared louder than normal, more protective of their would-be killers, the dark more absolute. The men seemed to work loudly, too loudly; they heard them sigh, grunt, they heard their sweat fall on the ground. And yet they didn't dare speak, they scarcely dared breathe.

Asha barely noticed the others in the cart. She held on to her stomach, tried to still its churning. She began to feel a warmth between her thighs, a spreading clammy wetness. Slowly her hand felt under her long *kameez* shirt, softly she lifted it back up to under her nose. Even this was full of danger. The cart was quiet, and she was scared of attracting attention. For a moment she didn't register the smell, and then, as her mother darted a furtive look in her direction, she breathed it again. It was the same as her monthly blood. Her eyes clamped shut, she shivered into the heat of the night. She held tightly onto the earrings she had placed inside her fist. She fingered them fervently, turning them like so many rosary beads as she whispered her desperate prayer. '*Bhagwanji*, please,' she said. 'Please, please,' but there were no further words inside her, even here, even as her voice disappeared into the air.

Mataji looked her way again, squeezed her shoulder. 'Don't worry, *Beta*,' Asha heard her whisper. '*Bhagwanji* will take care of us.'

The blood had begun to trickle down her starched cotton *salwar*, and once more she tried to will herself to stay calm. It was nothing. These things happened. She had bled before. She looked at her mother, wondering what she had heard and how much she had guessed, but the clouds had moved and the dark had too complete a hold of her. A soft, slow tear fell down her cheeks and through to the pooling wet in her *salwar*, and as she felt its warmth diffuse into her thigh, she couldn't be certain if she cried from sadness or relief.

I

1

Asha's first memory was of trying to scale the wall that separated her house from Nargis'. She had fallen forward, scraped her palms, and been rewarded for her foolhardiness with rose-scented milk and gram flour *laddoos* still warm from the pan. Nargis' earliest recollection was of knocking on Asha's heavy wooden door with a bowl full of fat, cool, milk-sodden *rasmalai* disks in her hand. 'Ammi sent these,' she had announced with a smile, and this introductory gift became a tradition between the two families to the extent that any time a delicacy was prepared in one house, it found a way over to the other in the hands of its daughters.

There were secret exchanges too. They ate from one plate and drank from one glass, though it was forbidden for Hindus to so much as touch their lips to a Muslim utensil. Mangoes were pilfered from the landowner's groves, early morning dips were taken in the fast-flowing Ravi. Nargis' father's study proved a particular treasure trove for the two. As police inspector of Suhanpur, his desk yielded all manner of contraband: pistols, explosives, powders, home-brewed alcohol and, thrillingly, hand-rolled *beedi* cigarettes. These last were inspected with some fear and great expectation on furtive misty nights atop the inspector's roof.

Both girls were followed from a young age by local Romeos attracted by Nargis' aloof, sharp-featured beauty,

7

and it was Asha – darker, shorter, and yet to achieve the fleetness of expression that would be her chief attraction – who proved an effective counterfoil to amorous proposals. '*Dhat*,' she would cry as a youth proclaimed his love for the sweep of Nargis' brow, 'I threaded them myself. I'll thread yours too if you let me.' Another would swear to die of his love, and she would take off her slippers. 'You miserable worm,' she would thunder. 'Endure a beating from my slippers and then tell me if you're still prepared to die.'

United as the two were by food and mischief, the secrets appeared to dry up during the holy month of *Ramzan*, when Nargis and her family fasted through the day. The landowner's mangoes were safe from pilfering hands. Nargis joined her family for dawn breakfasts instead of swimming in the Ravi; her rooftop was full of relatives breaking their fast as evening fell. But Asha would find her way to the jasmine-scented roof as her neighbours gathered for the *iftaar* meal, and as they broke their fast, so did she. She fasted through the month with her friend, remaining undetected by her mother, who assumed her daughter's appetite shrank when the heat rose.

At seventeen, Asha began to keep the annual *Karva Chauth* fast to pray for her future husband's long life, and Nargis kept her company. This was the first time a secret separated the two friends, a secret they were both aware of, for though Asha insisted she fasted without an object in mind, Nargis knew there was someone she thought of as she prayed.

They gathered early one October morning to mark the fast. Asha's home hummed with activity. As soon as the locality's menfolk grew busy with their work, palanquin *dolis* began to arrive at the Prakash house. They carried fasting women who wore satins and silks dyed a bridal red. Their arms jangled with gold bangles, tiny gold thread *gotas* sparkled on scarlet *dupattas*. They streaked the parting of their hair with vermillion. Their foreheads sparkled with red *bindis*. They walked through a hall decorated with auspicious red *swastikas*. This surfeit of red was their ode to fertility, that emblem of marital bliss. Waiting artists inked upturned palms with intricate henna tattoos, and this ritual completed, the women began to prepare for the evening's festivities.

It seemed the cruellest sort of anticipation, to organise a meal while unable to so much as drink a sip of water, though a portion of the ladies' pain was mitigated by being able to delegate their tasks. Servants – some belonging to the Prakash household, others who had carried the fasting women across in *dolis* – took over the endless chopping and churning. The women gained some small comfort from reclining and being fanned with long bamboo fans. They waited for their henna to dry, and complained bitterly about the heat as they oversaw the preparation of the feast. Dishes were infused with spices, warming *daals* were tempered for hours over an open fire, Mataji's famous chutneys were prepared. The women, some in their fourth decade of fasting for their husband's longevity, grew impatient as the day wore on. The smell of the evening meal's *masalas* assaulted their palates, saliva gathered on fatigued tongues until a small cup of tea carted to Asha's father in his office grew to seem like a personal affront, until the matriarchs did the only thing they could – vent their frustration at the domestic help.

The unfortunate retainers – male and used to

uncomplainingly toiling in hot kitchens – bore the brunt of the starving women's anger. '*Jaldi*, quick!' they were scolded as they scurried with tea and deep-fried vegetable *pakoras* to the office. A client would call on Asha's father, Pappaji, and a summons would arrive for fresh cups of tea. 'Today of all days, have they no mercy?'

Asha and Nargis, unburdened as they were by years of sacrifice, stayed out of the way of the other women. In any case they were met with a mixture of bemusement and pity. Some of the younger women found the girls' fasting romantic – 'Do you know who you're marrying?' and 'Is he handsome? Is he rich?' followed by the unvarying, 'Do I know him?' The older women were more phlegmatic: '*Hai* Shiela,' Mataji was asked repeatedly, 'Why do you make her fast? Isn't there time enough for all that once she's married?'

'Yes,' echoed Nargis as the two made their way out of the kitchen. 'Why fast? And why fast now?'

Asha shrugged. It was just past the lunch hour, and her hunger was at its height. It wasn't the food itself she missed, but water. The worst was feeling her saliva scratchy and sparse on her tongue. It was a tease, the saliva, a heartless tormentor, like a *purdah* curtain over a desired object. She smiled at the thought, and hurried to answer her friend. 'I never should have fasted. It's too much, this thirst . . .'

'No,' insisted Nargis. 'You can't worm your way out of my question. Why are you fasting? Who are you fasting for?'

Asha smiled again. She refused to meet her friend's eye, and Nargis crowed, 'I was right, I knew it! There is someone.' She frowned, tapping an impatient slippered foot on the marble of the floor. 'But who?'

The bell rang, and a client of Pappaji's entered. He was walking towards the office when he heard the girls' noise. He looked up, momentarily nonplussed, and blinked rapidly before folding his palms together. 'Asha-*ji*,' he said in a solemn tone. '*Namaste*.'

Asha folded her hands in her turn, and softly murmured her greeting.

'What is it, Asha-*ji*? Are you unwell?'

'No, no, Om-*ji*,' replied Asha, and then, with a slight incline of her head, she added, 'I'm fasting today.'

'Oh,' said Om. He seemed uncertain, unsure of whether to commiserate or applaud, and after a pause, he asked, 'Why?'

'It's *Karva Chauth*.'

'Oh.' The significance of the day hit Om, and he coloured. 'Oh.' His gaze fell towards the floor, he cleared his throat nervously, and repeated, 'Oh.' He indicated towards her father's study with his briefcase before striding rapidly away from the girls.

Nargis was convulsed with laughter. 'Oh,' she cried, 'Oh-oh!'

'Shhh,' scolded Asha. 'The whole house will hear you.' She herded her friend towards the courtyard, but Nargis darted back indoors.

'I'll be quiet,' she promised. 'But let's listen outside the door. Maybe he's asking for your hand in marriage.'

'It's not him. No, Nargis,' said Asha. 'It's not him,' but her friend wasn't listening. She squatted and leaned close to the door.

'*Hai Ram*, Nargis' implored Asha. 'Get up now. Someone will come along.'

'Shh,' said Nargis. 'I can hear them.'

'Or Pappaji may open the door.'

11

'Are you going to listen or not?'

Asha shook her head. Nargis shrugged, returning to her eavesdropping. '*Oof*, you're impossible,' said Asha, but she too squatted and strained to overhear the conversation.

There was a long silence, and Asha complained, 'I can't hear a thing.' Nargis held her finger to her lips, and after a moment, they heard Pappaji's voice.

'And you're sure?'

'Absolutely, Sir,' said Om in English. 'The troubles have started. You saw what they did in Bengal in August.'

'It won't happen here, Om. Not in Punjab.'

'I'm not so sure. The Muslim League is gaining in strength. And they insist on Partition.'

The room fell quiet, and Asha knew her father was shaking his head. She knew he had closed his eyes and rested his hand on the polished wood of his writing desk; she knew his forehead was marked with his disagreement. Her hand slipped into her friend's, and together they waited for Pappaji's next words. 'When are you leaving?'

'In a week, Sir. Two at the most. Ma has left already.'

'Hmm,' said Pappaji. 'I've got your papers here.' There was a rustle of files being sifted through, of pages being turned. 'The shop's sale has gone through, and the buyer has agreed to your terms for the sale of your house. All seems to be in order.'

'Thank you, Sir,' said Om.

'He'll be going now,' said Asha, pulling her friend up, but as they rose, Om began to speak again.

'Sir,' he was saying. 'I can't persuade you to leave?'

Both fell to their knees again.

'No,' said Pappaji.

12

'Sir . . .'

'I will never leave Suhanpur!' Pappaji said sternly. There was a lull, and when Pappaji spoke again, he was gentler, more measured in his words. 'What is India to me, what is Pakistan? I was born here, child, and I will die here.'

'What about . . .' began Om, but he seemed struck with uncertainty, for his speech trailed off. The two were quiet for another while, and the girls heard a chair being scraped back. They looked at each other, started to rise, when Om spoke, 'Sir, your daughter.'

Nargis jammed her elbow sharp into Asha's ribs, and the girl almost fell on the floor. 'Quick,' she said, as she righted herself, 'Did I miss anything?' Nargis' finger rose to her lips.

'If you don't mind, Sir,' Om was saying. His throat was cleared nervously, the girls heard him pace the floor before he resumed his request. 'You haven't arranged her marriage as yet?'

'Asha's?'

This seemed to floor Om. 'Yes,' he replied in a high pitch, before recovering his vigour. 'Yes, Sir. Your daughter Asha's.'

'No, no,' said Pappaji dismissively. 'Of course not.'

'Sir,' continued Om, and Asha's hand tightened around her friend's. She shook her head, exhaled deeply, and softly she murmured, 'Please say no, Pappaji.'

'Under ordinary circumstances my mother would have come over to have this discussion with you, but Sir . . .'

Nargis felt her friend's hand squeezing hers and looked across with surprise. 'Really?' she asked. 'It's not him?'

'Shhh . . .'

'Sir, what I want to ask is . . .'

13

'Really?' Nargis smiled widely now. 'It's really not him?'

'Sir . . .'

'No,' hissed Asha, her eyes firmly on the door. 'No, no, no.'

'Sir, what I want to ask is if . . .'

'*Beta*,' Pappaji interrupted. 'Asha is too young.'

'Of course, Sir . . .' They heard him clear his throat in preamble, when Pappaji spoke.

'Let me make myself clear. I won't have her living so far from me. You're moving to Delhi. It won't work.'

'Sir,' said Om, and initially the two friends thought he meant to argue his case, but they heard footsteps approach the door, and they scampered upstairs to Asha's room.

Once they were in and the door was safely shut, Nargis turned to her friend. '*Mashallah*,' she teased, 'Such persistence from your admirer,' but Asha wasn't listening. She held her hand over her heart, and as calm returned to her, she breathed deeply. 'A million thanks to God,' she said. 'That was close.'

'*Arre*,' purred Nargis. 'So this Om isn't your heart's desire?'

'Of course not,' smiled Asha. 'And thank God it's your father and not you who is the police inspector, or no crimes would get solved in all of Suhanpur.'

'But seriously,' said Nargis. 'I didn't say anything before, but I couldn't imagine how you could like a man like that. Short, dark, stocky.'

'I didn't like a man like that,' said Asha severely. 'I don't.'

'Who is it then?'

14

Asha turned and walked to her bed. She perched on its edge. Her embroidered leather slippers brushed against the floor, the flounces of her *salwar* kissed the ground. The floor was littered with outfits she had tried on earlier in the morning, and though Nargis raised an eyebrow at the mess, Asha remained distracted. Her *dupatta* slid off her head, and she occupied herself with rearranging it. She was impatient though, laying it hastily at the crown of her head without wrapping the fringed ends around her shoulders, tutting as it slid readily off, and finally, flinging it towards the rest of her mess at the foot of her bed. Nargis moved to face her and repeated her question. 'Who is it, Asha? You know I won't tell.'

'*Oof*,' replied Asha. She leaned forward, cupping her face in her hands, and Nargis dropped onto the floor to receive her friend's confidence. 'This thirst,' she said at length, 'and the weather too!'

'Asha!'

Asha continued with her complaint. 'When will it turn cool? There's no wind even. And to think of all the food they're cooking downstairs, why, it's cruel. It's a torment, it's like . . .' She trailed off, then sighed, 'It's like a *purdah* curtain over a desired object.'

She leant to recover her *dupatta*, but it was Nargis' turn to sigh now. 'What did you just say?' she asked.

'What?' asked Asha. She looked up at her friend, bit her lip, and answered earnestly. 'Oh no, that was nothing.'

'It's like a *purdah* . . .'said Nargis slowly. 'It's like a *purdah* curtain over a desired object. Where have I heard that before?'

'*Arre*, who told you to turn inspector?' scolded Asha.

15

She flushed deeply, but maintained her bluster. 'You must have heard it on your new transistor radio.'

'Ha!' Nargis clapped her hands. 'It's what *Bhaijaan* said the other day. We were talking about how hot it still was, and he said almost exactly the same thing.'

'*Bakwaas*,' said Asha stoutly. 'Rubbish.'

'No, no, he did. I remember because we all laughed at him. And now you too.' She bent down to her friend, took her hands in her own. 'Tell me, Asha, is it my brother?'

'No,' said Asha, but she spoke in a soft, half-hearted manner.

'Is it him?'

'No.'

Nargis smiled and began to hum a tune. '*Jawan hai mohabbat . . .*' The lyrics began to trip off the girl's tongue, the words of the latest hit tune, 'Love is young . . .'

'*Arre*,' scolded Asha. 'What's got into you? Didn't I tell you it wasn't Firoze?' She realised her mistake the moment she spoke his name. She coloured, but Nargis only sang more clearly now. 'The world is beautiful . . .'

'That damn transistor radio of yours.'

Nargis clutched at her heart, pretended to swoon. 'My heart's looted the treasure of happiness . . .'

'Shhh.'

'Love is young . . .'

'Stop, you tuneless cat! Someone will hear.'

This gave her friend pause. 'Does anyone know?' Asha shook her head, imperceptibly at first and then steadily. 'No, Nargis,' she said to her friend. 'No one knows. And,' she added, 'They can't know. Not yet.'

Nargis reached out. She caressed Asha's hair slowly, and asked in wonder, 'What will they say?'

16

Asha shook her head.

'Don't worry,' said Nargis. She embraced her friend, whispered softly into her ear, 'Don't worry, Asha. My friend, my life, my beloved, beloved sister, don't worry.'

The next morning Firoze took issue with Asha.

'Why did you need to tell my sister?' he asked. 'You know she can never keep her mouth shut.'

They stood in Pappaji's office. Firoze, studying to be a lawyer, often dropped by on the pretext of borrowing a book, and Asha generally offered to help with his search. They were constantly on the point of being caught, and jokes had long been made in both houses. Firoze was accused of being unduly scholarly, and Asha of knowing Pappaji's library better than its owner did.

The two were circumspect while in the room, terrified of discovery. Their arms brushed together as they moved through the bookcases, they walked in matching steps, they heard the other breathe, they smelt the soap on the other's morning skin, but they dared not touch. They barely dared look at each other; there was danger there too.

Their greatest fear was of Chotu walking in. Chotu, or the little one, was the aged family retainer, as old and as creaky as the family furniture. He had been inherited by the family from Pappaji's mother, and had been in the house for longer than anyone remembered, and long enough certainly for him to have outgrown the diminutive name that had been conferred on him. He had seen Firoze grow up, and was sure to bring him his favourite spiced lemonade. Chotu never knocked, never announced himself, and it was this, the tyranny of Chotu's ancient familiarity, that terrified the two.

Now, as Firoze scolded Asha, she looked up at him.

17

She pursed her lips, furrowed her brows, and he smiled at this change in her placid features.

'What are you smirking at?' Asha asked angrily.

'I can never stay angry at you.'

Asha flashed a quick glance at the door. She had suspected a noise, but all remained quiet, and as she turned towards Firoze, she scolded, 'Do you think I have no right to tell Nargis? She may be your sister, but she is also my best friend.'

'But, my dearest,' explained Firoze. 'Just think. She'll tell all to Ammi in her excitement, and then where will we be?'

Asha's *dupatta* looked like slipping. She turned back, as if at a sound, and slowly rearranged the cloth over her head. She heard Firoze move towards her, felt his breath over her head, and she whispered, 'Then where will we be?'

'Come on, you know it won't be easy.'

'I don't know any such thing!' Her voice rose, and as Firoze indicated towards the door, both paused. What was that, a creak? Were those ancient knees bending down to eavesdrop? Was that a door knob being turned? Firoze lifted his finger to his mouth, tiptoed to the door, gently pulled it open. It was safe; they were alone and undisturbed.

He returned to her, and with a rueful smile, said, '*Arre,* Asha, I've told you this before. There won't be a problem for me. It's your family who'll be against the match.'

'I don't see that they will. My cousin, Dilip, the one who lives in Lahore, well, he married a Muslim girl.' Firoze shook his head, and she said insistently, 'Look, no one liked it to start with, but now we've accepted her. She's part of our family . . .'

18

'That's just it,' he spoke over her. 'It's ok for a Muslim girl to marry into your family. She will live as a Hindu; her children will be brought up as Hindus. That's why my parents won't mind me marrying you – after all, my children will remain Muslim. It's your family who won't like it. Just imagine,' he said, but now he was leaning in again, and Asha had to remind herself to focus. She blinked hard, told herself they were in the middle of a disagreement. 'Do you see them agreeing to you living as a Muslim?'

She tutted.

'To see your children – their grandchildren – being brought up as Muslims?'

'Pappaji's not like that . . .'

The door burst open, and the pair sprang apart. Chotu entered, one hand on aching hips, the other holding a silver platter aloft. His progress was slow, and painful for more than just his audience. '*Beta*,' he wheezed as he reached Firoze, 'I brought you some *nimbu pani*. Sweet, as you like it, with some roasted cumin ground into it.'

'Thank you,' smiled Firoze. 'But you shouldn't have.'

'*Nahi*, Firoze *beta*, no,' said Chotu. 'It was nothing.'

Firoze smiled, took a sip, and this act on his part was seen as an invitation to converse. 'But why do you spend all day long in this musty library? You're young, you should be enjoying yourself.' No one spoke, but it appeared that no reply was expected, for Chotu went on, 'And this girl,' – indicating Asha with some disapproval – 'What work do you have with libraries and books? I've told your father a hundred times . . .'

Asha giggled, and though Firoze pretended to frown at her, her reaction was sufficient for Chotu to retreat. 'These are bad times,' he muttered loud enough for all to

19

hear. 'There's no telling anyone.' He retrieved the glass from Firoze's hand, placed it carefully on his platter, and shuffled slowly back towards the door. 'And,' he grumbled at the girl as he closed the door, 'Mataji asked me to tell you that your lunch is ready.'

2

When Nargis was late, which was often, Asha waited for her by the old *Sheesham* tree stump on the western bank of the river Ravi. Nargis would reach their meeting spot using an unsanctioned route through the back of her house, and the two would proceed together to school. Their meeting by the river had an additional advantage: they shook off Asha's younger brother Savan, who followed Asha as far as the *bazaar* before turning right on his journey to the boys' school.

It was this circuitous route that had allowed Asha her first contact with Firoze. It happened on the morning Nargis fell ill; a few months before the Karva Chauth fast with all its revelations.

Savan seemed bent on his sister's company. They had both risen early. A cockerel had been brought into the house for the evening's meal, and its final lamenting cries had woken the children before their accustomed time. By the time they left for school, Savan had eaten two breakfasts and appeared keen to exercise.

'Come,' he said with a curious combination of entreaty and bluster. 'I'll walk with you today.'

Asha studied her brother. At twelve, he was already towering above her. He bore his self-professed brilliance awkwardly – with thick-rimmed spectacles, an untucked shirt, scuffed shoes and an unwieldy gait. Nargis jokingly referred to him as a grasshopper, but Asha asked him impatiently, 'Won't you be late for school?'

'Ah,' he shrugged. 'They don't teach anything new there.'

Asha could picture the walk to school. Nargis would continually bait the boy and Savan would grow increasingly belligerent. Besides, there had been some excitement about a new bride moving into the neighbourhood, a tall, impossibly-groomed Delhi beauty who refused to cover her head, and Nargis – foresightedly named after the Narcissus flower – was sure to have an opinion. There would be no discussing the newcomer with Savan around.

They entered the *Meena Bazaar*. Though the shops would not open for hours, the jewellery traders were beginning to gather. Boys in faded Pathan suits ran through the *bazaar* with frosted glasses of freshly churned *lassi*. Men squatted up and down the street, sharing gossip and sugared milk *barfis* they crumbled into their *lassis*. The first convivial refreshment taken, the final rails against the ungodliness of the hour registered, tasselled velvet pouches were opened and bright, sparkling gemstones poured out onto waiting palms. Asha strained to catch closer sight of the jewels, but Savan looked unimpressed. 'Ah,' he complained wearily. 'Such vulgarity.'

'Listen,' said Asha, seizing her opportunity. 'Won't you get bored walking with us? All you'll hear is gossip.'

The boy considered her argument. 'You're right,' he said, and with a nod, he stalked off towards the end of the *bazaar*.

Asha had no way of knowing how long she waited. She carried no watch, but she knew Nargis was late. It was the height of the monsoon season, and she passed her time sounding out the cadence of the thundering Ravi. *Dham-dham-dharak, dham-dham-dharak*, she tapped into the damp earth, until she lost track of her rhythm. Next she picked up a twig from the ground and traced a hopscotch pattern on the earth. She skipped until she tired, then moved to rest against the gnarled *Sheesham* stump.

Dham-dham, she heard, *dharak-dham-dham*. Was that the river, its thunder muted with familiarity, or were those finally her friend's footsteps? She looked at the water, felt its force anew and turned towards the steps. '*Dear*,' she began. 'Do you know how late . . .' but she tailed sharply off.

It was Firoze. He was walking towards her. She raised her eyebrows in surprise, then looked back towards the water. It was loud, the noise deafening, and she didn't know what to say. The two had only previously met at Nargis' house, and they invariably passed each other by with a demure greeting. They'd never been alone before. They'd never had occasion to address the other.

'A thousand apologies,' he was saying. She looked up briefly, noticed thick brown hair gleam against the sun. 'Nargis isn't well, she asked me to let you know.'

Asha spoke softly. 'She should have sent a message. Chotu *Chacha* would have taken me to school.'

'I know,' he said. 'But it just happened. She twisted her ankle, and by then . . .' She saw him squint against the sunlight. There it was again, that loud rush, water bursting downstream, and she closed her eyes. 'She said you'd be waiting here.'

'Oh.'

'I can take you to school if you'd like.'

'No, no, there's no need.'

23

'I don't mind.'

She rose from the stump. Walk alone with a boy? What if someone was to see? In her panic, she said, 'I don't want to waste your time.'

'I'm not so busy, you know,' he smiled. 'We college boys don't have much to do.'

The next day he met her by the river again, and though Asha fretted her mother would learn of Nargis' indisposition, Firoze calmed her. 'Nargis won't tell. She thinks your Chotu is dropping you off at school.'

Asha glanced up. There it was again, the glint of brown hair against the sun, but she refused to look directly at him. She had a measure of his features, but a closer inspection was beyond her. 'So,' she asked softly, her words faint against the surge of the river, 'why are you here?'

'Don't you know?' And as she remained silent, 'Can't you guess?'

She didn't reply. She bit her lip, aware her mouth was reddening. 'It's like the lipstick those Bombay actresses use,' Nargis had claimed. The two had practised in front of the mirror: biting their lips, pinching their cheeks into colour. They had seen pictures in the papers of movie heroines, and even in black and white they spied signs of embellishment. They pointed out plucked brows; they sighed at bee-stung lips. Such magic these actresses had at their command, was it any wonder that the world fell at their feet?

Firoze was standing a breath away from her. His hands were by his side, he smiled politely, but it was clear he was waiting for a response. He inclined his head, as if to spur her into speech, and she felt herself freeze. Why was he talking with her, anyway? There were a million girls he could choose from. Nargis had been talking, just the other day, of the proposal from a Lahore beauty. 'Her eyes are like almonds,' Nargis had said. 'Her skin as pale as milk. And as for her lips, *hai,* her lips!' She had peered at her reflection in the mirror, had smiled at Asha valiantly biting colour into her lips. 'And that's without all the tricks we try.'

Why then was he coming after her? Why look at her, dark, flat-featured and unexciting, when he had his pick of milk-skinned beauties? '*Oof,*' she said in irritation. She turned, starting to walk towards school. The thunder of the river was full against her. She didn't know if he followed, didn't know if he had moved away. Asha didn't turn; she told herself she didn't care. It was silent, absolutely mind-numbingly full of the river for a minute, then longer, and she paused. She bent as if to straighten the fall of her *salwar* when she saw a long, lean shadow waver by hers. She smiled, she huffed, then straightened herself and began to walk again.

'Tell me,' he was saying. 'Are you going to stay quiet all the way to school?'

'You shouldn't be here,' she answered. 'It isn't right.'

'Don't you want to know why I'm here?'

'No,' she said firmly. She told herself he was toying with her. 'It's of no interest to me.'

'All right.'

She slowed her steps slightly, but couldn't hear anything. She looked to her right, but there was nothing: no Firoze, no long shadow next to hers. 'Good,' she thought. 'He's finally gone.' Her steps slowed further. She looked towards the river, but still couldn't hear him. He had left by now, surely. There was no danger in her stopping. She saw a speck of dust on her slippers, grew suddenly fastidious. She bent, cleaned them. As she straightened herself, she cast a quick glimpse backwards. He stood still a few metres behind her. Their eyes met, and before she looked away, she caught sight of a broad smile. 'Tell me,' he said as he caught up with her, 'Is it really of no interest to you?'

'*Dhat*,' she said. 'I'm late for school.'

Firoze accompanied her for the rest of the week. Nargis' ankle was slow to heal, her brother solicitous in advising complete rest, and no one – not the easily panicked Mataji, not Pappaji, not Chotu, nor Savan with the reaches of his imagination – suspected the two were meeting and falling in love. By the time Nargis returned to school, the routine was established. Codes had been set, times when both could be alone, and as others played, worked and dreamt India free, Firoze and Asha discovered a different purpose for their dreams.

3

Savan would never have considered himself a creature of habit. As he grew, he took care to leave his childish pastimes behind, though one tradition remained undisturbed. Every Sunday morning after breakfast, as the rest of the household busied itself with its chores – Pappaji with his newspaper and correspondence, Mataji with overseeing the grinding of the week's spices, and an increasingly distracted Asha with readying her slate and clothes for school – Savan would descend to the courtyard behind the house. Here, under the yawning branches of the *Peepal* tree, he would invariably find Chotu smoking a *beedi* cigarette on a break from his labours in the kitchen.

'Uncle,' he would begin, 'Chotu Chacha . . ..'

'Let me smoke my *beedi*, son.'

'How are you, Chotu Chacha?'

The man would shrug, his brow furrowing with contemplation. A thick plume of smoke would escape his broad nostrils, and he would look up at the boy, speaking with an assumed gruffness, 'Older than when you last asked.'

'And how old is that?'

'*Arre, beta*, how many times have I told you? I'm older than God.'

'Which God is that?'

This question always spurred an irreverent smile. Chotu would look around the yard to make sure they weren't overheard before continuing. 'Any God you can think of – Hindu, Sikh, Muslim, Christian, even the merciless Japanese one – I'm older than them all.'

If the boy, too old now for all the frivolities of childhood, didn't understand why a Japanese God would be merciless, he didn't let on. Instead, he would lower his lanky frame onto the ground, lay his head on the old man's starched cotton lap and inhale the musky-sweet scent of *beedi* smoke. They would lapse into a silence that would remain uninterrupted until Mataji discovered another spice they had run short of, or a visitor called and fresh *lassi* needed to be churned. Then Chotu would dust the remains of his smoke off his clothes, unfurl his knotted brow and creep arthritically back indoors.

Their routine had played out for years, and though Savan pretended he enacted his part for Chotu's gratification more than his, he was visibly upset when, one Sunday morning in March – early in the year of India's independence – he went into the courtyard to discover the *Peepal* tree deserted.

Savan searched for the retainer all over the house. He went first into the kitchen, where he ran into his mother. She was supervising the work of her staff, but the minute she saw her son, her complaints started, '*Arre*, Savan,' she cried. 'What are you doing here? It's hotter than hell today, son!'

'Chotu Chacha?'

'*Haan*, where is he?' Mataji looked around the room, expecting the truant to magically materialise, and when

28

he didn't, her anger rose. 'That man, he's never there when there's work to be done. He'll be outside now, smoking his *beedi*, polluting my yard.'

'Ok, Mataji.'

'*Haan*,' she huffed. A hand was raised to her brow to simulate the wiping of sweat, and she continued, 'And if you see that man, tell him there's work to be done.'

'Ok, Mataji.'

Savan hurried out and went upstairs. Chotu was nowhere to be seen – not in the hall, not in any of the bedrooms. He paused before Asha's room and then entered without knocking.

'Savan!' scolded his sister. 'Can't you knock?'

Savan swept a pile of clothes off the bed, sat down. 'Have you seen Chotu Chacha?'

'Why?' answered Asha cruelly. 'Does he have to sing you to sleep?'

'Don't be silly,' Savan said. He held his arms across his chest, viewing his sister in lofty condescension. 'Mataji needs him in the kitchen, and he's nowhere to be found.'

'All right then.' Asha rose and patted her brother on his shoulder. He squirmed at her touch, and she laughed. 'I know, I know, you're too big for all that.' He looked like protesting, so she carried on, 'But how about I help you look?'

They scoured the house, searched through the yard, and still there was no Chotu. Asha was about to give up when Savan asked, 'What if it's about the troubles?'

'The troubles? You mean the rioting?'

'Yes. Do we even know what religion he is?'

'He's Hindu, of course,' answered Asha, and then she paused. 'He is, isn't he?'

'He never answers when I ask. And then he calls God *Rab*, not *Bhagwan*. Does that not make him Sikh?'

'But there's no turban.'

He nodded. 'There's no turban.'

They were by Pappaji's study now. Savan indicated the door to his sister, inching slowly in its direction. 'No,' said Asha. 'We're not sneaking around,' and stepping ahead, she knocked loudly.

'Come in.'

They entered. Pappaji sat behind his writing desk, a file in his hand. He looked up at them with a smile of enquiry, but the siblings had turned towards his visitors. Chotu stood near the door, and a younger man stood with his hand on the retainer's shoulders. The siblings didn't recognise the newcomer – a slightly built man with a dense moustache on an earnest face – but there was something familiar about him. He had the same deep set eyes as Chotu, the same burgeoning brows. His shirt and trousers were creased, his face marked with travel, and he gave the children a deep, respectful nod before turning back to Pappaji.

'Come in,' called Pappaji, and the two walked in. '*Bachche*, children, do you know who this is?' he asked, and as Asha and Savan shook their heads, he explained, 'This is Bhole.' Blank looks reigned on both faces, and Pappaji said, 'Bhole, children, Bhole. Chotu's son.'

Namastes were exchanged and Bhole repeated his nod. 'How are you?' he asked Savan. 'I saw you when you were just starting to crawl.'

Savan shrugged. To Chotu, he said sullenly, 'I was looking for you.'

'I know, son. But I have work with your father today. You see Bhole comes with troubling news . . .'

Bhole interrupted gruffly, 'No sense bothering the children.'

'No,' said Pappaji. 'If this is true, what you are saying, then it's important the children know about it. It's their future too.'

Asha looked expectantly at Bhole, but he refused to explain the reason for his visit. Instead, he said tersely to Pappaji, 'Sahib, you have taken care of us all our lives.'

'Yes, yes,' said Pappaji. 'But you no longer feel safe.'

'Sahib, they were out to kill.' Again he cast a quick glance at the siblings standing by the door. 'If it hadn't been for our neighbours . . .'

'Muslims?'

'Sahib?'

'Were your neighbours Muslims?'

Asha's pulse quickened and she felt her throat go dry. Nargis had told her of the news she had heard from her father: of children kept home from school, of curfews and rioters, of a campaign for the creation of Pakistan. Firoze hadn't mentioned a word. Things were still the same between them. They met when the households slept – in the study, on the jasmine-strewn rooftop, or else when Nargis arranged to be out of her room – but there was no talk of trouble. She knew he was active in the struggle for freedom. There were rallies he attended, and some mornings afterwards she found him hoarse-voiced. She had laughingly accused him of rabble-rousing, and he had turned serious. He had closed his hand into a tight fist. 'We will have to snatch our independence,' he had said, and she had smiled indulgently at the fire in his eyes. 'They won't just give it to us for the asking.'

There was still no mention of marriage, but then there was no mention of the obstacles they faced either.

They were no renewed proposals from milk-skinned, almond-eyed Lahoris. There had been nothing to cause her alarm, but when she had been in Nargis' room the week before she had seen a Muslim League pamphlet. She had pointed to it, and Nargis had sighed, 'Oh, that's Bhaijaan's. I have no time for all this *politics-volitics*.'

'Sahib, the rioters were Muslims too.' Bhole's voice had risen, and Asha gave a start. 'Sahib,' he added in a conciliatory tone. His head was bowed now, out of deference to his father's employers, but he spoke asser-tively. 'We can't continue here, Sahib. We have family in Delhi,' he added, nodding towards Chotu, 'and they'll find us work. It's not safe for us in the village.'

'You've made up your mind,' said Pappaji softly.

'Sahib,' said Chotu. This was the first time he'd spoken during the exchange, and his voice was plaintive. 'Sahib, I have grandchildren. Four boys, two girls. What will become of them?'

'Chotu, you know how I feel.'

'How can I leave you, Sahib?' cried Chotu. Tears spilled down his weathered cheeks, his voice grew choked. 'And how can I let them go so far from me?'

'Do you trust me, Chotu?'

'With my life, Sahib.' The words were spoken, and as their import sunk in, Chotu went down on his haunches and began to howl. 'But Sahib,' he wailed, 'How can I choose between you and my family?'

Chotu's cries gathered in vigour. He raised the end of his *kurta* tunic and wiped his cheeks with it, but continued to blubber. Bhole bent down to his father and put an arm around him. Savan opened his mouth to speak and then thought better of it. Asha motioned him

32

towards her. He came silently, and the two stood side by side, holding hands, wishing themselves elsewhere.

'*Bus*,' said Pappaji gruffly. 'Enough crying.'

Chotu's noise rose.

'Please,' repeated Pappaji. 'That's enough.' He rose from his chair and walked to where Chotu squatted. He squatted too and put his hands in the retainer's aged ones. '*Bus*, Chotu,' he said, as the man began to wail even louder. 'Enough.' He patted the servant on the back. 'Please, please, for my sake, don't cry.'

'What do I do, Sahib?'

'Go,' Pappaji said. 'Your life is with your loved ones.'

'But . . .'

'We've kept you too long as it is. I've been thinking of a pension for you, but I've been lazy.'

Chotu bowed his head, fresh tears fell on the floor. 'Sahib . . .'

'No, no, there'll be no talk of money. But you'll be taken care of.'

Bhole cleared his throat. 'Sahib,' he said tentatively, and as Pappaji looked at him, he added, 'Won't you move? To Delhi, to Amritsar. You must have somewhere you can go . . .'

There was a pause as Pappaji considered the question. Asha squeezed her brother's hand, but she permitted herself no further reaction. She refused to speak, refused to so much as breathe for fear of attracting attention. Pappaji began to nod and she closed her eyes. 'Child,' he was saying. 'There is magic in this soil. It's taken good care of me so far, and I know it will take care of me till I die.'

'Well said,' hooted Savan. He jumped from his sister's side and ran into his father's embrace. The men laughed at his exuberance and Bhole began to wind his *pagdi* turban round his head. He had a long journey back home and was keen to prepare for the move to Delhi. He bent down, touching his hands to Pappaji's feet.

'Thank you,' he said to the older man. 'Thank you for all you've done for us.'

'Of course, *Beta*,' smiled Pappaji. He lifted Bhole up, hugged him affectionately. 'We'll see you soon,' he said. 'In Delhi, or Suhanpur, as soon as all this madness is behind us.'

'*Bhagwan kare*, Sahib,' replied an unsmiling Bhole. He looked steadily at Pappaji and folded his hands in farewell. 'God willing.'

4

Asha was called out of class early the next day.

'Your mother is unwell,' her teacher, Mrs Sodhi, told her. 'Your servant is waiting outside to take you home.'

She was escorted out to the school gate, where a tall, bearded man waited for her. He wore a dusty tunic over loose-fitting trousers, and Asha stared hard at him. Mrs Sodhi looked to her for signs of recognition, then prompted, 'Asha, is this your servant?'

They had heard of horrors in the last few months – of rapes, abductions, of girls lost forever. She stared hard at the stranger. There was something familiar about him. But then, Mrs Sodhi had called him a servant, and she frowned in confusion. He definitely didn't work inside the house. The man cleared his throat and bent his head in deference, as if waiting for instruction. Asha shuffled uncertainly and turned to Mrs Sodhi. 'Ma'am?'

'*Namaste* Asha Didi,' the man said in a rasping voice.

'Wait,' said the teacher. 'Asha, do you know this man? Is he not your servant?'

'Ma'am,' said Asha. She looked at the man again. He raised his head, smiled reassuringly, and Asha moved closer to her teacher.

'He's not?' asked Mrs Sodhi. She looked worried and her voice rose in alarm. 'You don't know this man?'

'Didi,' said the stranger, but Mrs Sodhi cut him off. She reached forward, putting a protective arm around Asha. The stranger stepped back, and the sun glinted brown on his head. Now Asha smiled, 'Oh no, Ma'am,' she said. 'I know him.'

'Now you know him?' asked Mrs Sodhi doubtfully.

'Yes Ma'am.'

'You're sure?'

'Of course, Ma'am,' said the girl confidently. 'He's our gardener.'

Mrs Sodhi seemed unconvinced. 'Why didn't you say so earlier?'

'Ma'am,' she gulped. She looked at Firoze for an answer, but he had bowed his head. 'Ma'am,' she floundered again, then quickly, as the teacher eyed her suspiciously, she said, 'I was worried about my mother. Tell me,' she spoke imperiously to Firoze, 'What happened to her?'

'Asha Didi,' he croaked. 'It's her back.'

'Her back?' She looked across at Firoze, took in his discomfort, and smiled. 'Tell me,' she asked. 'What happened to her back?'

'Didi . . .'

'Well?' She was ready to laugh, but Firoze nodded sharply, and she remembered they were being observed.

'I don't know,' he answered, and with an apologetic look at Mrs Sodhi, he added, 'I was just told to get you. It's all chaos at the house.'

The teacher looked around anxiously. 'It's not the mob, is it?'

'No,' said Firoze. 'There's no trouble in Suhanpur. But Ma'am,' he added, grimacing at his use of the English term, 'I think Mataji is in a lot of pain.'

'Right, then,' said Mrs Sodhi uncertainly. 'Tell me this, boy, how long have you been working with the Prakash family?'

'For years,' he said with his head bowed. 'My father was the gardener for the family, and after he passed away . . ..' His speech tapered off, and he looked into the distance.

'Ok then,' Mrs Sodhi said. 'You'd better hurry.' To Asha she added, 'Let me know if there is anything you need.'

'Thank you, Ma'am.'

'Do you want me to come see you after school? I'd like to talk to your mother.'

'No,' said Asha quickly 'No, Ma'am.' Mrs Sodhi frowned, and she added, 'If Mataji isn't well, it's better for her to rest. I'll be back tomorrow, or I'll send word through Nargis.'

'*Chalo*,' urged the servant. 'Come quickly, Didi. Mataji is waiting.'

They were off. They walked at a sedate pace, not looking back to see if they were being watched. After a while, they thought they heard a gate shut, but they were too distant for certainty. They turned a corner, reached the banks of the river, and it was here that Asha dared to speak.

'Well?' she asked as she feigned displeasure. 'What business have you pulling me out of school?'

'A husband's business.'

She laughed. 'I thought you were my servant.'

'Husband, servant, it's the same thing these days.' He pulled off his beard, smiling down at her. His voice took on a gravelly whine as he pretended to stoop with

37

Chotu's age. 'These,' he complained, 'are bad times.'

'*Arre*,' she huffed, 'Leave it. Imagine if someone sees me here with you?' She strode off ahead. The Ravi was calmer at this time of year, silty and sluggish, and there was no hiding the sound of his steps following her. He caught up with her in a moment and took hold of her arm.

'No!' His hand was cool on her, but she trembled as she shook him off. 'It's the last week before the summer holidays. I want to spend time with my friends.'

'Not with me?' He spoke with a smile, but his voice was serious, and she knew she had wounded him. They walked in silence for a while. Their hands brushed together, and now she didn't push away from him. He didn't ask her about school, she didn't ask him about the question that tormented her. It had been months since they had started seeing each other, and the stress was telling on her. She was less certain than Firoze of any objection to their match, but he insisted they couldn't tell anyone. 'But,' she said, and as he looked at her in surprise, she betrayed her unhappiness with a downward tilt to her mouth.

'You think I should talk to your father.'

'You talk of husbands and wives, you pick me up from school without any worry for my reputation, and then you refuse to talk to my father.'

'My life,' he said with infinite tenderness. 'You don't understand.'

'Make me understand, then.'

They stood still opposite each other. He smiled, his lips stretched thin, but she refused to budge. 'I don't understand,' she continued. 'I know I don't. We like each other. Our families like each other. I don't see what the problem is.'

'If only it was as simple as that.'

Her hands were on her hips. She refused to smile, her face with its calm, even features refused to yield, and he said baldly, 'I'm Muslim. You're Hindu. That's the problem.'

She shook her head unhappily.

'Asha,' he said. 'Your family won't like the idea of our match. And the country, and Punjab right now . . .' He paused, looking towards the river. The water flowed gently, but he seemed caught up with its rhythm, for his head moved slightly with every crest and fall of the waves. 'Punjab has been set alight,' he said at length. 'It's burning with a call for freedom, with a call for Partition.'

'A call you favour.'

'There's no room for Muslims in a free India.'

'That's not true.'

'It is,' he said firmly. His chest rose, his eyes shone, and Asha was struck by how closely he resembled Nargis. They had the same high cheekbones, the same proud forehead. They had the same curl of the lip when impassioned. 'And we will not live as second-class citizens.'

'What about us?' she asked. 'What about the Hindus and Sikhs in Punjab?' He turned to her with a frown, but she continued. 'And what about me?'

'It's your Punjab too,' he said slowly. He grew more confident, and repeated, 'It's your Punjab too.'

'Then,' she added smugly. 'Why won't you talk to Pappaji?'

'*Oof*,' he laughed. 'The country is crying out for life, and that's all you care about? That I talk to your Pappaji?'

'I'm crying out for life too.'

'Ok,' he said. 'OK, if you insist. He's not going to like it, but I will speak to him.'

She lit up like a child. 'Promise?'

'Promise.'

'And we'll be married?'

He smiled too then. 'Yes, my darling, we'll be married.'

He reached out to Asha. She shook him off again, but he held onto her. Slowly he turned her around to face him, and when she wouldn't look at him, he lifted her face to his own. 'We'll be married,' he said. He spoke softly, but she felt each syllable burn against her. It was absolutely silent. There was no noise from the road above them, and miraculously no passers-by. The river inched past, a slow wind looked like picking up before falling away. The sun was near its zenith, and Asha struggled against an urge to close her eyes. 'My darling,' he said, and now his lips brushed against her head. Her heart surged, she felt his breath on her hair, felt the sun, felt herself sway. 'Do you really promise?'

'Yes.' He was nuzzling against her now, his mouth warm on her skin, and she had to remind herself to speak. It was her only defence.

'Really?' she asked again as he looked at her with a smile. 'You really promise?'

He didn't reply, and as she struggled for speech, he bent again to kiss her. His fingers slipped under her *dupatta*, he felt the warmth of her hair, and he sighed feverishly against her. '*Oof*, this distance,' he complained. 'I will banish all *dupattas* once we're married.'

'*Hunh*,' she said, but her protest was largely for form's sake, and he carried on with his embrace. 'I'll tell you what,' he said, 'I want half a dozen children. At least four sons . . .'

'Half a dozen!' she squealed. 'What will we do with so many?'

40

'Fill the house up with them. I want our home to be full of people, of laughter, of our children racing up and down passages.'

She looked up at him, and for the first time, she permitted herself an unhurried survey. He was smiling down at her, his mouth warm, his eyes heavy-lidded. There was a crease in the corner of his eye, and she wasn't sure if it came from his smile. She reached up, smoothed it out, smiled as it reappeared.

'Come,' he said, and leading her by her hand, he took her to a clearing by the banks of the river.

They were alone. The clearing was cool with the shade of Sheesham, and though Asha was alert for noise, all was quiet barring the gentle lull of the Ravi.

'Six children,' he was whispering to her, 'Do you understand?' and she smiled and hid her face in his chest. He lifted her face again, looked deep into her eyes with his own smiling, crease-edged ones, and she found she was forgetting to breathe. She was forgetting to smile, forgetting to turn away, forgetting to be afraid. He bent towards her again. She felt his hands under her *dupatta*, felt them under her *kameez*. She felt him against her bare skin, and she found she was forgetting to lodge any protests at all.

5

They sat where they felt themselves alone – on the balcony outside Nargis' room.

It was the first day of the school holidays, and it felt like the height of summer. Ancient sun umbrellas offered them shade, but they still complained about the heat. It was too hot, too sunny, the air was too still. They were sure to burn black. And yet they refused to decamp indoors. They applied a cooling Multani mud mask to their skin. They found a giant brass basin lurking redundantly in the corner of the balcony, and dragged it slowly over to where they sat. They filled it with water, rolled their *salwar* legs up, dipped their feet in the basin. '*Oof*,' sighed Nargis. 'Finally some relief.'

They heard some noise from the road below, and stood up on their brass basin to watch a crowd of youths surge towards the square. 'Hindustan,' they shouted, 'Hindustan *zindabad*.'

'*Oof*,' complained Nargis. 'Will they never stop?'

'Hmm.'

'Hindustan-Pakistan all day long. And now the Pathans arriving to make trouble.'

Nargis fidgeted. Her hand rose to her ears, to her long, straight hair. Asha saw her lick her lips, saw her cross and uncross her legs. She wouldn't sit still. Asha, with her secret burning inside her, fought her own silent battle for composure. She struggled most against the urge to re-imagine her friend's home. 'We'll fill the house with children,' Firoze had said, and she pictured their daughters growing up in Nargis' bedroom. There would be a cricket pitch in the garden. They would plant Sheesham trees in the back, an eternal reminder of their love. They would cover the deep well in the courtyard. She herself had almost fallen into it once, and if anything happened to one of the children . . , 'Hai Ram,' she gasped. She shivered, making a mental note to remind Firoze of the danger. As she took her feet out of the basin, she saw her friend studying her.

'The water's too cold,' she complained, and Nargis nodded.

It had been a long, interminable, unbearable week since Firoze had taken her out of school. She tutted in frustration. There was no way of describing all that had passed. 'This,' she thought as the luscious shame of the deed washed over her anew, 'This is the real Partition.'

'Yes,' Nargis was saying. 'But it's still refreshing.' She shifted again, broke into a smile. She scraped her hair back into a ponytail before letting go. 'Asha,' she said finally, and her friend's name filled her with resolve. 'I'm not sure,' she said, 'but I think Ammi and Abba are thinking of my marriage.'

'Why Nargis!' exclaimed Asha. She hugged her friend, blushing at her plans to give away the girl's room. 'Who is it?' she asked. 'What do you know?'

'He's in the police,' said Nargis. 'He's been to the house before for work.' She paused, colouring at her friend's scrutiny. 'Then last night his parents came to the house. I was called in, and was made to sit next to his mother.' Nargis smiled and Asha reached across to clutch her hand. 'They were very nice,' said Nargis, 'They said I was beautiful.'

'It's no more than the truth,' said Asha.

'They were very nice,' repeated the girl, faltering. Asha looked at her, nodded encouragingly. 'I know I've met him before,' said Nargis at length. 'But for the life of me I can't remember what he looks like.'

'Surely . . .'

'No,' Nargis insisted. 'It's no good. I've tried all I can, but I just can't remember what he looks like.'

Asha stared. The girls paused, then slowly began to laugh.

'What if he's ugly?' asked Nargis.

'You would have remembered if he was ugly.'

'But why can't I remember his face?'

'Don't worry,' counselled Asha. 'These things . . .'

'I don't want what they have in the movies,' cut in Nargis. 'I don't need him to be dashing or romantic. And in the end, what matters in a marriage? Friendship, kindness, a bit of luck.'

Asha breathed in deeply. 'You'll have that,' she said. 'All the kindness you need, all the luck, and more.'

Nargis smiled. 'His mother gave me a pair of *balis*,' she said. She rose and went indoors. Asha heard her feet slap on the marble of the bedroom floor. A dressing-table drawer was opened, a pouch carefully extracted. Nargis returned and handed the pouch to her friend. 'Open it,' she said.

Out came a pair of thin gold *balis*. At the bottom of each earring was a tiny, gold bell. Asha shook the earrings, and the bells chimed a frail peal. She leaned forward to put the earrings on Nargis. She lifted her friend's *dupatta*, wrapped it around her head. '*Arre*, Nargis,' she smiled. 'Now you're looking like a bride.' She touched a finger to her lower lid and removed some *kohl* powder. This she applied behind her friend's ear. 'To keep you safe from the evil eye,' she said as she embraced Nargis again.

Both were crying. 'It'll be you next,' whispered Nargis.

'I know,' said Asha softly. Any day now, Firoze would talk to her father. He had begun to work for Pappaji, and the two were often closeted together in the study. She passed him occasionally in the corridors. He would be rushing in with files, and would quickly look at her with his crease-edged, knowing smile, but that would be all. There were no words exchanged, no caresses, no brushing of hands, and she would have to live off that hurried look till they next saw one another.

Nargis ran a hand down Asha's back and repeated. 'Mark my words, Asha. It'll be you next.'

'I know,' replied Asha. She looked out onto the street, onto her house where Firoze diligently applied himself to his work. Her attention was caught by the noise of the youths, and by the ancient banyan tree that splintered the street in front of them. They had played there as children, she and Nargis, losing each other behind its massive trunk, climbing its branches in search of play. It gave them shade, it gave them grazed knees and the platform to imagine themselves pirates, adventurers or wasting princesses. Every so often a resident worried about new branches bending in incursion of the neighbourhood's properties, but these concerns were always swept away. The banyan was older than Suhanpur itself, it was older than Chotu, older than Asha and her eternal love. It was sacred to the city, and it would remain protected for as long as it chose to spread it sheltering branches over Suhanpur.

'*Arre*,' scolded Nargis. 'Of course you'll be next.' She moved away, singing. '*Love is young . . .*'

Asha hid her smile. 'Stop it.'

'*The world is beautiful . . .*'

'Someone will hear, Nargis.'

'*My heart's looted the treasure of happiness . . .*'

'Yes,' said Asha. There was silence outside. The protesting youths had moved away. It was still again, the air at once unmoving and heavy with rain. The banyan's branches rustled softly, as if echoing with a thousand whispered promises. Asha smiled. She dipped her feet into the water, and as Nargis' voice rose, she lent her own to the music.

6

Violence fanned across the land like a flame. Trouble seeped into dry, parched plains from the arid north, and the Punjabis – excitable and valiant at the best of times – found that any spur – a look, a word, a shove – was like kindling to the fire.

Suddenly those who read, those who had access to news, learned to differentiate. People spoke of 'those Muslims' and 'those Hindus', of separatists and patriots, of a Hindustan for Hindus and a Pakistan for Muslims. They spoke of two nations, they mourned the martyred, the *shaheed*. Reports came in from elsewhere – always from elsewhere – of violence. Throats were slit, men were shot, houses were torched, innocents from the wrong religion ambushed, and revenge was paid in kind. Partition seemed a certainty, and those who could move – those without elderly parents, those with assets they could monetise, those with friends in Delhi or Ambala or Amritsar – moved. Om and his mother were long gone, and in May, he returned to Suhanpur to help his cousins move across. He visited Pappaji, offered help, and haltingly, offered himself again as a son-in-law, but both offers were politely refused. One morning Asha and Nargis learnt that Mrs Sodhi – the teacher who had been so suspicious of Firoze – had left for Karnal. She never came to see Mataji, and though Asha joined her friend in mourning the loss of her teacher, she couldn't help but breathe a sigh of relief that her truancy would remain undiscovered.

The migrations turned Mataji nervous. She cried the day Chotu left. A strong-willed matriarch who seldom betrayed emotion, she took Chotu's weathered hands in her own on his last day in the Prakash household. 'You were here when I came to this house as a bride,' she said. 'How am I going to manage without you?'

'You'll manage, Mataji,' smiled Chotu, though he wasn't far from crying. His skin seemed slacker in the days since his departure had been announced, his hair coarser, whiter. He clung on to his mistress' hand. 'You've always managed everything, Mataji.'

'And who'll handle the children? You know Pappaji lets them run wild. He'll send the girl to college . . .'

The servant looked up with a creased forehead. 'Mataji, you should get her married. Send her to Delhi. These are bad times.' And as Mataji nodded, 'You know that boy Om Sharma. He was here a few weeks ago, back from Delhi. Surely he's a good match for our girl?'

'Now who's to talk to Pappaji?' asked Mataji. 'Who's to make him see sense?'

They parted – the two erstwhile kitchen adversaries – with ostentatious grief. They cried for each other, and a little for their own fading selves too.

Then there were those who refused to believe. Pappaji shrugged as those around him – the Hindus, the Sikhs – upped and left. He nodded as the Muslims in his acquaintance bristled at being unable to form a government in the state, he batted away Hindu paranoia about

Muslim League-sponsored rioting. Even as Chotu packed his bags and set off tearfully to join his family in Delhi, Pappaji refused to believe.

Mostly, they waited. The summer was hot, the land dry and aching for relief. The days felt long, and as unbearable as the wait. They knew Independence was imminent; they knew a new Viceroy had been appointed to effect the handover, but beyond that they dared not hope.

The air crackled on the evening of the 3rd June. A radio announcement was to be broadcast, and all the major leaders were to speak: the British Viceroy, Mountbatten; the advocate for Partition, Jinnah; the charismatic Congress leader, Nehru; the Sikh leader, Baldev Singh. Rain was predicted, a good portent. Crowds emptied out onto the town square armed with umbrellas, with tarpaulin hoods draped over their bodies. A loudspeaker was set up over the clock tower, and all eyes were set to the time. They waited in their thousands, the men of Suhanpur – impatiently, hopelessly. The clock didn't work, or at any rate, it didn't work quickly enough. The rain didn't fall. The sun refused to set. It grew hotter, the square more packed. And still, they smiled at each other in the crowd. Thin lipped, nervous smiles, smiles of youth, smiles of an expectation that consumed them.

Pappaji, on his way back from court, had intended to listen to the broadcast in the square, but he found the air too close, and instead, he returned home and sent a servant over to the house next door to see if he could listen to the broadcast on Inspector Khan's radio. The servant returned with a warm invitation, and Pappaji crossed the fence that divided the two houses.

The mood at the inspector's bordered on the festive. The air was still, the voices hushed, and yet, all were counting on victory. It was the same in houses up and down the country. In later years, those who were there would struggle to explain the atmosphere. The closest comparison would be the tone during an India-Pakistan cricket match – that air of bravado prior to the event, the claims made, the hopes expressed; and while the match was taking place, the absolute silence, the rapt, worshipful, unblinking attention. India stood on the brink of life and death that evening, on the cusp of promise and despair, and the hammering heart of the nation beat as one.

No one remembered details afterwards, no one could remember any particular sentence, the tone of any voice, but all in the inspector's room – Hindu friends, Muslim relatives – all remembered the minutiae surrounding the event. Pappaji remembered the condensation on his iced *sharbat;* remembered focusing intently on a teardrop of water on the glass pool slowly down to the inspector's side table as Mountbatten spoke. 'The decision of the Indian people,' the new viceroy said, and Pappaji put his hands around the glass and lifted it to his mouth for a deep draught. It was hot, he was thirsty, and he remembered being surprised at the connection. Next, it was Nehru's turn to speak, and Pappaji found himself mesmerised by the mother-of-pearl detailing on old Khalique's walking stick. It was this, the colour around the edges of the broadcast that stayed with him, and afterwards, as everyone embraced in celebration, they found they had more questions. When would they be independent – in less than a year, in 1947 itself? Had the date been set? And the question that was starting increasingly to occupy them – what about the Partition?

Firoze insisted on seeing Pappaji back home. It wasn't a long distance, and no great danger lay in wait between the houses, but the young man was adamant, and Pappaji was happy for the evening – so fragrant with promise – to last a little longer.

As they turned into the Prakash compound, they saw that tiny earthenware *diyas* lined each window. A tentative lick of light burst out from each, fragile but vigorous, and the men paused to admire the display.

'That's quick,' said Firoze, looking up at the unlit bedroom windows on the upper floor. 'They've heard already?'

'It'll be one of the servant boys. A couple of them wanted to go down to the square to listen to the broadcast.'

From somewhere down the road, they heard the sound of fireworks being set off. A spark flew across the sky, the sound of loud revelry followed. The branches of the ancient banyan blushed bright.

'Just imagine,' said Firoze, 'We'll be free soon.'

Pappaji shook his head. 'Even now,' he said. 'Even while they were saying the words on the radio I refused to believe. I almost refused to listen. I concentrated on my drink, on my neighbour's clothes. Independence so soon – can we dare hope?' Another spark rose to the sky, and he smiled ruefully. He looked across at his companion and extended his hand towards him. 'Don't listen to me,' he laughed, clapping the younger man on the back. 'We'll be independent. The world will belong to you, Firoze – the principled, the young.'

They both thought then of the calls for a separate Pakistan. A look passed between them; Pappaji turned towards the door, and Firoze said, 'Sir . . .'

'Yes, child?'

'I was wondering.' He stalled for a moment. The night sky was ablaze again, and Pappaji had turned to face him. His face was smooth, unmarked by age, his features similar to his daughter's – gentle eyes, neat mouth. He was smiling at him, happy, tired, and Firoze stumbled, 'Sir, I wanted to ask you something.'

'Is it about work?' asked Pappaji.

Firoze swallowed hard and inclined his head, mumbling something about a case they were working on. Pappaji pretended to frown at the boy, 'Chotu was right about you. You work too hard. Thinking about a case on a night like tonight.'

'Sorry, Sir.'

'*Bhai*, history is being made tonight.'

There it all was; Asha's smile, Asha's bright eyes looking at him trustingly. 'I promise,' Firoze had told her, 'I'll talk to your Pappaji.' He looked at the ground now, suddenly miserable, suddenly as frightened as a child at a spilt pot of milk. 'Sorry,' he said, 'Sorry, Sir.'

Pappaji let out a full-bellied laugh. He clapped Firoze on the back, prepared to go back indoors. '*Chalo*,' he said, 'Alright.'

Firoze nodded his farewell, and then, as the door opened, he blurted out, 'Sir, I wanted to ask for your daughter's hand in marriage.'

'Asha's?' asked Pappaji, and then, 'You want to marry Asha?'

'Yes Sir.'

'But . . .'

'Sir, I believe,' began Firoze nervously, but Pappaji had raised his hand. He stood on the threshold of his house, and his face was bathed with the gentle light of the *diyas*. He looked calm in the light, benign, a friend. 'Firoze,' he said coldly, and the younger man knew instantly he'd been right to be afraid. 'I know you well enough to know you don't mean to insult me.'

'Sir, no.'

'And you know we're Hindu.'

'Sir . . .'

Pappaji spoke over him. 'These things aren't done.' Firoze looked like speaking, and Pappaji waved him silent. 'These marriages aren't accepted.'

Firoze's voice wavered, 'Sir, I hope . . .'

'Son,' asked Pappaji. 'What do you think of the calls for Pakistan?'

'I believe,' Firoze said slowly, 'that they're inevitable.'

'Where does that leave things?'

The night settled back into silence. Firoze paused for thought, then said firmly, 'Sir, you know there is no space for Muslims in India.'

'I know no such thing,' said Pappaji. 'But even if I take you at your word, what about the Hindus? What of us if Suhanpur lies in Pakistan?'

'Sir, this is your home too.'

'That's very kind of you . . . '

'No Sir,' said Firoze. His face shone with the excitement of the evening, but he spoke earnestly, and his voice carried. A hush fell down the street. They heard voices bidding farewell to each other. Firoze's front door opened as the inspector embraced a departing visitor. 'Tonight,' they heard him boom, 'Tonight the entire country is happy.'

Firoze spoke again, urgently and softly. 'Sir, there will always be room for Hindus and Sikhs in Pakistan.'

'Then listen to this, son,' said Pappaji. 'If there is room for me in this Pakistan of yours, then we can talk of marriage. Until then, I don't want you to breathe a word of it to anyone. I don't want you to so much as talk to Asha.'

Firoze heard his name being called, and footsteps approaching them. His head was spinning with the heat, with the older man's words. 'Sir?'

'You heard me. I don't want you talking to Asha until we're safe.'

7

There were a million things to do. Nargis' trousseau had to be readied for the wedding – a dozen new *salwar kameezes* stitched, her wedding outfit embroidered, her jewellery organised. Pashmina shawls were to be covered with intricate *jama* designs. Two craftsmen came down from Kashmir's valleys to prepare her clothes. They laboured through the day in the backyard beside the Sheesham trees Asha had imagined into existence, stopping only for prayers and the fading light. They embroidered the bride's blood-coloured wedding *salwar kameez* with stiff, unyielding thread made of pure gold. They asked for topaz stones, for garnets and tourmalines, and used the gems to ornament the outfit. The inspector complained about the expense, but he was shot down by his wife. 'We only have one daughter,' she said. 'We have to do things with style.'

New jewellery was bought. 'Besides,' Ammi explained to her husband. 'The price of jewellery is low right now. With all the people looking to migrate, there are real bargains to be had.' An ornate *navratan* necklace was purchased, as was that most subtle of treasures, a gold set, heavy with uncut diamonds.

'Just imagine,' said Nargis to Asha. The two were alone in Ammi's room. Nargis set down her *dupatta* to hold her new diamond necklace against her skin. 'They say it belonged to the granddaughter of a *Maharajah*.' A hundred minute lights danced against her skin, and her friend clapped in delight. 'Nargis,' she exclaimed. 'You look like a queen!'

'I know,' Nargis replied. 'And to imagine wearing a diamond necklace!' She stared at herself dispassionately in the mirror. She hollowed out her cheeks, bit her lips into colour, gave herself a stiff, regal bow. 'Ammi said I needed high-class jewellery. She said *he* is destined for greatness.'

Nargis never referred to her husband-to-be by name. They still hadn't met, not properly, not since the marriage had been arranged. She still couldn't remember what he looked like, but she was certain he was handsome. She was certain he was kind, or Ammi wouldn't have arranged the wedding. She knew he was involved in politics, knew he was known to Firoze. 'He and Bhaijaan go to the League meetings together,' she told Asha. Asha nodded. They still hadn't spoken, she and Firoze, and now she had the distinct impression he was avoiding her. He didn't even look at her when they passed each other. She told herself she was being paranoid. A Muslim family – distant relatives of the Khans – had just arrived in Suhanpur. They spoke of violence, of bloodthirsty Hindus rampaging through the countryside. She had heard Ammi vow to keep her relatives safe. 'Those faithless Hindus,' she had heard her curse, but she knew Firoze was different. He wasn't going to turn on her.

Nargis went on, 'They say he'll be a minister after the Partition. His family are big landowners, and he's been so useful to the League.' She squeezed Asha's hand. 'And

Insha'Allah, Bhaijaan will do well too. They've both been politically active.'

Asha's mind swam. Politically active. Useful to the League. A minister in the Pakistan Government. But she smiled at her friend's excitement. '*Insha'Allah*,' she said. 'God willing.'

8

Summer blazed through the country. It was hot outdoors, impossibly hot indoors and, it seemed to Mataji, hottest in the kitchen. The *jaali* screen was shut against the sun, lattice fans were used to provide a welcome breeze, but still she suffered. She sat on a rattan stool in the coolest, darkest corner of the kitchen, and she communicated with minute motions of her hand. She didn't speak, didn't move more than she had to. Flies, fat with waste, buzzed around her half-heartedly, and though she clapped her hands together on one, she soon gave up the effort. It was too hot to bother. It was too hot to move, too hot to complain. It was too hot even for recrimination, and for once the servants went about their work without being scolded.

It seemed that the suffering was universal, for quiet as it was in the kitchen, it appeared to be equally silent outside.

'Mataji,' Riaz, the Muslim boy hired to replace Chotu, said hopefully. He looked up at her, his small, sharp teeth dull. A smile was attempted, abandoned then resuscitated. 'It's like everyone has fallen asleep.'

'Or died in this heat,' thought Mataji, though she didn't bother articulating her opinion. Instead, she motioned towards the flame, and the boy began listlessly stirring the pot of *daal*.

'*Hai Ram*,' said Mataji, lifting the end of her *dupatta*

to her face. She wiped it of its moisture, blew into the air, and settled against the wall. '*Oof,*' she said, 'Will this day never end?'

The *jaali* screen flew open at once, knocking against Mataji's stool. She rose, a string of curses ready on her lips, but she held them once she saw the newcomers. It was Om, Asha's rejected suitor. He held Savan by the arm, and rushed him firmly indoors.

'*Hai Ram,*' Mataji started wailing as soon as she saw her son. 'Who did this to you, child?' Savan looked tousled – his shirt was dusty and torn, his spectacles missing, and his hair more dishevelled than usual – but otherwise unharmed, and he shrugged at his mother's hysterics.

'It's nothing, Mataji,' he said, and as the matriarch continued to cry, he added, 'It was just a small disturbance. I shouldn't have got in the middle of it.'

'Small disturbance!' scoffed Om. He held his hands out to indicate a mob. 'There were twenty of them, thirty maybe. They had set a poor Hindu fruit-seller's cart on fire. The wretched man tried to run for his life when some passers-by tried to help him out. That's when this Mister here got involved.' He smiled wearily at the boy's bravado. 'There, there,' he said. 'There's no point wasting your bravery on a mob. They'll kill you in an instant, and then where will you be?'

'Yes,' cried Mataji. All the heat she had complained about seemed forgotten, 'I was saying this to Riaz. I was, wasn't I, Riaz?' and as the servant dutifully nodded, she added, 'I said it was too quiet. No good comes out of such silence. And for you,' she cuffed her son sharply on his head. He yelped, jumping away from her, but she cuffed him again, 'for you to be getting mixed up in all this trouble!'

'Mataji,' said Om soothingly. 'It's not his fault. These are hard times.'

'They are. You're right, child,' and noting for the first time the identity of her son's saviour, she said with surprise, 'But aren't you meant to be in Delhi?'

'I am,' he said. His mouth extended in a grimace. 'My aunt's boy, his shop was attacked last week.'

'In Suhanpur?'

'No, no, closer to Lahore. I've come back to take them to Delhi, and I thought I'd check in on our friends in Suhanpur.'

'Oh, I see.'

'Tell me,' said Om. He addressed himself to Savan, but his eyes were on Mataji. 'You don't think of moving?'

'No,' Savan spoke in a muted voice. 'Pappaji says . . .'

'This Pappaji of theirs,' railed Mataji. 'I've been telling him for so long. The world is turning on its head, and he refuses to see sense. Everyone is leaving. You, the Sodhis, even the Rajpals from across the street. *Arre*, our servants are leaving too. Our man Chotu, he was with me when I came to this house . . .' Mataji trailed off. Her hand rose accusingly towards Chotu's replacement, who began to stir the *daal* with fresh gusto.

'Tell me,' said Om. He and Mataji looked at each other for an unwavering age, and both seemed to recognise an ally. 'Tell me how I can help.'

Mataji sat slowly down on her stool and put a hand to her head. 'I want to be prepared,' she said. 'I'm sure we have to leave, but I don't want to do it in a panic. I've heard of those who've had to leave everything behind – jewellery, lands, everything.'

'Would it be Delhi you would come to?'

60

'Yes, I think so.' She considered her words. 'Yes, it would be Delhi. Pappaji's uncle lives there.'

'Then,' offered Om. 'I can carry something for you. Any jewellery you have.'

'We have silver too,' said Mataji. She compiled her list of valuables. 'And our plates. My shawls and *saris*.'

'Mataji,' counselled Om. 'If I may.' He drew closer, whispering, 'It's best to take things you can transport quickly. Something light and precious. Jewellery is best.'

'But . . .'

'I'm sure everything else is valuable too.' He put up a hand to silence her. 'As and when you can, sell what you have. Change it to gold, and bring it with you when you come. In the meantime –' Here the door opened from the hall, and Asha walked in.

She first took in her brother in his disarray. Next she looked to Mataji and Om huddled in their corner. 'Mataji?' she asked, and as Om turned to her, she folded her hands together. '*Namaste*,' she said. '*Namaste*, Om-ji.'

Om rose, bowed low in response, and explained, 'Mataji is worried.' If Asha was surprised at his informal manner in addressing her mother, she didn't let on, and Om continued. 'I was advising her to plan for your move to Delhi.'

'Oh.'

Asha tried to disguise her anger. This little man, this dark, short, unctuous trader with his broad nose and endless teeth, this man here in her home, going round Pappaji and preying on her mother's worries. Mataji, he called her, as if she was his own mother. *Mataji is worried, I am worried.* 'Yes,' he was saying now, turning towards Mataji. 'Give me your jewellery and I will take it to Delhi for you.'

61

Mataji rose with a grateful smile. '*Beta*,' she said. 'Child, I don't know what I would do . . .'

'Mataji!' Asha said sharply. 'Wait a minute.'

Her mother frowned. 'Don't worry, Asha,' she said, 'Om's only thinking of us.'

'Have you spoken to Pappaji? Does he know what you're doing?'

'Asha-ji,' said Om. 'I'm just taking care of some jewellery. Think of it as insurance. If all goes well after independence, I'll bring it back. But if you need to start afresh in Delhi,' She shook her head. '*If* you need to come to Delhi, you will find it useful.'

Mataji was at the door.

Asha flew after her. 'Mataji,' she said. 'Think this through. Is it wise?' Mataji carried on upstairs, and Asha tried again desperately. 'And how do we know we can trust him, this Om?'

'You can trust those we don't know,' hissed Mataji. 'The Muslim League, the leaders carving up our country. You and your father trust those who will outnumber us, but you won't trust one of our own.'

'What if –' said Asha wildly, 'what if he's here to steal our belongings?'

'Yes,' scoffed Mataji. In the dim light of the stairway she appeared frail. Her hair was greying, her laughter lines etched deeper into her skin, and Asha wondered when her mother had grown old. 'He's come here,' Mataji was laughing, 'all the way from Delhi just to rob me of a few rupees. Yes, that's worth his effort, isn't it?'

'You don't know, Mataji,' insisted Asha. She looked around, hoping to see someone – Pappaji, Firoze – who could stop Mataji, but the house was quiet. They were in the upper floor now, in Mataji's room. Her mother lifted a set of keys from the skirt of her *sari* and opened a heavy steel cupboard. 'Here,' she said, pointing to a parcel wrapped in cloth. 'Hold this.' She took out another cloth bundle and locked the cupboard. She took the parcel out of her daughter's hand and hurried towards the stairs. 'Well,' she asked as Asha hung back. 'Are you coming or not?'

'No, Mataji,' she said. 'No, I'm not.'

She rushed downstairs first. The study was empty. There was no Pappaji, no Firoze. Asha remembered there was a new case her father had taken on and that he wasn't expected back until late in the evening.

She wandered back to the kitchen. Hushed voices came from inside, and she was sure the bundles of cloth were being passed from hand to hand. 'Asha won't,' she heard Om say. She turned and hurried out to the front of the house.

She opened the door. Heat flew at her like an unwelcome caress, and she stumbled back for an instant. Then her eyes adjusted to the light, and she moved towards her friend's house.

She saw Firoze by the fence that separated the two houses. He smiled, lifted his file and made to walk on. Day by day, his house was filling with wedding celebrations. Two mournful musicians piped their *shehnais* the moment day broke. The lawn – her children's future cricket pitch – had been given over to a large *shamiana* tent. A *halwai* sat out as the sun set, frying *jalebis*, gram flour *pakoras*, lamb-stuffed *tikkis*. It was the month of *Ramzan*, and the guests, arriving as the failing sun relieved them from their fasting, polished off entire trays of snacks while waiting for their meals.

63

Mataji claimed she couldn't sleep any more. The smell of the food kept her up at night, and the din from the *shehnais* attacked her in the morning. She didn't allow Asha to attend any of the festivities either. 'There's too much bad blood between the communities,' and though Pappaji rolled his eyes in response, he didn't contradict his wife.

Firoze had begun to move. He reached the banyan tree, and as she ran towards him, he frowned. 'Asha,' he said. 'We can't.'

It was the first time they had properly met since their truancy of a few weeks ago. Asha feared he had lost interest in her, fretted she had been too careless with her virtue, then that she was worrying without cause. He wasn't like the boys Mataji warned her about, he loved her. They were planning a life together. He had promised to speak to Pappaji, had promised to ask for her hand in marriage. Now though, he shook off her hand. 'I can't,' he said. 'I have to go meet your father.'

'I have to talk to you.'

'I can't,' he repeated. He darted a quick look at her, then he glanced at his watch, tucked his file under his arm, and nodded his farewell.

'Pappaji,' she said. There was a high note to her voice she couldn't control. 'Did you talk to him?'

He was moving away now. 'I can't stop,' he repeated, and he was off. She smelt spices being roasted in preparation for the evening's festivities and her stomach turned. Her mouth filled with a taste at once sharp and bitter. It was hotter than it had been all summer long.

'Firoze,' she called. He didn't look back, didn't answer her, and as the sky grew brighter, and then in an instant, darker than black, he didn't turn to see her fall.

9

Asha was on her own when she knew for certain that
her body was changing. She walked to the mirror in
her room, lifted her tunic *kameez* to display a taut, flat
stomach. She patted it softly, then slowly cradled it with
the palm of her left hand. She stood in this position for a
long while, as the dark gathered around the room, until
she heard a sound outside her door, and she quickly
pulled her *kameez* down and walked towards the door.

Riaz was standing by the door. Asha raised an eyebrow
at him. The male servants never entered her room, and as
for Riaz – pubescent and Muslim – he would be thrashed
for his audacity.

'What are you doing here?' she asked as he stood
silently grinning at her. 'Have you lost your mind, boy?'

He shrugged. He didn't appear embarrassed, and if
anything, he laughed at her wonder.

'Riaz, didn't you know this was my room?'

He leaned forward. His teeth were small and uneven,
a little like the jagged amber beads she'd once won at
the annual town fair. Asha had been thrilled with the
trinket, but Mataji had sneered when she'd seen them.
'*Chee*,' she had said. 'What rubbish you pick up.' Riaz
had moved closer. She smelled raw onion on his breath,

that and spiced salty *lassi* as he said, 'You're very beautiful.'

'Riaz!' she protested. She was suddenly nervous, thinking of Chotu's constant admonishment – *these are bad times*. At night, they shuttered all the windows, and for the first time she could remember, they locked the front door. A grim-faced Pappaji would go out into the night himself and bolt the gate to the property. All these precautions, and still they weren't safe from the calls of the night: the march of a dozen, no a hundred or more League miscreants; the insistent tapping of *lathi* sticks on the parched earth; then the slow, rising call of *Allah-ho-Akbar*. God is great, our Allah is great.

Riaz took hold of her wrist. He brought it up to his face and laid her palm against his cheek. Asha balled her hand into a fist, and he smiled at the resistance. 'Spirit,' he said, licking his lips. 'This should be fun.'

More people were leaving. Pappaji scoffed when Mataji reeled off the numbers, but there was no hiding the sense of panic. *Allah-ho-Akbar* went the nightly chant on quiet, empty streets, and it was the non-Muslims who paid heed. Hindus, Sikhs from all over Suhanpur were travelling in any manner they could – by bullock cart, by cars, buses, trains, by foot if they had to – but they were leaving. Possessions were abandoned, and all over town, warehouses stood empty, houses, factories and shops lay deserted. They were beginning to recognise new owners, and the friends and partners of the departed took charge, or else the opportunistic amongst the new arrivals from the East found a warm welcome in newly vacant premises.

Riaz lowered Asha's fist and opened it, stroking it softly with his calloused fingers. She took in the hardness of his skin, the roughness of his touch, and found herself shivering. He noticed the tattoo on her wrist. 'Om,' he laughed. He pressed his thumb on the symbol. Asha howled at his touch, but Riaz went on laughing. 'The magical, mystical, Hindu Om.'

'Riaz,' she cried. 'Riaz, what madness is this?'

'*Arre*,' he smiled slowly. 'You see me outside the kitchen and you call it madness. What about what you Hindus are doing to us? Do you know my sister was murdered on the train from Sonipat?' Asha placed an instinctive hand over her stomach, and perhaps he noticed, for he added, 'She was expecting, did you know that? Her stomach was big as a balloon, and still the savages showed no mercy.' He grinned again, and Asha was struck by how composed he was. His voice was soft, his words rational, free of expletives or hyperbole.

They'd heard, of course. There had been trains pulling in from the other side, all empty, all full of the dead. Those who made it over, the lucky few who had simply witnessed the carnage, spoke with a terror that was worse than death. Women had their breasts sliced off, men were made to watch their loved ones being stripped, raped, then carelessly murdered. Children were orphaned, brides widowed. And these were the lucky ones, the survivors who lived to tell their stories.

'No mercy, do you understand?' Riaz paused for her answer, and as she stood silent, his gaze fell again on her wrist with the offensive tattoo, and he rubbed at it with his thumb, as if to sandpaper it off.

'I know, I know,' she said quickly. She tried to twist her hand free, but he wouldn't slacken his hold. 'I know.' She didn't know what else to say, so she spoke the words to calm herself as well as the boy. 'It's all the Partition.'

Where was Firoze? Defending the Muslim League, advocating Partition, and now, abandoning her when she needed him. He wouldn't speak to her, wouldn't let her be in the same room as him. She wasn't even allowed to leave the house. 'Things will return to normal,' Pappaji had told her when she had argued, 'It's just that passions are raised at the moment.' Mataji had tutted at his insouciance, but Asha had been satisfied with his explanation. This would pass, things would revert to normal. 'We live together,' he had said, 'We're all the same people,' and she had taken hope at his words. But there was no Firoze to talk to, no Nargis even to meet, and now this servant boy assaulted her and she didn't know where to turn for help. *You Hindus, You Muslims*, she said to herself silently, and where does that leave me? To Riaz, she said cheerfully, 'It'll all die down in a week or so, after Independence. See, we're not even leaving Suhanpur. Life will carry on as it always did.'

'Not for my sister,' he said. He looked distracted for a moment, and Asha found herself feeling sorry for him. He was young, no more than thirteen or fourteen, and this was not a time for the vulnerable. 'Not for her unborn baby,' he said now, springing up and backing her into her room.

'No,' she screamed, and though he was laughing with his beadlike teeth, and though he looked like an overtired child at the end of an evening's celebrations, she howled as loudly as she could. Then all was quiet, and she strained to hear some movement. It was *sandhya*, the hour of dusk. Mataji would be downstairs finishing her prayers. Savan would be with Pappaji, talking politics, talking him into convincing the authorities to reopen the schools. As for Firoze . . .

68

Riaz was inside the room now. He no longer laughed. He looked around, taking in her bed, the pile of clothes on the floor, her panelled mirror and mother-of-pearl brush and comb set. He seemed to take courage from these possessions, from the privileged debris of her life, and he pushed her further inwards. 'Stop it,' Asha said. Her *dupatta* slipped off her head, but she tried to speak authoritatively. 'I understand this is a hard time for you. It's horrible for all of us.' He stepped forward, and as he did, she screamed, 'Pappaji!' No one replied, Riaz laughed his jagged-toothed smile, and she called out for her mother, for Savan, for Nargis, even for Chotu in her desperation. Suddenly, Asha heard the rush of footsteps, and Pappaji was running in, a stern-jawed Firoze behind him. Riaz slackened as soon as he heard them enter, and though his eyes were bright and his face unashamed, he didn't resist as they heaved him out of the room.

10

The inspector came over as soon as he found out about Riaz. He held Pappaji's hands between his own and apologised for the servant's transgression.

'*Arre, Bhai*,' smiled Pappaji. 'I grant that you're responsible for law and order in Suhanpur. Are you also responsible for all the world's Muslims?'

'Your daughter . . .'

'Yes,' said Pappaji, and both men looked away. Pappaji asked hesitantly, as if the shame of the question was all his, 'Is it safe for us here?'

The inspector smelt of his daughter's wedding festivities. There were patches of sweat under his arms, his moustache gleamed with exertion, and they knew they had been celebrating in the other house. The *shehnai* players had been joined by a *dholak* drummer, and even now, they heard the noise of wedding songs. 'Prakash *sahib*, you know my view,' he said, 'but things are very tense at the moment. Trains are full of Muslims coming from the East, and those who haven't been hacked to death talk of rapes and abductions. It's stoking passions here, and there's no knowing what the mob will do.'

'This is it then,' said Pappaji sadly. His head drooped, and his hair, luxuriant and black, seemed suddenly lifeless. He looked around the room he'd grown up in

70

and filled with possessions, and it was as if he didn't recognise anything. 'This is Partition.'

'No, *Bhai sahib*,' said the inspector. '*Bhai sahib*, please listen to me. They won't listen to reason now, I give you that much. It isn't safe here for you. But once all this has passed – once we're independent, once the Indians are in India and the Pakistanis in Pakistan, then it will be the same as always. And you're a Pakistani as much as I am.'

'I wonder.'

'Please *Bhai Sahib*, repeated the inspector. 'This is your home.'

'Of course,' said Pappaji. 'That much is clear.' Firoze, who stood quietly in the corner of the room, nodded his agreement. 'Yes, Sir,' he said. 'This is your home.'

'This is my home,' Pappaji said thoughtfully. 'It's just that I can't stay here.'

'*Bhai Sahib*, it's just for the moment,' the inspector repeated earnestly. 'Please believe me. Go to Delhi, go somewhere safe while people work through their savagery. Come back once they have recovered their senses.'

Pappaji shook his head. 'But this is home,' he repeated, and as the inspector nodded sadly, he added, 'Who do I know in Delhi? You might as well ask me to go to the moon.'

Mataji entered the room. Pappaji barely noticed her presence, but the inspector rose. 'Please, sister,' he begged, 'Please help me convince *Bhai Sahib* that it's not safe here.'

Mataji walked up to her husband. She spoke softly, but with such coldness that Pappaji gave a start. 'What do you wait for?' she asked. 'Today your daughter almost lost her honour. Yesterday your son was beaten

71

up. What more do you want to see before you believe what everyone is saying? Do you want the house to be burnt down? Do you want me to be killed or worse?'

The gardener was going through the house lighting the lamps for the evening. He entered, bowed to those seated, then went about his work. Pappaji waited for the man to leave. No words were exchanged between husband and wife. He didn't even look at her, but she knew she had her way at last.

They packed quickly. 'Only take as much as you can carry,' instructed Mataji. Pappaji was quiet now, obedient, and she came into her own. She threw away Savan's socks, packed for a subdued Asha. 'Just two changes of clothes,' she instructed. 'God knows there are shops enough in Delhi. You can buy new provisions there.'

The servants were dispatched. Chotu had been gone for months; the other Hindu retainers hadn't been to the house for more than a week. The roads were too unsafe, they had said, and Mataji had grumbled about truancy. She had threatened to hire new staff. 'I'll get in Muslims,' she had warned. 'What do I care who they pray to?' Now she settled accounts with the Muslim gardener, patting him on his back as he hung his head in shame. 'Mataji,' he said. 'I had no idea. If I did – ' He balled his hand into a fist, shaking it angrily.

Mataji patted him again. '*Bus*,' she said. 'That's enough.'

The Khan house was primed for celebration. Lights from dozens of tiny clay *diyas* played out a reckless, heedless dance along the edge of the lawn, bowing, wavering, then bursting forth with every capricious change of air. Two bored little girls, no older than six or seven, sat unobserved on the wet grass, following the play of light. The *shamiana* itself hummed with noise. A crowd of nearly a hundred revellers thronged around the lone male servant bravely bearing snacks. 'Too good,' was the lamenting verdict. 'It's too hot, but really, these are too, too good.' Nargis stood at the edge of the crowd near the seated girls, sombre in a pale green *sulwar kameez*. She wore her new *navratan* necklace and the gold *balis* gifted by her mother-in-law, and she appeared distracted. Her eyes darted towards the fence, and a cousin teased her. 'Have patience,' she counselled. 'You'll be married in a few days, and then your wait will be over.'

Nargis coloured. She had a denial ready on her lips, but there was some noise by the fence, and she saw her father leading the Prakash family in. She ran towards them and hugged her friend. 'I heard,' she said. 'I'm so sorry.'

'It's not your fault,' said Asha. She looked over her friend's shoulder at the party. The guests had paused in their feasting. Some stepped forward now to express their regrets to Pappaji. Others stared. There were refugees from the East in the gathering, and they subjected the newcomers to a dispassionate, unhurried survey. 'It's worse in Hindustan,' Asha heard someone say. 'They're such heathens.'

'Come,' said Nargis. 'Let's get you upstairs.'

She slept the night in her friend's bed, and it was as if all was normal again. A better, festive version of normal, as it was when the grown-ups were distracted and they were allowed to make their own mischief. When they swam in the Ravi, when they stole mangoes from Lalaji, when, like the two little girls outside on the wet grass, they watched the dancing lights.

Riaz was in jail, Mataji had recovered from her shock, and the rest of her family had settled into their room next to Nargis's. Asha had been coddled and scolded for not shouting sooner and louder. She hadn't been left alone, and Mataji said she was never going to be alone again. Not long enough for her to blink. The *halwai* had cooked her *samosas* and tangy potato *tikkis*, her favourite snacks. Ammi had sent up rose-flavoured milk and soggy, sweet *rasmalai* disks. She had been allowed to sit with Nargis until both had tired. They had caught up on all the festivities of the previous week. Nargis was almost certain she'd caught a glimpse of her husband-to-be. He was tall, she said, with a moustache. 'What if he kisses me?' Nargis had asked, as her friend began to giggle. 'What do I do if it tickles?'

Asha wasn't sure when they had fallen asleep. 'I'll miss you,' she remembered saying. 'I will hate missing your wedding.'

She woke in the middle of the night. She heard a noise near her, thought she imagined a spark overhead. It was dark in the room, but she knew he was near. She smelt the *lassi* on him; she was sure she saw the dull gleam of his teeth. His chest rose, he moved his arm towards her. Asha uttered a strangled cry. His arm was over her now, and as she squirmed under it, the clouds shifted. The moon shone into the room; she saw it was Nargis who slept next to her.

Nargis, not Riaz.

She went to the room her family slept in, got into the bed they all shared.

All was back to normal.

Yet she was unable to sleep.

It was hot, still unbearable, and sticky too now that the monsoon was in full force. They had cracked the dusty window in the room open, and even this air, hot and turgid as it was, was a relief. She heard the dull, persistent beat of the rain, then another beat over it – that of young feet, like a febrile army marching. It was nearly the 14th August, and at that day's end, one country would be made anew, and two torn asunder. It was the end they all waited for, the night of Independence and that of Partition. Another noise rose, and though initially she was sure it was only the rain growing in strength, she was struck by its staccato bursts. Mataji turned in her sleep, patting her daughter reassuringly. '*Bus*,' she muttered. 'All will be well now.'

A fiery spark rose to accompany the sound from the crowd. The rain was silenced now, and in its place, the sky burnished bright. She moved out of the bed, looked out through a chink – she dared not risk exposure, even here, even in the inspector's house – but she couldn't be sure if the Prakash house had been party to the bonfire that raged outside.

11

Asha was woken by an insistent drumming. Its tempo was like the river racing downstream. *Dham dharak dham*. Slowly, other sounds were added to its noise: the stamping of feet, the slap of metal. The noise came from directly below her. She heard a voice ring out in time to the beat, and ran downstairs to find all the women of the wedding party crowded on the floor. They sat cross-legged, one and all, even though many complained of advancing age and creaking joints. They wore clothes as bright as an infant's palette: gold-flecked orange, peacock blue, fuchsia pink. Their reserve vanished in the all-female gathering. *Dupattas* slipped, revealing *henna*-stained heads and ageing bosoms. They hammered at two *dholak* drums with the base of their palms, and those without access to the instrument improvised. They tapped at the floor with the backs of spoons, they stamped their feet hard on the ground, they clapped and sang.

Nargis was seated near the centre of the throng. Seeing Asha, she patted the floor next to her. Space was cleared, ancient knees shuffled unwillingly backwards, and Asha threaded her way to her friend.

A new song started up. '*Piche piche aanda*,' sang a woman in a loud, cheerful voice, and the rest of the party answered, 'You follow me, you follow me . . .'

'Tomorrow's the henna ceremony,' Nargis whispered to her friend. 'And the day after that is the wedding.' She squeezed her friend's hand. 'Asha,' she said. 'I'm so glad you're here.'

The music turned mournful. 'Father,' sang the clear-voiced soloist. 'We must fly . . .' Her voice quivered and dozens of hands were lifted to tearful eyes. Everyone was transported back to the house of their childhood, to rela tives sobbing uncontrollably as skittish brides boarded palanquin *dolis* to head to their husband's home. They had grown in age, in experience and in girth in the intervening years. Their father's house was now just a memory, as removed and as precious as their time in pigtails. Their life was where they lived now, with their husbands, with their husband's families. This was where they had brought up their children, this was where they were growing old. This was home. And yet, as the song's refrain rang out, 'There's no return . . .', there wasn't a single dry eye in the room.

Asha returned Nargis' pressure. 'And to think I would have missed it all.'

'*Bus*,' complained Ammi. She rose, scolding the singer. 'No sad-sad music.' She began to clap her hands. The inspector entered, a sheaf of papers in his hand, but was faced with scores of piercing eyes. He stared uncompre-hendingly for a moment, then bowed his head.

'Forgive me,' he apologised as he began to back away. The seated women laughed and wiping their tears, began to crow. 'See,' said one. 'Even as great a man as the inspector of Suhanpur is afraid of us.'

Nargis rose now, fuelled by the gathering's camara-derie. 'Sing that song,' she said to the woman manning the *dholak*, 'Love is young.'

An instant hoot broke out. 'Why?' asked a broad-hipped grandmother. She revealed a gap-toothed smile. 'Did your sweetheart sing it for you?'

A dozen voices added their calls to the cacophony. Nargis sank quickly to the ground. '*Oof*,' she huffed. 'They won't give up.' A fleshy matron lifted her hands and began to clap out a tune. 'And the old ones are the worst.'

They began to sing. '*Love is young*,' they trilled. They laughed as they sang, pointing at the bride, acting out the exchange of longing glances. '*Hai*,' they sighed, and '*Oof* no,' as an older lady lecherously pulled the *dupatta* off a young girl's chest. Nargis kept her head down, conscious of the crowd's attention, but her hand was firm on her friend's. She felt Asha tremble, and she smiled. '*Arre*,' clucked the matrons. 'Look, she smiles,' and Nargis buried her face in Asha's shoulder.

Mataji came to join the singing. 'This song,' she smiled. 'It's one of my favourites.' Now they were laughing again, clapping and pointing at the bride. They made room for Mataji, who innocently proceeded to sit next to her daughter. She began to sing, smiling at the two girls next to her. She leaned forward, fingered Nargis' diamond necklace in admiration and extended her hands to the bride's face to ward off the evil eye. Then she exclaimed, '*Hai Ram*, Asha, did you bring the jewellery?'

Asha was blank. 'Mataji?'

'The jewellery. You know, the rubies I bought, the *balis*?'

Asha shook her head.

'You didn't pack them?'

'Mataji, no.'

'*Arre*, I sold everything. Our armchair was exchanged for a bangle, our silverware for *balis*. And then, the rubies for your dowry.' A new song had started, another cheery number, and several of the women in front of them began to sway. Mataji grew more hysterical. She shook her daughter, asked, 'Don't you remember, girl?'

There *had* been unusual visitors in the past few weeks. Potbellied traders would come into the house when Pappaji was away for work. Lanky assistants would trail clumsily behind, carrying heavy wrought-iron scales. Asha didn't think anything of the visits. She was preoccupied with Firoze and her changing body, and she didn't pay attention to missing furniture or empty chests. There had been one morning though, when Mataji had brought in a heavy velvet pouch. She had seated herself on her daughter's bed and taken out a ruby set. 'You'll wear this on your wedding day,' Mataji had promised as she placed the jewellery around her daughter's neck. The rubies had fallen down the gentle swell of her breasts, tiny diamonds had twinkled against her skin. All at once she had been radiant, luminous. 'We won't have you looking like a refugee,' Mataji had said, and though Asha had blushed and tutted away the suggestion, she had turned to observe herself in the mirror.

Pappaji was unmoved by his wife's deception. She described each lie, every carefully hidden treasure, and he just shrugged.

'Are you listening?' Mataji screamed, pulling at his sleeve. 'We've lost everything. All the jewellery I saved up, it's all back in the house.'

'It doesn't matter,' Pappaji said reassuringly. 'What's money at a time like this?'

'What's money?' Mataji laughed shrilly. 'All these degrees you have, and not an ounce of sense. What's money? It's comfort, that's what it is. It's your son's education. It's your daughter's dowry, that's what it is.'

'We're not the only ones affected by this.'

'No, we're not,' shouted Mataji. 'But I planned for it. I saved, I siphoned, I exchanged. I gave up all the memories, all the treasures of our life, and all for nothing.' Her arms were flailing in her agitation, and now she began to slap at him. She hit at his sleeves, at his arms, finally at his turned back. *Dham-dham*, went her hands against his clothes, *Dham-dham-dharak*, and Asha was transported to her first thundering, sun-drenched encounter with Firoze. Where was he now? In the next room, in the corridor? Was he close enough to hear her breathe, to smell her skin as he had that last, fateful morning? Where was he? She heard a loud noise. Mataji had fallen on the ground crying, Pappaji had turned towards the room. 'I'll be back in a minute,' Savan was saying, 'It's just across the road.'

Pappaji followed him within seconds. Mataji didn't speak. They remained in the room, and as it grew lighter overhead, it grew darker indoors. They couldn't mark the time, couldn't occupy themselves. Asha irritated herself by counting out her *Dham-dham-dharak* routine, but still there was no movement from outside, and no sound from within the room.

After a while, she looked towards her mother. 'Mataji,' she started, but the older woman silenced her with a glance. She waited another while, then tried to speak again. 'Mataji . . .'

'*Chup*,' snapped her mother. 'It's all your doing, you miserable girl. If it wasn't for your dowry, both of them would be back here. It's all your fault.'

80

'You don't mean that.'

Asha felt the heat rise. Her mouth filled with water, with the sharp taste of metal. Mataji turned to her, eyebrows raised. She heard a noise, a scratching, and she knew they both did. They looked at each other, took in a sharp breath and moved towards the door.

It was Firoze.

'A thousand apologies,' he was saying to Mataji. 'But the situation is really bad,'

'But my son . . .'

In came a new family. It was the Maliks from the next street; a widowed mother and her teenage daughter. They wore dusty, torn clothes, and for an instant Asha was repelled by how dirty they looked. The women fell on her. 'If he hadn't been here,' sobbed the mother, 'Firoze *Beta* . . .'

'But my son,' Mataji was saying again. 'Savan, and his father . . .'

Firoze looked towards Asha. 'Where are they?' he asked.

'They went back to look for our jewellery,' she replied.

The Malik women renewed their crying. '*Hai Ram,*' she heard them invoke, and she was hugged closely against their dusty clothes. Firoze went out, shutting the door. The heat rose, as did the taste of metal, and she realised they were looking at her strangely. Mrs Malik sat her down and fetched her water. She fanned her, told her all would be well, and wiped her cheek as Asha began to cry.

'It's all the shock,' explained Mataji. 'And it's so hot.' She pointed at the window Pappaji had forbidden her from opening. 'You never know who's watching,' he had said.

'We can't breathe, we can't leave,' Mataji said. 'Outside, they're getting ready to celebrate Independence, and we're left to die.'

81

Mrs Malik nodded. 'I'm telling you,' she said. 'I almost preferred it when we were subjugated. At least there wasn't this indignity.'

Patriotism was at its height in India. People were beginning to think of themselves as masters of their own destiny. Heads were held high, shoulders pulled smartly back. Sweets were distributed in the street, people smiled at strangers. But here Mataji was, agreeing with Mrs Malik. Asha looked across at the daughter, a tall, gangly girl called Roopa, who raised an eyebrow in amusement.

Mrs Malik was back to focussing on Asha. '*Hai* Shiela,' she said to Mataji. 'What a beauty your daughter is!' Asha was examined from head to toe. Mrs Malik looked rapturously at her face, sighed as she touched her cheek. 'What flawless skin.'

Asha turned away in embarrassment. She touched her hand to her face, thought of the last time her skin had broken out. She *had* been in good looks recently. Even Mataji had commented on it. 'You're glowing,' she had said grudgingly.

'Thank God I don't have a son,' Mrs Malik was saying, 'Or else he would have spirited your daughter away!'

'Ma!' said Roopa.

They thought then of the girls they had known; neighbours, acquaintances, school friends, who were lost to them forever. Some were abducted, others ravaged and left for dead, still others murdered as their families cowered in the background.

'*Arre*, what have I said?' countered Mrs Malik. 'Their daughter is beautiful, that's it.'

'*Haan, behenji*,' hurried Mataji. 'I understand, sister.'

'See,' Mrs Malik exulted. 'Asha's mother understands.'

12

Pappaji and Savan returned empty-handed.

It was Firoze who shepherded them in. 'I found them outside the house,' and as Mataji held her hands out, Pappaji shook his head silently. His hair was matted with dirt, his shirt was creased and stained, but he did not seem to be aware of his appearance. He just stood by the doorway shaking his head.

'Sit down, *Bhai Sahib*,' Mrs Malik said. 'You've had a shock. Tell me, is it bad outside?'

They sat him down and gave him water. New clothes were found for him and Savan, and it was the latter who supplied the details of their adventure. The entire street had been razed. The mob had passed by in the early evening applying red paint on the doorways of all the Hindu homes, and as night-time fell, they came out again to burn and loot.

'They all knew,' said Firoze. 'Even that damned Riaz knew that the street would be destroyed in the night. That's why he had the guts to make his move.'

They looked at Asha as she came to sit beside her father. She stroked his hair, and as he inclined his head to her touch, she asked, 'Is there nothing left?'

He didn't reply.

'Speak please, Pappaji.'

'Nothing,' said Savan. He sat down next to Asha and Pappaji. 'The banyan has been felled. It's been wrenched straight out by the roots. There's a hole in the ground now, as big as . . .' He extended his hands in demonstration. He looked out at the room, then at the shuttered window that hid the street from view. 'No, no,' he insisted, 'It's bigger. Its absence is larger than the tree ever was.'

'*Bus*,' said Mrs Malik. '*Beta*, it doesn't do to think about these things.'

'All the houses are rubble. Nothing is left.' He shook as he spoke, and his hands, long-fingered and animated in speech, trembled. 'I went in to see what I could recover, and there was nothing left. There were no rooms, nothing. Mataji!' A tear fell down his cheek, and at this sign of emotion in the boy, they all began to cry. Mataji was quickly cocooned by the Malik women, and Asha clung to her father. Pappaji sobbed soundlessly, his chest heaving.

'Mataji,' Savan was crying, 'There was a body there.'

'A body, child?'

'I don't know whose it was,' he said. 'It was too burnt . . .'

'But the servants,' pointed out Mataji crossly. 'They'd all left.'

'I know . . .'

'We'd locked the house . . .'

'Mataji, I couldn't see whose body it was.'

The crying erupted again. Savan tried to give details, to worry out who he had found, to try and remember which part of the house it was in and Firoze came towards him. He put his arms around the boy and patted him roughly. 'Come now,' he said. 'We can't think like this.'

'There were bodies everywhere,' continued Savan. 'On the streets, in doorways. Children, women, men.'

'Enough,' said Firoze. 'Please, Savan, there's no point upsetting the others.'

'Part of me wanted to stop and examine. They didn't look real, so many bodies.'

'Think of your mother. Think of your sis . . .'

Savan spoke over him, his voice tremulous. To Asha it was as if her little brother was trying to work through a problem. It was how she would find him in his room as the evening closed in, too engrossed in his studies to worry about the fading light. She shut her eyes, trying not to think of their house. 'So many people who looked like they'd died screaming,' Savan said. 'It was like a painting, a painting of a massacre.'

'*Bus,* Savan,' said Firoze.

'Like a Mughal miniature,' expanded Savan. He brought his thumb and index finger together in a pincer movement to indicate a tiny painting. 'Everything was so bright. It wasn't real.'

'Savan . . .'

'It just wasn't real.'

Mataji was crying louder, and Mrs Malik joined readily in the orgy of grief. 'Those Muslims,' she said. 'Those savages.'

Firoze gave no indication of having heard the remark. He slid across to where Pappaji sat, and fetched him a fresh glass of water. 'Is there anything else I can get you, Sir?' he asked. 'Is there anything that will make you more comfortable?'

Pappaji didn't move.

'Speak, Pappaji!' Asha cried. 'Please,' and as the rest of the room took Mataji to one side to care for her, she

85

reached her hand across and squeezed his. 'Pappaji,' she sobbed, 'Speak, speak! You must speak.'

Pappaji shook his head. He looked at Firoze bending down at his feet, and put his hand on the younger man's head. He didn't say a word, and Asha couldn't be sure if Pappaji's gesture carried a deeper meaning. They exchanged a quick glance, Firoze and Asha, and despite the horror of the past day – despite the attack and the move and Pappaji's silence – they smiled. She shut her eyes, thinking of her burgeoning womb. She thought of the noise of the wedding, of the *shamiana* set up on their future cricket pitch. A door opened downstairs, and a stray snatch of song reached them. 'You follow me, you follow me . . .' She looked briefly back at Firoze. He was still crouched at Pappaji's feet, but his eyes were fixed on her.

'You'll speak, won't you, Pappaji?' Savan asked again. Pappaji refused to budge. He refused to lift his hands from Firoze's head, but there was no life in his eyes, no warmth in his face. There were no words on his lips.

13

They had to move. Suhanpur was no longer safe, and while the adults worked out their plans, Firoze took the girls to Nargis' room.

It had only been a few hours since she had last been out of the room. She had slept much of the previous night with Nargis, had sung smutty wedding songs a little while back. Now she paused by a window in the corridor, trying to make out her house. There was nothing she recognised, no neat row of whitewashed houses, no proud, balconied home mirroring the one she was sheltering in. Then she saw the remains of her house. It was rubble now, all broken plaster and ground brick. Branches poked out of the wreckage, but nothing was recognisable. She couldn't see any furniture, couldn't see a single book or stick or mother-of-pearl inlaid comb, couldn't see a single kitchen utensil. And then she saw the remains of the uprooted banyan tree. 'It will destroy all our homes,' she had heard the Principal say to Pappaji. He had come in one evening to enlist Pappaji's support in having the tree torn down. 'It keeps spreading,' he had argued. 'Our foundations are compromised.'

There was no tree now, no threatening, spreading branches taking root. It was replaced by a hole, a lack of presence so profound that it consumed her vision. It filled her, this loss, it led her to utter a cry so primal that Firoze turned to her at once. He held his hand to her shoulder, allowing himself to lean close. '*Bus*,' he said softly. 'Don't look out.' Then he was holding her, helping her turn towards Nargis' room. His hand remained on the small of her back as they walked, and though she was soon steady, he didn't let go. He didn't look at her or attempt to initiate conversation, but he didn't let go. '*Bhai Sahib*,' Roopa was saying. 'Are we definitely going then? And leaving today?'

'Yes,' Firoze answered. His hand tensed against Asha's back 'But it's only for a bit. In fact, I'm not certain there's any need for it at all.' He laughed, a high-pitched sound new to Asha, and she knew then that he was afraid too. 'I'll take you myself – to Amritsar or Delhi or as far as I have to. Amritsar will remain in India, I'm certain of it. But there's no need for the move, and of course you'll all be back once things have settled down. This is your home.' She thought of the first time they had been alone in Nargis' room. Nargis had pretended to hear Ammi calling and had sped away before Asha could call her back. And so they had stood, Asha and Firoze, at opposite ends of her bed. 'I'll show you the rest of the house one day,' Firoze had said. 'The sooner you're familiar with your new home, the better.' Asha had thought of the endless games of hide-and-seek she had grown up playing in the house. She knew each corridor, she knew each forgotten, dust-filled cupboard. But this was a new, tantalising discovery she had been promised, and she had looked away, uncertain how to respond. It had still been early in their courtship. Their hands hadn't yet brushed together, she hadn't grown familiar with the contours of his face. 'This is your home,' and she had looked away in delighted confusion.

88

They were at Nargis' door. Firoze knocked, Nargis answered, and they were quickly rushed in.

Firoze was about to go back into the corridor, when Asha whispered to him, 'Did you know?'

He looked at her, then at the room beyond. Nargis was with Roopa, making her comfortable. 'Know what?' he asked.

'About last night,' she said. He looked surprised at her question, so she added, 'About the attacks on the Hindus.'

'Of course not,' he hissed. He came closer to her. His breath was on her again, his eyes on hers. She noticed the glint of brown in his hair, the curl in his lip. 'I knew there was trouble to come, that's why I made sure I was at your house all day yesterday. There wasn't much work to do, and your Pappaji was surprised that I had come over this close to the wedding. But it was all I could do to try and make sure you were safe. I promise you I didn't know. I wanted Pakistan, of course I did, but this . . .' He gestured towards the street, his voice rose, and the two girls looked their way. 'I promise I didn't know,' he whispered. Firoze turned and went out, closing the door, but as he walked away, Asha heard him say, 'Of course I didn't know.'

It was instantly clear that Roopa had inherited her mother's genius for directness. She was in school with Asha and Nargis, and was soon pronouncing judgement on their classmates.

'Such an ugly nose-pin,' Roopa laughed about a hapless acquaintance. She touched her own broad nose. 'Now who will marry her?'

Nargis shrugged and Asha looked away. Neither was

in any mood for conversation, but Roopa hadn't noticed. 'And Rashmi?' she asked. 'Where is she now?'

'In Ambala,' answered Asha softly. 'They left last month.'

'And Sita?'

'They don't know,' said Nargis. There were many, too numerous to count, who had left. Some had announced plans for travel, others had stopped being allowed out by nervous parents, and others still – the unenviable few – now formed an infinitesimal part of the statistics of the missing or martyred.

Roopa seamlessly shifted gear. 'And why do I never see you both on the way to school?'

Here the girls smiled. Both thought of the gnarled Sheesham stump on the banks of the Ravi. They looked towards the corridor, and for an instant, they were bound together in their secret knowledge. She was just a breath away, Nargis. She just had to lean across, find the words to explain the events that separated them. 'I'm carrying your brother's child,' she thought, and as Nargis looked at her, she smiled and imagined herself safe in their shared understanding. This was enough for now. This would have to do.

'Well?' asked Roopa. 'Why don't I ever see you?'

'*Arre*,' explained Nargis. 'It's just us trying to get away from Asha's grasshopper of a brother.'

The two friends giggled. Nargis said, 'He never lets us talk. It's long division and general knowledge all the way to school.'

'Thank God then,' sighed Roopa, 'that I have no brother.'

'Join us,' offered Nargis impetuously. 'Once school restarts.'

Asha looked up, and Nargis added uncertainly. 'And once you're back.'

'Once we're back,' echoed Roopa softly.

Nargis said to her friend, 'You'll be back within the month.'

'I just wish I didn't have to miss your wedding . . .'

'Pah,' sniffed Nargis. 'That's just one event.' She walked to her dressing-table and retrieved a large velvet pouch. A pair of gold *balis* was removed from its warm embrace. These were handed over to Asha.

'Nargis,' protested the girl. 'How can I accept these?'

'Take them,' said Nargis, and as her friend continued to refuse, she began to cry. 'Can't I even give you a gift?'

'But Nargis,' said Asha. She pretended to smile. 'Your mother-in-law gave you these.'

'Just think it through,' Roopa counselled. 'She'll want to see them on you.'

'*Arre*, who's giving them to her forever?' replied Nargis petulantly. 'Return them to me once you're back.' The *balis* were unfastened and carefully placed on Asha's ears.

'I can't carry them with me,' said Asha. 'There will be thieves or worse.' Tears flowed down Nargis' cheeks, her mouth was set in a frown, like a child bent on a treat, and Asha finally relented. Smiling, she turned to the mirror. Tiny golden lights flickered on her skin. Nargis lifted Asha's *dupatta* and wrapped it around her head. She took some kohl powder from her lower lid, as Asha had done all those weeks ago, and patted it behind her friend's ear to ward off the evil eye.

'You'll be married next,' Roopa predicted.

'You're not getting married without me, do you understand?' said Nargis tearfully. 'Asha, promise me you'll return here for your wedding.'

Asha didn't reply but the other girls imbued her silence with their own meaning, and both were swiftly on her with whistles and wedding songs. Roopa had a clear, tuneful voice, and she launched into the previous year's hit song. '*Love is young . . .*'

Nargis and Asha looked at each other.

'*The world is beautiful . . .*'

'No, Roopa . . .'

'*My heart's looted the treasure of happiness . . .*'

'No,' said Nargis forcefully, and Roopa trailed off in surprise. She looked at Nargis, and then at a sorrowful Asha. 'My voice isn't that bad, is it?' she joked.

'*Nahi*,' smiled Nargis, though her voice grew choked. 'I'll sing that song myself,' she said, 'But I'll sing it next at Asha's wedding.'

The day seemed endless. The noise of the street grew louder, and all three were conscious that as the day drew to a close, Suhanpur would be a foreign land to two of them. They longed for the day to last as they ached for its end. They ached for rest, for sleep. They ached for peace.

When Firoze and Savan knocked on the door some hours later – as a spent sun threw out a final, burning salvo through Nargis' shutters – they cried, especially the two childhood friends. They wept and swore to wait for the other, but their grief was catharsis. This – this heartbreaking move – this at any rate was better than their wait had been.

14

The *tonga* cart jolted hard and came to a stop. A wave of muted panic rose from the passengers. Some sighed their frustration, some were roused from a restless sleep, others – older, in painful consciousness of what lay in wait – held in a mounting hysteria at the back of their throats. The horse, dark as the night they were travelling in, snorted through steaming nostrils before pacing back. The cart lurched to one side, the crowd jostling along with it.

Asha felt a fresh wave of nausea well up. 'No,' she prayed silently. 'Please no. Not here.'

She needn't have fretted. Someone from further up the packed cart – Roopa perhaps, or her mother – retched and leaned noisily over the side. A new wave of frustration rose, and now people began to voice their irritation. Firoze stood up. He held his hand high, urging restraint. 'Brothers,' he said. 'You don't know where they are lying in wait. We must be silent.'

'Why have we stopped then?' asked Mrs Malik.

The back – filled largely as it was with Asha's family – started complaining about the halt. Firoze counselled calm – too late for frayed nerves – and the debate looked like turning lively when he jumped off his perch. All fell silent at once, watching anxiously as he bent to the road to inspect the obstacle.

'*Yah Khuda*,' he invoked. 'They've placed a huge boulder on the road. There's another further ahead. They must be nearby.'

They worked quickly. Pappaji and Savan joined Firoze and together they set to moving the rocks to the side of the road. The cart had become still, and now the night seemed to heave with noise. A cricket chirped in the distance, and the crowd shrivelled in their fear. Was that the sound of gunfire? Savan stepped on a twig, and all turned towards the night – was this them, was this the Muslim butchers? The wind appeared louder than normal, more protective of their would-be killers, the dark more absolute. The men seemed to work loudly, too loudly; they heard them sigh and grunt. And yet they didn't dare speak, they scarcely dared breathe.

Asha barely noticed the others in the cart. She held her stomach, to still its churning. She began to feel a warmth between her thighs, a spreading clammy wetness. Slowly her hand felt under her long *kameez* shirt, softly she lifted it back up to under her nose. Even this was full of danger. The cart was quiet, and she was scared of attracting attention. For a moment she didn't register the smell, and then, as her mother darted a furtive look in her direction, she breathed it again. It was the same as her monthly blood. Her eyes clamped shut, she shivered into the heat of the night. She held tightly onto the *balis* she had placed inside her fist. She fingered them fervently, turning them like so many rosary beads as she whispered her desperate prayer. '*Bhagwanji*, please,' she said. 'Please, please,' but her words disappeared into the air.

Mataji looked her way again and squeezed her shoulder. 'Don't worry, *Beta*,' Asha heard her whisper.

'*Bhagwanji* will take care of us. We'll be in India soon.'

The blood had begun to trickle down her starched cotton *salwar*, and once more she tried to will herself to stay calm. It was nothing. These things happened. She had bled before. She looked at her mother, wondering what she had heard and how much she had guessed, but the clouds had moved and the dark had too complete a hold of her. A soft, slow teal fell down her cheeks and through to the pooling wet in her *salwar*, and as she felt its warmth diffuse into her thigh, she couldn't be certain if she cried from sadness or relief.

15

It was daybreak, and independent India's first glittering dawn when they reached the bus stop. It was absolutely still. There was no noise from the one solitary hut in the distance, and mercifully, no sign of the violence that had so regularly punctuated their travel. A flock of birds stirred in the tree nearest them, and they smiled to hear their noise fill the air. They were quiet in the *tonga* for a moment. No one moved, no one spoke. Then Mataji and Mrs Malik bowed to the sun, giving thanks for their safe delivery. 'We're nearly there,' they repeated to each other. 'Another few miles and we're in India.'

Firoze jumped off his perch and helped the passengers down. He held each one by the waist to steady them. This was it, their one last chance for a word, for a lingering look that wouldn't be monitored, but Asha was too frightened for eye contact. Her clothes were drenched now, her *salwar* stiff from the drying blood. She felt her legs wet as she moved. She wrapped her *dupatta* protectively around herself, even though the morning's chill was fast dissipating. He would notice, she knew, he would feel her back to be damp, he would sense that something was amiss. He would know, surely he would know their loss. She didn't look at him, didn't dare to, and as he reached out towards her, she looked away and stumbled. Firoze reached out to catch her, as did Pappaji, and then she was on solid ground. The moment had passed, and Firoze turned instead to Mataji to help her down.

They were escorted to the bus stop. The ground was wet from the monsoon and several times they nearly slipped into potholes. They were all uncomfortable, all tired and dirty and afraid, but they didn't speak. They made their way in a solemn single file, and no one, not even the voluminous matrons, dared to give voice to their feelings. Firoze accompanied them, made sure they were safely seated. He brought out a stack of potato pancakes wrapped in cloth. 'Ammi sent these,' he said, and now the women began to weep silently. 'You go back,' said Mataji to Firoze, but he shook his head.

'Beta,' said Mrs Malik. 'You must go.' There were Hindu miscreants as well as Muslim ones, and Firoze was safer back at home. Besides, the horse, their brave saviour, was sure to be hungry and in need of his home. The horse whinnied, Mataji and Mrs Malik urged his return, and Firoze finally agreed. He looked towards the rest of the group. Savan came forward, met the older boy in a roughish hug. 'Don't get so emotional,' Firoze scolded. 'You'll be back before you know it.'

They were all crying now, the Maliks, Mataji, Savan and Asha. Firoze looked at Asha, then as she hid her face in her *dupatta*, he moved on to Pappaji. The older man put his hand on Firoze's head in benediction once more, and now Firoze succumbed to his grief. 'You'll be back,' he repeated hoarsely. 'Of course you will. Who else will teach me about the law?'

'It's all yours now,' said Pappaji. They were the first

words he'd spoken since he'd been outside to see the
ruins of his house, and they all looked at him. He was
older than he had seemed in the benevolent light of the
inspector's house. His hair had greyed, lines marked his
face. He smiled, or attempted a smile, but it seemed that
cheer was beyond him. 'Take care of it.'

'You'll be back,' Firoze said again, but Pappaji just
removed his hand from the younger man's head. 'You'll be
back,' he repeated, 'Before the year is out you'll be back.'

'*Chalo*,' urged Mrs Malik. 'Please Firoze, it isn't safe
for you either.'

Asha missed her *balis* the minute he was out of view.
She aired out her *kameez*, unfurled her *dupatta* in the
air. She let loose a clump of wet earth, and as they all
turned to look at her – the Maliks, Mataji, Pappaji and
Savan – she bent to the ground and began to rake the
earth for any trace of her lost earrings.

'What is it?' asked Mataji.

'My *balis*,' said Asha. She glanced at her mother, then
began to search the ground again. The earth was wet,
her nails soon full of mud, but she went on searching,
crawling towards the *tonga* cart, like an ungainly infant,
but there was no tell-tale twinkle of gold to give her hope.

Mataji stormed up to her. Asha was wet through, and
she was briefly grateful that her bloody *salwar* was no
longer so conspicuous. 'What are you doing?' Mataji
hissed. She let go of the girl. 'You're a mess!' she said.
She pointed at Asha's mud-splattered slippers. 'What are
you thinking?'

Asha began to cry. 'My *balis*,' she sobbed, lowering
herself onto the ground again to continue her frantic,
hopeless search.

'*Beta*,' said her mother. She bent to where Asha knelt and put a hand on her back. She promised Asha a new pair of *balis* when they got to Delhi, but Asha was hysterical. 'Nargis gave them to me,' she wept, and in the end, Mataji gave in.

'Go,' she scolded. 'Go get those damned *balis* of yours. But don't wander far or some savage will carry you off.'

Asha ran. She heard the rearing of wheels in the distance, heard the horse whinny, and was sure she had missed Firoze. She turned the corner, reached the clearing, and he was still there.

He looked up as she walked towards him, her heart suddenly light, and it was as if the horror of the past few months hadn't taken place. It wasn't the fifteenth of August and she wasn't in a hostile land. Firoze hadn't turned silent. She hadn't lost their child, she hadn't lost her dearest friend's only keepsake. The sun still glinted brown on his head, he rose as she reached him and smiled, his generous, crease-eyed smile of old. Then he remembered where they were, what they had been through, and he said, 'Please, Asha.' He indicated the little mud hut in the distance, said, 'Please, Asha, let's not do this.'

Her voice wavered. 'Don't you want to say goodbye?'

'No,' he said.

Asha was in tears. She looked down at her soiled clothes, at her sodden slippers, and then she trembled with anger. There was no danger of him suspecting anything. He didn't even want to talk to her. 'Why this silence?' she asked. He looked at her, lifting his finger to his lips in warning, and she shook her head. A paranoid tone crept into her voice, 'You changed the minute we . . .'

She paused, and as he looked at her uncomprehend-ingly, she added, 'You know, after we,' and in some confusion, 'you know, that morning, when you took me out of school . . .'

He smiled then, leaned forward and squeezed her hand. He brought it to his lips and let it rest there. 'My Asha,' he said. 'I made a promise to your Pappaji. I spoke to him of our marriage, and he made me promise not to talk to you until after the issue of Partition was resolved. I didn't want to go against his wishes.'

'And what of mine?' she asked.

'Don't fight,' he said. 'Please, not now.'

They remained as they were for a brief, precious moment. The sun shone lustily. She was still dirty, still filthy from her blood, but now she didn't feel any discomfort. Her eyes grew heavy in the brilliant light, and she found herself leaning towards him. She was full of his touch, of his hand warm on hers, and everything else – India, Pakistan, her meddling Pappaji, the *balis* – everything else felt distant and unimportant. This was all that mattered, she and Firoze and the bright, smiling sun above them.

She heard a noise, and turned to see Savan striding towards them. She looked at Firoze, saw him pause. 'Come with me,' he whispered. 'Be my wife,' but she shook her head.

'I'll talk to Pappaji again . . .'

'No,' she said, 'We'll be back before the year is out.' Still he looked uncertain. 'Asha,' he began, but the foot-steps grew nearer, and Asha turned a pleading face to him. 'Please,' she said. 'Just go.' He lifted her hand to his mouth, and she shivered as he brushed against her skin. Savan drew nearer. 'Go,' she said, and he picked up the reins of his *tonga* and was off.

16

'I told you,' said Mataji as she returned. 'I told you the *balis* will be somewhere in Suhanpur. Probably on Nargis' dressing table.'

The party laughed at the thought, and it seemed mirth was needed, for Mrs Malik launched into a joke. When it ended, they laughed loudly, more generously perhaps than the joke itself warranted, and Mrs Malik was soon encouraged by her success to launch into another.

Her hands rose in illustration, a thick bangle jangled on her arm. It cast a glow on her clothes, then on the earth, and for a while, Asha was mesmerised by its play of light. She was hot now, and heavy in her clothes. She watched her companions, saw them smile, saw them frown as they worried out a riddle Mrs Malik threw at them.

Pappaji sat a little way away from the rest of the group, and she couldn't be certain if he listened to Mrs Malik. He didn't look up, didn't smile. He huddled instead against the shelter, head bowed, shoulders slumped. Then he looked up and saw his daughter watching him. He smiled slightly, patting the empty seat by his side, but she walked instead to where her mother sat. He bowed his head again, but she was in no mood for tenderness. She wasn't going to talk to him, not yet, not after the misery he had caused her.

Mrs Malik's joke was soon over, and as silence returned to the party, the mood turned sombre.

'If we are parted,' said Mataji. The Maliks tutted, and Mrs Malik promised to stay by Mataji's side. 'I'll be your shadow,' she said, 'I'll be your tail,' but Mataji was not to be distracted. 'If we are parted, I have some money saved up with Om Sharma.'

'Who?'

'Om Sharma, you know, whose family owned the printing press?' The materialistic matron in Mataji reasserted herself, and she added, 'And also the sweet shop and the book shop.' Mrs Malik nodded in awe, and she added, 'They left it all behind to go to Delhi.' Mataji looked up at the heavens, sighed. A philosophical aside followed on the transience of worldly possessions, and then she carried on, 'He took across some jewellery for me. If you get lost, look for me in his house.'

Mrs Malik protested again. They weren't going to get lost; they weren't going to need to be reunited, but Mataji was firm. An address was given, a house number in a new Lutyens enclave no one had heard of, and though the Maliks shrugged, they were made to write down the address. 'And you two too,' said Mataji, turning to her children. 'The Maliks aren't the only ones who can get lost.' She lifted up each child's tunic sleeve, and just below their shoulders, she put down Om's address with the last ink of Pappaji's fading pen.

They waited. Their shadows grew longer, the clouds threatened rain, but the sun raged on. Every few minutes one of the women repeated their question, 'When will the damned bus come?' and it fell on the trembling young Savan to assuage their worries. 'Don't worry,' he told his mother, then jumped as a new shadow was cast in the distance. He kept a watch for buses, for saviours and traitors, and he found he could never stay still for long.

Asha felt her *salwar* grow increasingly uncomfortable. Her thighs stuck together. The day grew more humid, and they all grew a little impatient. Mataji snapped at her for moving too much, Savan pushed when she fidgeted, and she grew increasingly conscious. The smell rose, she was sure. Her clothes were dark – which added to her discomfort in the heat – but she wasn't convinced they provided sufficient disguise. The blood had stained surely, and as she shifted again and saw her mother look at her strangely, she whispered to her, 'Mataji, my clothes.'

'*Hai Ram*, what is the matter now?'

Mataji looked stern as she explained her predicament. 'Blood?' she asked. Asha imagined her mother working out her trouble. She blushed scarlet with shame, explaining her period had come early. Mataji's voice rose, and Asha knew her truth remained undiscovered. She invoked God and scolded her daughter for travelling without supplies. 'And you only have one spare set of clothes. What will happen if you soil these?'

Mrs Malik was consulted. It emerged that Roopa had some spare cotton, and both girls made their way over to the clearing where Firoze had stopped the *tonga*. Asha cleaned up as best as she could manage. There was no water, and she dared not go to the hut for help, so she remained feeling unclean. She was petrified the bleeding would resume. She knew she had stained the cart, she knew she had bled more than she normally shed in a day, but she wasn't sure if there was more to come.

103

'Hurry up,' Roopa was saying. 'It's not safe. They'll know us for Hindus at once.'

'I wonder,' said Asha, and the other girl laughed at her naiveté.

'Of course not,' she jeered. 'Muslim girls would be out and about at this hour, wouldn't they? They'd be seen around bus stops heading towards India, wouldn't they?' Asha's face fell, and Roopa added more gently, 'A million things give away our faith, Asha.' She turned her hand to reveal the name of the God Ram tattooed on her wrist. 'I bet you'll have something similar.' She turned Asha's hand and fingered the symbol Om.

Asha remembered the stab of Riaz's touch, she remembered his fascination with her tattoo. She straightened her *kameez*, listening for noise. There it was again, another crack in the air. 'All right,' she said, and the two prepared to return to the bus shelter.

They were a turn away from their families when they heard the noise.

'Pappaji!' cried Asha, but there was no answer. She heard it again, a loud clap of thunder. It was safe, of course it was. She had been worried about nothing, had been as restless as Savan. She took a step forward, then as she heard it again, that intangible dread, that unfamiliar step, she turned to look at Roopa.

The older girl forced her down into a crouch. They remained hidden, but they heard everything. Another step, another crack, then *lathi* sticks on the soil. Mataji cried out first. She mistook the noise for the girls and began to scold them for having taken so long, and then, as she saw her mistake, Asha heard the terror in her cry. There were other voices: Savan, serious and reasoned,

Mrs Malik panicking. They heard pleading, begging, screaming, the noises all blending into each other, then the systematic, unrelenting blows of wood against bone.

Asha rose to go to her family.

She would be able to help.

She would provide a distraction, she would run to the hut for help, but as the noise continued, the rhythm of the slaughter, she found herself unable to move. Her feet were paralysed, and at the base of her throat, she felt the strangled choking of a scream. She sank back down. It was beginning to rain now. The air grew fuller for a moment, then the temperature dropped. They heard feverish laughter, and then the beat of footsteps charging off into the distance.

17

They remained hidden for what seemed an age. Asha rose a dozen times, and each time she was sure she heard a noise, a return of the rain, the slap of a *lathi*, and Roopa pulled her back down.

'They've gone,' she told the older girl. 'We must go to them.' She was sure she heard breathing. She was sure she heard the wheezing of Savan's monsoon cold, then as Roopa shook her head, she was certain it was the wind, or the panting of exhausted killers. It was too quiet for hope, and then too loud for safety.

They remained where they lay, a step away from slaughter, until the rain died down. The sun fell lower in the sky, like a stricken bird, and the air was suddenly silent.

Finally Roopa let them move. They tiptoed towards the shelter, alert for any noise. The soil was wet, the morning's potholes were back, and Asha lost her footing more than once. The shadows grew around the bus stop. Suddenly they were unsure. Had the shelter been this high before? And had there been a tarpaulin awning or a metal roof? Had the shadow looked like it did now? They moved tentatively, suspicious of each unfamiliar sound. They were petrified of what they would see when they reached the shelter. They didn't speak to each other.

Asha saw *salwar kameezes* trailing in the mud, knew the wearers were women, but any further knowledge was impossible. She was too far away, and for a moment, she ached to go back to the shelter, to smooth out limbs and torn clothes, to restore some peace to the bodies of those she had loved. She remembered Savan saying the Suhanpur massacre looked like a painting. She had thought him melodramatic, but now, as she struggled to identify a limb or a feature, now she understood.

She heard Roopa call out to her. 'Asha,' she cried, 'Asha, please!' Her voice grew dimmer, and as she turned to run, the man lunged forward and took hold of her by the hand.

'Now, my nymph, my queen,' he said, 'No escape for you.'

How distant it all felt, Firoze, Nargis, her wedding, her gift of the *balis*. How stupid she had been in the morning, scrambling about in the dirt for the earrings. They should have been on the lookout instead, they should have saved themselves from this monster.

He pulled her round to face him, lifted her so she was looking him in the eye. 'Yes,' he was saying, 'I have plans for you.'

'Please,' she said. 'Please, just let me go,' and as he smiled his languid smile, she cried, 'Don't you understand I'm not Hindu?'

Again he laughed. His was a beautiful face, all inflection and warm tone, but his eyes were cold as he studied her. 'Please,' she tried again, then raised her head suddenly and spat at him. He let go of her in his surprise, and she quickly scrambled to her feet. She could no longer hear Roopa now, but she hurried in the direction her friend had run.

108

He was soon after her. She ran as fast as she could, but she was no match for his speed. Within moments he was with her, laughing as if it were all a game. He grabbed her hand and dragged her back to the shelter.

'Now, now,' he said cheerfully. 'Didn't I say you weren't to run away?'

She thought of her bag in the shelter. 'I have money,' she said desperately, pointing to where her family lay, and as he laughed, she added, 'I'll give you all I have, just let me go.'

He didn't reply but once more turned her to face him, and now he brought her wrist up. He spotted the Om tattoo, and his smile broadened. 'Not Hindu?' he purred, and as she squirmed and tried to free herself, he said comfortingly, 'Don't worry about that, my queen. It doesn't matter.'

He dug into the pocket of his tunic with his free hand. 'We can set this right in a second.'

He brought out a pocket knife. The blade was dull as an extinguished *diya*, and caked thick with blood.

'No,' she found herself begging, 'Please, please no,' and as he dug a thick, deep line into her flesh, she found the earth closing in on her again. It grew dark, burning dark, darker than the falling sun, darker than the bleakest, most enduring night.

II

1

She heard a sigh, she felt the caress of the breeze, as
tender as a lover, as tender as Firoze that distant,
sun-filled morning. She moved an inch, and her head
drummed with thunder. *Dham-dham*, she heard, *Dham-
dham-dharak*, and then the sound of a wedding song.
'*You follow me, you follow me . . .*' She smiled drowsily.

'Nargis,' she whispered.

The song picked up in tempo, and now a *dholak* drum
beat in time to the music. '*You follow me, you follow
me . . .*'

She needn't have worried. All was well. She was back
in Suhanpur, back in time for her friend's wedding.

All was well, all was well again.

She tried to sit up, and there it was again, the unrelenting
march of thunder pounding in her head.

'Lie down, please, child.'

The noise grew louder, and she struggled to place the
voice. Was it Mataji? Perhaps it was Nargis' mother.
Perhaps she was in Suhanpur, and married to Firoze.
Maybe she was about to give birth. That would explain
the pain. Her eyes opened a little and a blurred room
swam in front of her. She tried to move her hand to her
belly, but found she wasn't equal to the effort.

113

'*Bus*,' said the voice. 'That's it, child. Don't strain yourself.' Then it faded again, the voice, the room, the pain.

When Asha next woke, someone was massaging her. She kept her eyes shut for a while, luxuriating in the touch, in the gentle rubbing of her forehead, her hands, her wrist. A little warm oil was applied to her skin, and as its fragrance wafted towards her, she inhaled deeply. There was a floral note, jasmine perhaps, a smell so heady and reminiscent of night-time escapades on the inspector's rooftop that she smiled.

'*Beta*? Child, can you hear me?'

She opened her eyes. The room swam around her, but the pain had eased, and slowly the person in front of her came into focus. It was a woman, middle-aged or more. Her skin was dewy, her face glowing with contentment and with the orange *dupatta* she wrapped around her. She nodded at Asha cheerfully. Her smile seemed to be offered unconditionally, without judgement, and all at once Asha remembered. There was to be no Suhanpur for her; no family or Firoze or Nargis. There was to be no baby. She felt her wrist being turned, felt a sharp burst of pain where her tattoo had been.

Suddenly the events at the bus stop came into focus. Her inability to move, to shout out for help. Roopa running fast, and that beautiful, hateful Pathan moving to hide the massacre from view. Her darting to catch a glimpse, not being able to identify anything – glasses, watch, a head heavy with grey. Her stomach had turned, and she had ached to run to her family, but her host had prevented her. And then her new clothes filing with her child's blood, Firoze's touch still warm on her skin, and the loathsome Pathan stalking forward, smiling and offering her the world. Her wrist being turned over, her tattoo visible, the knife blade caked with her family's blood. Asha's head reeled. She looked down. It was still there, the Om on her skin, but over it – as if staking greater claim – was a thin, jagged red line. The wound was livid, the flesh around it raw and tender. The room swam before her again, she felt her vision turn dark, felt her eyes grow heavy. The woman continued with her ministrations, slowly and firmly moving up her arm, and Asha forced her eyes open.

The lady cupped a fresh supply of oil onto her palm before massaging it onto Asha's skin. She worked with a thorough, unhurried motion, massaging her elbow, then the soft inside of her arms. Asha stared at her, trying to identify tell-tale features. She tried to remember what the Afghan had looked like that morning. Tall, fair, with angular features, but this woman – of the right age to be his mother – didn't resemble him in the slightest. Her skin was darker, earthier; her features plump with age and peace.

Who was she then – friend or enemy - and where were they? Was this India or Pakistan? Would she even be able to look out of the window and tell the difference? Where was Roopa, and what had become of her?

The woman raised the sleeve of Asha's tunic and began massaging her upper arm. She began to hum the wedding song Asha had heard before. 'Sorry, child,' she said. 'It was my daughter's wedding the week before, and I can't get the song out of my head.' She used the Punjabi word for daughter, and Asha ached to ask which country that placed them in. Punjab had been rent in two. The woman's *dupatta* was wrapped tight around her

115

head; she had cupped her hand in the Muslim manner of giving thanks when Asha had opened her eyes, but still she couldn't be sure.

She was the same age as Mataji. She had a smooth, round face, and soft, doughy circles under her eyes. Her hair was beginning to show white, and Asha said, 'You must be the same age as my Mataji.'

'Then you must call me Ammi.'

She lowered her eyes. Firoze's mother was to have been called by that name. Ammi opened her mouth to sing, and Asha asked, 'Where am I?'

The woman stopped singing and asked kindly. 'Do you remember anything, child?'

Asha didn't answer. She met the older woman's gaze with a blank look. 'Maulvi Sahib,' Ammi began. She paused, qualifying her words, 'My husband, the Maulvi, had heard some disturbance out by the bus stop. He picked up a *lathi* stick, called our son, and together they walked down to the shelter.' Ammi began to massage her again. Her hands worked on the girl's elbow, smoothing oil over the skin, rubbing it in gently in slowly growing circles. Her hands trembled, and Asha felt oil spill on the bed. 'That wastrel,' she said fiercely. 'That coward. One sight of a *lathi*, and off he ran.' She smoothed more oil up Asha's arm. 'They're all the same, these heroes, these guardians of Pakistan.'

'My family,' said Asha. She attempted to rise, but sank back in pain. She pointed out of the window, though she wasn't sure which direction they faced. 'My parents,' she said. 'My brother. They . . .'

'Child . . .'

'And Roopa,' she said, and as Ammi looked blank, she added, 'My friend. She ran to get help.'

116

'Child,' said Ammi tenderly. 'We never saw anyone else.'

She was lost then to her, Roopa, like all the others she had known. Pappaji, Mataji, Savan, Firoze, Nargis, Chotu, her unborn child, Mrs Sodhi even, and Roopa too now, erased from her life like her school slate washed clean. Asha lifted her hand and pointed again in the direction of the window. Tears fell, but she paid them no attention. Ammi leant forward to wipe her face, and she shook her head angrily. 'My family,' she repeated, 'My parents, my brother . . .'

Ammi placed her arms around Asha.

'And I never even tried to help . . .'

'No, child.'

'My legs wouldn't move.' Ammi was looking at her with troubled eyes. 'I couldn't even scream . . .'

'Hush,' Ammi was saying, and as Asha's chest filled with sobs, Ammi stroked her back. She wiped her tears, she cried with her. '*Bus*,' she said, 'Enough, child.'

'But,' cried Asha. Agitated, she tried once more to rise. 'I need to arrange their last rites.'

'We didn't know their religion,' said Ammi soothingly. 'We buried them.' She extended a hand slowly towards the girl. 'We thought it best . . .'

Asha held her hand out, and Ammi began to massage it. The older woman applied pressure on her joints as she ran her fingers across the girl's skin. A tear slipped down Asha's face, and intent as Ammi was on her work, she missed it. Now Ammi bent to the little earthenware pot by her feet. She poured more oil onto her palm. She shifted in her rattan stool, so similar to the one Mataji had used in their Suhanpur kitchen; she arched her back. Soon she was singing again. '*You follow me, you follow me . . .*'

117

When she noticed Asha's tears, she bit her lip. 'I'm sorry, child,' she said. 'I'll stop.'

Asha smiled sadly. 'No Ammi,' she said as she wiped her tears. 'My best friend is getting married. I'll sing for her.'

2

Noise built through the day like a desert storm. It was the festival of Eid, the celebration at the close of the long summer fast. Asha smelt gram flour *laddoos* being savoured, she heard the smacking of lips at the taste of ice-cold *sharbat*. She heard the fond slapping of shoulders, she heard the laughter in Ammi's voice as she greeted her guests. 'Yes,' she heard a guest pronounce. 'Pakistan's first Eid.'

Asha didn't leave her room during these visits. 'People aren't willing to think of Hindus as people,' Ammi's husband had told her hesitantly. He had looked at her sadly, his eyes heavy-lidded, his mouth stretched thin, and there was something about his wistfulness that reminded her of Pappaji. Of a silent Pappaji in his final days, after their home had been destroyed, after he had lost his words.

'Please don't worry,' she said. She thought of Firoze, of his final words to her. *Come with me, be my wife.* 'I have friends in Suhanpur,' she added. 'They'll hear of my plight, surely, or maybe you can pass a message . . .'

'No,' said the Maulvi.

There had been no further explanation, no eye contact, no apologetic grimace, and Asha had protested. 'But . . .'

119

'No, child. Everything has changed. There is no keeping a Hindu safe here anymore . . .'

He didn't understand. Didn't know what Firoze was to her. What Nargis was. 'But my friends . . .'

'No,' he repeated, his expression so full of pity that Asha lost heart. 'You've seen what they've done to your family. And we found no trace of your friend. There have been others.' His words were like gunfire. 'People killed in their beds.' These images filled her head, clouded her vision. 'Entire villages mown down.'

'Ok,' said Asha, more to stop his assault than anything else.

'Please,' said the Maulvi kindly. 'There's no going back.'

She heard the visitors speak from the safety of her room. Along with the friends came refugees from the East. They arrived in endless convoys, and spoke between silences that reverberated in the darkness of her room. Daughters had been raped and lost, breasts cleaved off. Men had been shot, robbed, maimed in body and mind. She heard of murders; she heard of massacres by the trainload. She heard in each anguished voice a yearning for revenge.

Asha did her best to make sure she remained undiscovered. She took care to be silent. She didn't speak, didn't sing, didn't turn the pages of a book or so much as unfurl the *dupatta* from her head for fear of being heard. She stood by her bolted window in the futile hope of a cool breeze and deliverance. When the main door opened, the window of her room rattled. She imagined a cooler breeze blowing in, but this brought with it unwelcome danger. Her curtain fluttered, and for a moment, before she ducked, her face was visible to any passer-by.

She saw a short man, wiry and dusty and sluggish in his movements, walking to the house. He mopped his brow, then let loose a long, gleaming stream of spittle. Asha dropped onto her haunches, worrying he had seen her, but in a minute she heard him at the door. She heard him utter his Eid greetings, and she sighed. It was all in her imagination. He hadn't seen her. *This, she told herself, is my punishment. I was immobile while my family was butchered, and while my friend ran, and now I must remain immobile still.*

She closed her eyes, thinking of Suhanpur. Wasn't Nargis to be wedded around now? The halls would be full of laughter, of hennaed hands clapping to the tune of wedding songs. The *shamiana* set on her future cricket pitch would be humming with revelry; the *shehnai* music players, that miserable, unstoppable pair, would finally pipe their culinary contentment.

The excitement, and Nargis' nervousness! There would have been another few sightings of her nameless groom, she would have fretted about his moustache, about whether he drank or smoked or gambled, about whether he would love her. *Friendship*, she had said, *kindness, a bit of luck*. They would have sat up late into the night if she had still been there, sorting through clues, imagining the bride's future happiness.

The sounds from inside the house grew louder. Asha heard a raised voice, then the Maulvi soothing. His voice was tender, uncomplainingly accepting of his audience's truculence. He was like the ancient banyan tree in Suhanpur. Storms had come, as had new conquerors, and it had simply dipped an enduring branch into grateful soil and spread its gospel. Then Asha remembered how

121

it had been felled, and remembered the emptiness it spawned afterwards. '*Bus*,' she heard the Maulvi say, 'Enough, child.'

'Just let me see one of them,' a man said. 'One single Hindu. Just let me near one of them, and you see what I do.'

Asha shivered. It was the man she had seen. Thin and ordinary and confounded by his grief.

'Come on, child,' urged the Maulvi. 'They're children of God too.'

'No, Maulvi *Sahib*,' spat out the man. Asha could picture him; young, wiry and spare, sitting cross-legged on the floor as a mark of respect to the Maulvi's scholarship. Had he seen her? Had he known her for a Hindu? He referred to the older man with respect, calling him Maulvi *Sahib*, agreeing wholeheartedly with his opinions, but here, on the issue of Hindu humanity, he turned vehement. 'No they're not,' he said. 'They're animals, the lot of them. They're *kafirs*. They're uncivilised unbelievers.'

'Child, please don't upset yourself,' reasoned the Maulvi. 'You've seen such sadness.'

'My mother,' insisted the man. 'She couldn't walk any more because of her arthritis. I had to carry her. And my new bride. Gunned down in an instant. Tell me, what danger did they pose to the infidels? Who had they raped, who had they looted?'

Asha leant against the wall. A breeze blew once more into the room, and the curtain took flight. She sank quickly down to the floor. Who had her family hurt? Who had she raped, who had she looted? And yet she cowered in the dark, invisible, unheard, an outsider in her own land. She thought of Firoze's confidence. 'This is your home now,' he had said. He had held her hand, had told her she would be back before long. She lifted her hand. Just below her palm, below where he had kissed her, were the remains of her tattoo. She felt it raw, the wound. She felt the blade on her, felt it carve its way deep into her flesh. She squirmed, covering her wrist with her *dupatta*. 'Om,' she said to herself softly in prayer, and then she jumped up. Om! She'd go to Delhi, retrieve her money, wait for Firoze to find her. News would reach him, surely, of her family's fate, and even if he didn't, he'd know soon, in a month, at the year's end, that there was no returning home for her family. *No going back*. He'd come after her then. He'd come to the big cities, to Amritsar and then to Delhi, to look for her, to bring her back home.

She ran to the door. 'Om,' she repeated. She lifted the sleeve of her tunic up, looking in vain for the address Mataji had written down. 'It must be the other sleeve,' she said to herself. She stood on tiptoe, craning her neck, but here too she saw only bare skin.

She stalked back to her bed, and then to the door again. She was about to open it, when she heard more guests enter. '*Eid Mubarak*,' she heard, and she sank down to her knees. The curtain waved in the breeze, a brilliant light momentarily fell into the room, and the noise of the crowd grew louder. She heard them laugh, heard them cheer the creation of Pakistan. 'There's no room for us in Hindustan,' she heard someone say, and she closed her eyes and waited for the noise to die down.

Ammi entered. 'A million apologies,' she smiled. 'But they refused to leave. You know what it's like on Eid . . .'

123

Asha nodded. She smiled at the plate of food held out to her. 'Eid Mubarak,' she said, and then, as the older woman looked back towards the door, she burst out, 'Ammi, there was something on my arm . . .' Asha patted the skin under her sleeve, but Ammi was distracted. Her skin was flushed from the festivities, and she smiled. 'So many people,' she complained. 'But it's only during Eid that we get so busy . . .'

'Ammi,' repeated Asha urgently. She lifted her sleeve, pointing at her bare arm. 'My mother,' she added, 'Mataji wrote down an address. Om Sharma,' she continued, and as Ammi looked uncomprehending, she said, 'He lives in Delhi, Ammi. He'll take care of me.' She looked up, saw she wasn't making any sense. She pointed again at her shoulder, mimed the act of writing, and she tried again. 'Om Sharma's address.'

'*Ruko, Beti,*' said Ammi. 'Wait, child.' She put a hand on Asha's to calm her, and turned towards the door. 'Ali,' she called out, 'Come fast, child!'

Asha heard footsteps rushing in their direction and a boy's voice ringing out. He came to the door, bowing respectfully. He had Ammi's round face and calm features he combined with an embarrassed manner. He refused to enter the room or to look at Asha. Ammi called out to him again, and now he looked once at Asha, his eyes darting to her scarred hand before looking away. 'You called, Ammi?' he asked.

'Child,' nodded his mother. 'Remember the words you noted down?'

The boy blushed scarlet. His eyes were on her sleeve, the tenderness of her upper arm, and once more he looked quickly away. A denial was on his lips, a resolute shake of his head, but Ammi spoke again.

'Ali wrote down the address,' she said, and as Asha pointed to her shoulder, the older woman repeated, 'Remember child, the writing on Asha's arm?'

Ali backed wordlessly out of the room. 'I'm sorry, child,' Ammi said. 'I can't read, so I had to show the boy your shoulder.'

Ali was back. He stood by the doorway, his eyes on the ground, his colour still high. He held a piece of paper in his hand. His mother took it from him and placed it ceremoniously in Asha's lap.

There was an address, an unfamiliar locality in an unfamiliar Delhi, and she asked, 'Is this what Mataji wrote?' As Ammi nodded, she asked again, 'But are you sure?'

Ammi turned towards Ali, who inclined his head. 'I wrote it all down,' he said. He recited the address, and Asha saw it matched the lines on the paper precisely.

'This *is* the address,' confirmed Ammi. 'Don't worry, child, my husband is trying to get you on a convoy heading to Delhi. We'll get you to safety soon.'

Ali disappeared once more. Ammi smiled and brought the girl into her embrace. The older woman smelt of jasmine, of the day's feasting, and Asha nodded.

She would be safe in Delhi soon, and within reach of Firoze.

3

They stood out in the beating rain all day long, from early, hopeful daybreak to the sultry, wet heat of the midday sun, to when the sun neared the end of its descent through the sky. They stood together, the Maulvi and his son, like a bridal welcome party in anxious wait for the groom.

They would have waited like that in Suhanpur, the inspector and Firoze. How nervous they must have been, how terrified of a no-show on the part of Nargis' betrothed. And how they must have smiled, how their faces must have strained with their delight when they finally heard a skittish neigh from a horse, and then when they heard the din of the groom's *shehnai* music She could see Firoze's eyes creasing as he smiled, she could see him rush forward to embrace his brother-in-law. 'Welcome,' the inspector would have boomed over the wedding music. 'Welcome to the family, son.'

The Maulvi and Ali stood anxiously too, but they remained silent. They didn't share jokes or exchange anecdotes. They didn't look at each other. They kept their eyes trained to the West, pointing out any movement they sensed. Often it was no more than a change in the intensity of the rain. Every now and then they would see a convoy approach them. What joy then, what hope!

126

But then, what fear they saw in the faces of the people who passed, what shock, what utter terror. They raised their hands, urging them to stop, but no one so much as slowed down. They saw eyes widen with fear, they saw the passers-by – Sikhs or the escaping Hindus they yearned for – look at the beards of the Maulvi and his son, then they saw them speed up and on to safety.

'It's no use,' said Asha to Ammi one day. The Maulvi and his son were outside, keeping their vigil. The women were in the tiny yard behind the hut, roasting spices for the evening meal. Asha wasn't allowed to do any work. Ammi insisted that nothing be allowed to interfere with the recovery of her wrist. She imagined an irritation from chopping an onion, the graze of a knife in Asha's unaccustomed hand, the strain to her healing skin from stretching her wrist. 'No, Beta,' she repeated patiently. 'You have the rest of your life for these chores. Now you rest.' Ammi would smile mildly in gentle expectation of Asha seeing sense, and Asha – used so often to setting her jaw at her own mother – would sit peacefully and capitulate.

Now, as Ammi worked, she said, 'I don't see how I'll ever get to India.'

'Leave it to God,' said Ammi.

'People are scared, don't you see? They see their beards, they know them for Muslims.' Asha picked up some discarded onion skin and began to play with it. It yielded as she bent it, then sprang back to its original curvature as she let go. At length, the skin tore, splitting across the line in a neat, crackling motion. Ammi looked up. 'Have patience, Asha,' she said. 'God will take care of things.'

Asha let the skin fall. 'But they won't stop,' she burst out. 'Not a single *tonga* or rickshaw or car. No one. They speed up when they see the Maulvi.'

'Come on,' said Ammi. 'They're scared, they've fled horrors. There'll be someone,' and as Asha raised her eyebrows, she added, 'Soon, there'll be someone who stops.' She rose to go indoors for a fresh supply of onions. From inside the hut, Asha heard the sound of Ammi singing, 'You follow me, you follow me . . .'

The wedding was sure to have taken place by now. Nargis would have sat before the Imam, wearing her high-necked red dress, the gold of her *gotas* like stars against her hair. She would have bowed her head as the Imam asked if she agreed to the match, she would have bashfully – and cruelly – kept her silence as he repeated his question, and finally, as he asked her if she agreed the third, most anxious time, and as her relatives, as her father and brother rushed to her side to give her resolve, she would have nodded, then whispered in a voice tremulous with anticipation, '*Qubool hai.*' I accept.

The clouds gathered above Asha. It would rain soon. A peal of thunder sounded overhead, like the thunder of the Ravi.

Dham dharak dham.

It was the sound of her falling in love. It was the sound of her choosing her happiness.

Ammi called out, 'Bring the food indoors, child.'

Asha rose. 'No,' she said firmly to herself. 'I don't accept.' She would make it to Delhi. If the travellers were frightened of the Maulvi, if they looked at him with his beard and saw a vengeful Muslim, she would go out on her own.

She thought of the last time she had been out alone.

She thought of the Afghan and his chilling advances. Asha took an end of her *dupatta* in her hand and held it over her disfigured wrist. She turned it over until it was facing inwards, until her tunic shielded it further from view, but still she thought of it. She imagined it livid, she imagined new skin splintering again – yielding to unkind manipulation like the onion skin.

'Hurry, child,' Ammi called from indoors. 'The spices will spoil.'

'Coming, Ammi,' replied Asha. She walked resolutely towards the hut, and as a soft, slow rain began to descend, she smiled. 'No,' she repeated to herself. 'No, I don't accept.'

4

She crept out in the middle of the night.

It was absolutely silent in the house, and she feared she would lose her bearings in the dark. She feared the noise from an opening door; she feared a loud burst of rain. Once outside, her worries resurfaced. She was alone now, and completely unprotected. And it was quiet. Still and dark and silent.

Asha waited. She could see the outline of the hut to her left, but beyond that, she couldn't place any landmark with absolute certainty. There was a broad structure in the distance, roughly where the shelter had been, but as she stared, she thought she saw it move. Perhaps it was a bush, disturbed by the night. She shivered, imagining the structure move closer to her. She blinked, stared again. No, it was definitely not moving. It remained where it was, inanimate, benign. It posed no danger to her.

The wind shifted and she thought she heard a noise. A cricket chirped, just as it had when Firoze had dropped them off in his *tonga*. She heard a howl, and froze. What was that, a dog or worse? Was it a human sound?

She looked at the ground. They had rested there, just yards away, her family, unsuspecting and innocent. They had expected to return to Suhanpur. 'This is your home,' Firoze had told them. How hopeful they had all been, how naïve. She laughed, then checked her noise, peering ahead. There they had lain, she was sure. Just by the broad structure, just by the shelter. Just by where she had stood, paralysed by her fear. There they had fallen like so many dolls, arms and legs askew.

And Roopa, where was she now? Lying dead in some dusty, unlamented corner? Or perhaps she had been lucky. Maybe she had been taken in by a local family, married off to a Muslim boy. She would live out her days as a Muslim. She wasn't beautiful, wasn't feminine, and so her chances of tempting a boy were slim. But still. Miracles could happen.

The wind picked up; Asha's eyes stung. She pulled her *dupatta* tight around her, and her hands grazed her belly. She thought of the death, the sudden bleed that had taken her to her safety. How grateful she had been, for that one instant. She thought of the people she had lost, of the affection, the smiles, the belonging she could never again take for granted. It was the end of a life, and as she stood there, shivering in the brief night-time chill, it dawned on her that it was the end of her childhood.

When a *tonga* did approach, she debated asking it to halt. But there was no seeing the riders, and there was no knowing their religion or their intentions. She watched it pass, and immediately regretted not stepping out onto the road. They were sure to have been Hindus travelling under the cover of dark.

Another *tonga* passed, another one was let go, and finally, as the sun showed signs of breaking through the dark, she heard a noise. It was muffled at first, and slow. *Dham-dham*, imagined Asha, and as the sound grew slowly nearer, she shook her head. No, this was a slower,

131

nearer thunder. The sun stretched a first tentative finger into the night; she thought she saw an outline against the sky. It grew closer, as did its sound, closer and full of possibility. The sun dipped low for a moment, then burst upwards lustfully, and Asha stepped out onto the road.

They might have been Muslims, so she almost stepped back into the shadows, but the car was slowing down, it was stopping, and a dark, dusty window was wound down.

They were Hindus.

They were the Kapurs – a newlywed couple – escaping from Lahore. The man leant across his wife, peered at her through the open window. They glanced warily at each other. The man had the beginnings of a beard, and Asha couldn't be certain if it signalled his religion or a lack of care. He had narrow eyes, a thin moustache and fleshy lips that he chewed thoughtfully as he studied her. Asha pulled her *dupatta* protectively over her head. 'What is it?' the man asked suspiciously.

'Bhaiya,' she said. 'Brother. I'm looking to get to Delhi.'

'Hindu?'

He was staring at her anxiously, unblinking. He could be Hindu, and she could be safe. Or it could be an elaborate trap. They might have heard locally that the Maulvi was harbouring a Hindu. He continued chewing his lips, and now his fingers began a rapid drum on his steering wheel. 'Well?' he asked.

Asha nodded. 'Yes,' she said. 'I'm Hindu.'

He sighed and turned to the woman in the passenger seat.

'Take her in,' she counselled.

He didn't look convinced. 'I'm not sure,' he said. His eyes reverted to the road in front of him, and now Asha brought her hand up to the window. He saw her wrist, took in her scar, and he nodded grudgingly. '*Jai Siya Ram,*' he invoked, as he leaned across to open the door to the back seat.

'Bhaiya,' she said. 'The people who have given me shelter . . .'

'*Siya Ram,*' Bhaiya was praying. He looked up, saw Asha standing, and gestured her in. 'Hurry,' he said impatiently. 'It's not safe.'

'I just have to tell them I'm going.'

'No,' she heard him say, but she'd already turned back.

Asha heard the couple arguing. 'I told you,' she heard Bhaiya spit out. 'No stopping, I said.' A car door opened then shut, the woman called out to her, but she hurried towards the hut and knocked on the door. She didn't turn back to the car, and part of her expected Bhaiya to drive away.

The hut was quiet, and she knocked again.

She heard the car rev up, and the woman call her to return, and still no one came to the door.

'Ammi,' she called. 'Ammi, please open the door!' Finally, she heard footsteps. The door opened an inch and the Maulvi's kind, faded face poked questioningly out.

The car began to move, and she cried out, 'I've found a ride' but the car was moving away.

'Run,' cried the Maulvi, and as Ammi appeared by his side, smiling and crying and waving at her, she turned and ran.

Bhaiya had begun to gather pace, and she ran faster, her *dupatta* trailing in the ground. She saw the car's fumes in front of her, she saw the bus shelter to her left, but now as she called out, 'Bhaiya!' he was slowing down. He was stopping, his car lights still on, and she was catching up with them. She hurried into the back seat, and they zoomed off again.

The bride turned to look at Asha and introduced herself as Bina. She was the same age as her, maybe a year older. She smiled shyly. 'Where are you from?'

'Suhanpur,' Asha answered, and as Bina looked blank, she added, 'It's to the West.'

'I don't know,' shrugged Bina with big city disdain. 'My family's from Delhi. That's where we're going now, thank goodness.'

Bhaiya sped up, and as Bina complained, he pointed to a burning shack behind them. 'I saw bodies,' he said. '*Hai Ram*, I saw burning bodies. We have to keep moving.' He kept praying as he drove, and any time he detected people in the distance, he turned pious. *Ram Ram*, she heard in the back seat. *Jai Mata di, Jai Siya Ram*, and then, as a young, powerfully built man strolled across the road in front of them, he switched allegiance. *Radhe, Shyam*, he invoked, *Radhe, Shyam*.

'You're so nervous,' Bina complained.

'Just look around,' said Bhaiya. From where she sat, Asha heard him invoke the Gods. 'It's a miracle we're alive.' He gestured to Asha. 'It's a miracle she is.' They passed by another burning hut, and he redoubled his invocations. Gods were switched again.

'It's lucky, isn't it,' laughed Bina, 'that we have so many Gods to choose from?'

'Yes,' smiled Asha. It felt a little to her like Mrs Malik's forced hilarity, but as Bina turned to her, she added, 'If one God abandons us, surely another will protect us.'

'Right,' Bina said to her husband. 'You can pray all you like, but I'm going to sit in the back with Asha.'

'*Hai Ram*,' protested Bhaiya. He pointed to where two women sat on the road, crying over a corpse. They beat their breasts in their grief, they held their hands up to the heavens, and he said, 'The world is ending, Bina, and you want me to stop the car?'

'Don't worry,' said his wife. She clambered over her seat; Asha held her hand out to steady her, and Bina was soon comfortably seated in the back. Asha looked across at Bina. Her skin was soft, dewy, her features plump and contented. She turned a flushed face to her, complaining about the heat, and Asha wondered if she was carrying her husband's child. This, she thought, is a girl on the brink of life. Nothing has happened to her, nothing has gone wrong. She saw Bina looking at her scarred wrist, and she quickly hid her hand under her *dupatta*.

Bina held her hand out. 'We've lost so much too,' she said matter-of-factly. 'My husband's family lives in Lahore. Lived,' she corrected herself. 'They came in one night as we slept. We had just been married, and I had prepared dinner for the first time. My *daal* had been too spicy, and I worried my mother-in-law would suffer from indigestion. So I went down to the kitchen at night to fetch a glass of milk for her. 'He,' she said, nodding coyly towards her husband. 'He followed me. We heard them enter, heard them go into the bedrooms.' She was silent now, her pretty, plump face suddenly expressionless. 'We saw them drag out his family, saw everyone – father, mother, sister – being killed in front of us. We just stayed crouching on the kitchen floor.'

Asha patted the girl's hand.

'No,' insisted Bina crossly, as if Asha didn't understand her words. 'We didn't even try to save them.'

'I know,' said Asha. 'I heard my family die too.' She looked away, and both were silent for a while. Her hand slipped from Bina's.

It had grown lighter, and now they saw more people on the road. They passed by more burning ruins, passed by miles of desperate, snaking convoys heading East. About a mile from the border with India, an elderly, turbaned man stepped out into the road in front of them. Bhaiya braked hard and wound down his window with a fresh invocation. 'Move,' he said to the man with authority.

'*Beta*,' said the man. He held an infant in his arms, whom he now held out to Bhaiya.

'What are you doing?'

'This is my grandson,' said the man. His face was caked with dirt, his clothes travel-stained. His long, straggly beard was matted, but he looked out with a clear, certain gaze. Asha peered at his grandson's listless body through the window. 'He's not moving,' she whispered to Bina, who shivered in response. The man saw the two women looking in his direction. 'Please,' he pleaded. 'Take him with you. He'll die out here.'

'*Hey Ram*,' Bhaiya was saying, and as Bina turned towards him, he called out to the old man. 'We don't have space, we don't have a home in India . . .'

'Please,' begged the man. 'Just do your best for him.' He moved towards the car, towards the women who looked like yielding, and at this, Bhaiya started up the car.

'Stop!' cried his wife, but Bhaiya began to move. 'How many can we take in?' he asked. 'Do you even know if this child is alive? Maybe he's carrying a disease he'll transmit to us. Now is the time to think straight. We can indulge in all the charity you want once we're safe in Delhi.'

They passed by another burning ruin, and Asha said, 'I've never been to Delhi before.'

Bina looked up with interest, 'Who are you going to stay with, then? Family?'

'No.'

'Not family, then?'

'No.' Asha fell silent.

'Then?' Bina prompted.

'They're friends of the family,' explained Asha. 'They're holding some jewellery for me.'

The bride leaned forward and tapped her husband smartly on his shoulder. 'Let me drive,' he said. 'We're nearly in Delhi,' and Bina leant back in her seat. 'You're coming with us,' she told Asha. 'We can't have you living with any stranger.'

'Bina,' said her husband, and both girls looked up to see him watching them through the rear view mirror. He smiled as he spoke, 'Just think, Bina, think of her,' but his voice betrayed his strain. 'Will she be comfortable?'

'Of course she will.'

'Bina . . .'

'But,' and here his voice grew shrill. 'What about her future? She should think about getting married. And if we keep her in our home, a young girl, what will people say?'

'What will they say?'

'*Arre*, Bina,' he cajoled now. He frowned and bit his lip. 'It doesn't look good, a young girl living with me. Who'll marry her?'

137

Bina shook her head, and Asha returned the pressure of the bride's hand. 'Don't worry,' she said. 'My friends will take me in.' Om would, she knew. And it wouldn't be for long. She just had to wait for Firoze to come looking for her.

'Take your money,' insisted Bina, looking firmly at the rear view. 'Then come stay with us. We'll take care of you. We'll get you married.'

'No, Bina.'

'What other options do you have?'

'Look,' Bhaiya nodded rapidly. 'She's got somewhere to stay.' He looked at Asha, smiled at her. 'You have, don't you, Asha?' Asha nodded, and he added, 'She'll want to stay with people she knows. Maybe someone in the family will marry her.'

Asha thought of Om, of his awkwardness around her, his stutter, his perpetual embarrassment. She smiled, and as Bina elbowed her playfully, she thought of his smile. She thought of his endless teeth, his broad nose and clammy hands. She shook her head at Bina, and said sternly, 'No, no, I have no thoughts of marriage.'

'But you looked . . .'

'No,' repeated Asha firmly. 'No.'

The landscape changed suddenly. Gone were the empty tracts of land, gone was the shade of a hundred bereaved Eucalyptus trees. Instead, they saw a long queue reaching out in front of them. People rested listlessly on bullock carts, on the shoulders of the more able. They walked miles, then crouched down for a rest. They fanned them-selves with the ends of turbans, they swatted flies. The air was close, and from where they sat in the car, they saw people in the procession call out for relief. They heard them curse the mosquitoes that came with the monsoon. Swarms of children ran about, gathering twigs, and one applied them to the rear end of a terrified goat. 'Stop it,' a grown-up cried. He ran up to the child and slapped his cheek. 'Really,' he scolded. 'You're no better than those pitiless *Mussalman*.'

They came to a halt. There were a few cars in front of them, but beyond that they could identify no obstruction. 'We're in Delhi now,' said Bhaiya. 'Thank God, we're safe.'

Asha fingered her scar. Om *would* take her in, Firoze *would* find her. She *would* be safe. As the couple discussed directions, she heard Bhaiya utter grateful prayers, and she turned to look out of the window.

The entire city seemed to have been turned into a refugee camp. All temples, all major monuments, every available space heaved with people. Women carried crying, emaciated babies on their hips. Crowds of boys milled around – laughing and slapping each other. Grubby-faced children ran out onto the roads unwatched; several ran up to their car. They banged their palms on the windows, offering up greasy sweets. '*Le lo, Bhaiya*,' they entreated. 'Take this. Mataji made it fresh this morning, just give us a few *paise* for it.'

Bina beckoned each child over, bought a few inedible sweets.

'*Bus*,' said Bhaiya, 'Enough.'

'These poor children,' replied Bina. 'They've lost everything.'

'I know,' he said, as she pushed more coins through the window. 'But how many can you buy?'

'This could be us,' she argued. 'If we didn't have

my parents' house in Delhi, this would be us.' She had stopped taking the sweets, was just handing out money. It had started to rain, and it ran in smears down the dirty windows of the car. More tiny, dirt-stained hands were pressed against the car, filthy sleeves were lifted to streaming noses, and though Bhaiya hit his head against the steering wheel, she carried on. 'Please,' she said, 'take pity on them.'

He was taken aback by her passion. 'Of course,' he agreed, 'But we can't solve all of India's problems, my darling.'

The children clamoured for more – for money for their sweets, for attention, for interaction with the kind, smiling Bina – but she was lost to them now. The road-block in front of them was cleared, the car resumed its slow progress, and the new bride blushed a deep red. Bhaiya had won the day; he had slayed her argument with a single, tender word. The two young women giggled nervously in the back seat, suddenly feeling themselves unequal to a reply.

Asha looked out. The rain fell harder now. Already puddles were forming on the streets, and tarpaulin sheets were being lifted in futile defence. This could be her. In another minute, in another couple, if Om chose to turn her away. If Firoze was unable to make his way to her.

Bhaiya turned in his seat. 'Do you have an address for your friends?'

'I'm telling you,' piped up his wife. 'She'll stay with us . . .'

'Come on,' remonstrated her husband, nervously chewing his lip, and then with his new knowledge, he added, 'Listen to reason, darling.'

Bina looked away, blushing, and now Bhaiya studied

140

Asha in the rear view mirror. 'Is there an address?'

Asha paused. She turned her hand over to reveal her scar. 'Of course,' she said. She was worrying about nothing. Om would take her in. He had wanted to marry her, had offered her family any assistance they wanted. She took out the piece of paper and read the address Ali had so carefully noted down.

'But that's great,' Bhaiya was saying. He broke into a broad smile. 'Then you won't be parted. Not really. Asha's home is ten minutes from us. We'll drop her off first.'

5

The queue in front of Om's house ran into the hundreds. The more fortunate – the early supplicants, those with the strongest claims, or else, those with the strongest lungs – clustered by the heavy wooden door. They counted on being seen by the family, by Om, or his mother, in a matter of minutes. Others formed a ragged, sorry line that snaked out of the front gate and onto the street. Every so often a car passed and an irate driver applied a loud horn, and the queue broke apart. '*Oof*,' those in the car would declaim. 'These animals,' but as soon as they passed, Om's petitioners would rush to reform their line. Some would sneak ahead, looking to gain a march on a rival claim, but others were vigilant. A festive village spirit would descend on the crowd, and dozens – men and women – would pick up their slippers and beat the culprit into returning to his rightful place in the queue.

'Savages,' Bhaiya said as they drove up. 'Taking up the entire street.' They saw children run out and grown men urinate onto the rose bushes of a neighbouring house. An elderly woman emptied the contents of her stomach onto Om's white wall, and Bhaiya grimaced. '*Hai Ram*,' he swore. 'What next?'

Asha got out of the car, and Bhaiya prepared to drive off. He nodded briefly at her. 'Of course we'll see you soon,' he said, but Bina stopped him. 'I'll go stand with Asha for a minute.'

'But Bina, your family will be waiting.'

Bina held a hand up. 'I'll only be a minute,' she said. 'I'll be back before you know it.'

They stood behind an elderly man who complained about the heat. 'And if the heat doesn't get me,' he had said, 'The rains will. Or the disease in the camps.' He took an earthenware pot out of the grimy folds of his *kurta*, and raised it to his mouth. '*Pani*,' he said, 'From the river, such as it is.' He lifted the pot high, tilting it until some sluggish brown water trickled out. 'Still,' he smiled, showing teeth stained with tobacco or river water. 'It quenches the thirst.' He held the pot out to the girls. 'Would you like some?'

Both shook their heads. 'Take your money,' Bina said to Asha. 'Then come to me. We're on Hailey Road.' Asha frowned, but Bina went on, 'I'll give you the address in case you need it.'

'Om will take me in.'

Bina looked behind her. Already the queue had grown, and another dozen or so families waited for their turn. Just behind them was a family with a lissom, doe-eyed daughter. 'We'll be fine,' her mother crowed. 'Om will marry our girl, and then our worries will be over.' The bride-to-be lowered her eyes, but a slow smile spread across her features, and Asha knew the mother was right to be confident. Their daughter was a superior specimen, milk-skinned, wide-eyed, arch-browed. She thought of Om proposing marriage to her, and stamped her feet. Of course she didn't want Om. But still, what chance did she have against a girl like that, with a smile as gratifying as it was gratified?

143

Bina tapped her arm. 'Find your way to Hailey Road,' she said. 'We're the house near the end, just past the haunted *haveli*.'

Bhaiya had begun to sound his horn. Another car was trying to get past, the queue was being made to splinter again, and the two girls were jostled out of position. 'Come on,' said Bhaiya to his wife. 'We're getting late.'

'Just remember,' said Bina as she ran to the car. 'Hailey Road, just past the haunted house.'

Asha decided to go to the front of the queue. 'But I know them,' she said as a squat, flat-faced matron turned to stare at her.

'*Akele ho*?' the matron asked. 'Have you come alone?'

'Yes.'

'No family, no husband.' This was a statement, not a question, and Asha didn't feel she was called on to reply. The matron gave a nod that was at once appraising and sympathetic. Then the door opened, and an ancient retainer thrust an unwilling head out. '*Rukiye*,' he said, as the crowd threatened to surge ahead. '*Sahib* will be here shortly.'

They grumbled then. The matron turned to Asha, 'It's not like we want to be here. We're not beggars, you know,' but Asha had already inched forward. She said to the servant, 'Please, I know Om-*ji*.'

'Of course,' he said coldly.

'No, really, I do.'

'So does everyone in this queue, apparently,' he said with a shrug. He inspected her from head to foot, took in her grubby clothes, the ill-fitting outfit she had been given by Ammi, and he frowned. 'Join the queue, please.'

'If you would only call Om-*ji*.'

144

'Yes,' said the retainer impatiently. 'He'll be here soon. Until then, you wait.' He pointed to the back of the queue; the matron reached forward and pulled her back. 'Wait,' she said. 'You wait your turn like the rest of us.'

The queue had reformed, and Asha saw she had lost the place she had occupied with Bina. She found the elderly man who had offered her his decaying water. 'Come, *Beta*,' he said to her. 'Stand with me.'

'But uncle,' Asha said. She pointed at the bride-to-be, who now waited in front of her. 'We were further ahead before.'

He shrugged phlegmatically. 'This is how these things work, child. The strongest, the loudest, they get ahead. The rest of us wait our turn.'

'No,' she said. 'That's not right. Come to the front with me.'

'Don't bother, child,' he said. 'Or we'll lose this place too.'

Another car announced its presence, another queue reshuffle was imminent. 'No,' she said. She remembered her bravado in the Maulvi's house. *I don't accept.* 'We can't let them bully us or we'll never be seen.' The man shrugged again, made way for the moving line, and Asha looked towards the front door.

She walked up to the front and was met with the flat-faced matron once more.

'Are you still waiting?' Asha asked in surprise. 'I thought you would have been seen by now.'

'*Arre*,' replied the matron. 'We're at their mercy now. They will see us when it suits them.'

I don't accept. 'How long have you been waiting?'

'Since morning,' said the woman proudly. Her face broke into something akin to a smile. 'I was at the back of the queue then.' She looked around her with considerable satisfaction. 'I'll definitely be seen today.'

'I won't,' replied Asha.

'No,' pronounced the woman. 'Probably not. But,' she added, leaning forward. 'You have to time things better. Arrive here early in the morning. Or,' she whispered. 'Use your youth, child.' Asha shook a shocked head, but the matron insisted. 'Let your *dupatta* slip. Give a man the chance to rescue you.'

'No,' Asha said. 'No.' The money was hers; she wouldn't demean herself. She would go to Hailey Road, she would make her way to Suhanpur, but she wouldn't wait night and day for Om to honour her with his presence. She knew she had fallen in the world. She didn't have her father's protection, she no longer had her home or her money, but this was too much. 'No,' she repeated aloud, and as the matron stared incredulously, she added, 'I don't accept.'

The front door opened. She saw Om look out and the matron stride ahead. '*Beta*,' she heard. 'Om *Beta*, remember what you said to me? Come to Delhi, and I'll help you . . .'

He nodded slightly and raised his hand to shade his face. His face broke into his toothy, broad-nosed grin. She shook with rage. The insincere fool, making promises to all and sundry! How he had tried to woo Mataji. *Let me take your jewellery; let me take care of you.* He looked out beyond her now, towards the edge of the crowd, sighing.

'No,' she thought again. *I don't accept.* Then suddenly, as she finally caught his eye, she turned and rushed past

146

the thrusting, desperate line, past hordes of scrapping children, past the bride-to-be, past her elderly friend with tobacco-stained teeth, and finally, past the end of the line that snaked onto the street.

'Asha-*ji*,' she heard Om call out, 'Stop, please,' but she kept moving. She ran past the house, turning towards an open space at the end of the street. This turned out to be a park built around a large water tank. She looked up and saw refugees in every corner: on the lawn, by the exit, on the stairs of the tank. Some of them saw her approach and began to surge towards her. She heard Om behind her and hurried towards the road, towards the noise of cars and safety. She looked around for signs of Hailey Road, for any marker that would guide her, but there was nothing. 'Come to me,' Bina had said. 'We're just past the haunted house,' but it was all haunted, this Delhi of hers, all full of echoes and ghosts and stench and disease. All full of grasping hands, all full of death.

She turned a corner and found herself facing another, smaller park. *So green Delhi is*, she remembered Mataji saying. Om had just been to see her, had just taken away the family's jewellery. He had whispered in her ears about the magic of Delhi. *It's safe there, Mataji. You'll be safe there*. That Om! There was no staying in Delhi, not for her. She'd make her way back to Suhanpur, and back to Firoze.

Asha turned again, and suddenly she was at the beginning of a residential area. All was quiet. She heard the sound of footsteps, and was sure it was Om. She squeezed herself into the gap between two houses. Footsteps rushed past. She heard a breathless cry of 'Asha!' but she stayed quiet.

She heard a commotion in the next house. Voices were

raised, possessions were flung against walls.

'There's a Muslim hiding inside,' someone shouted from somewhere near her, and there it was again, the same thudding feet as in Suhanpur, the same insistent knock on the door. She heard a door being broken down and a ragged voice call out in fear.

'Kill the bastard,' a man ordered, and then she heard his comrades' answering echoes. She heard the blow of metal against flesh; then an uncontrolled hammering. There was a crack, audible to her in the street, a little like the breaking of bone after the weekly slaughter of cockerel in Suhanpur. But even that had been more humane; a simple wrench of the neck followed by blessed oblivion. She didn't hear anything from the Muslim now, no plea, no cry for help. Instead, she heard laughter, the sound of a senseless, possessed army. For it was lunacy, wasn't it, what they were doing? Asha heard a window being opened, then the assailants relieving their bladders on their victim's corpse.

She waited, rooted to the ground, helpless and terrified. Just as she had been when her family was being slaughtered. There was no going back for her. They would know her for a Hindu at once.

There was no coming to Delhi for Firoze either. He wouldn't last one minute.

Footsteps approached her. She squeezed herself against the wall, but someone was turning into the lane and she saw that Om was upon her. 'Asha-*ji*,' he said, and for the first time, his voice rose in complaint. 'I've been looking everywhere. Don't you know it isn't safe?'

The murderers set the Muslim man's house on fire, and as it all came alight, as a sooty smoke began to rise into the air, Asha and Om stood still. There it was, finally, a Muslim made Hindu in death, and given the funeral pyre that had been denied her family. Om put a hand on her shoulder. Asha opened her mouth in a silent scream. She found she was letting him hold her, lead her back to his house. She found she was forgetting to register any complaint at all.

6

'I told you,' Asha said to the retainer. 'I said I knew Om-*ji*.'

Om had left her in the hallway of his house, beyond the echoing clamour of the crowd. 'I'll get Ma,' he had nervously said to her. 'I want her to meet you.'

It was over, her dream, her childhood. She had to forget about Firoze. She had to smile at Om now, and to let her *dupatta* slip.

'I'll just be back,' he had said, smiling his toothy smile, and she had nodded.

'Yes,' she had replied. 'Yes, take your time.'

'Well,' the retainer said uncertainly. He indicated the divan in the hall. He surveyed her unhurriedly, and she grew conscious of how long it had been since she had last bathed. Of how long it had been since she had last seen her mother-of-pearl brush, of how long it had been since she had last eaten. The retainer bowed his head, staring at her mud-splattered slippers, and she found herself muttering about the rain in Punjab. 'If you say so,' huffed the man. He indicated the divan again, but as Asha moved towards it, he winced. 'The upholstery is new. Maybe I'll fetch you a cloth to sit on.'

So Asha perched on a kitchen cloth in Om's house. 'I'm just waiting,' she said with more confidence than she felt. 'I'm going to meet Om-*ji*'s mother.' Her hand rose as she spoke, and she nearly knocked a priceless vase off its perch. The man rushed forward to protect the precious heirloom. 'You're sure,' he glared at her, 'you're sure you're to wait indoors?'

'Yes,' Asha replied meekly, and the man sighed. He picked up the vase, moved it to a table away from her and marched wordlessly off inside the house.

Even where she sat, in the dimly lit hall, she saw signs of careless prosperity. There was the tall screen inlaid with semi-precious stones, there were the twin elephant tusks that guarded the door to the principal rooms. An enormous brass chandelier hung low; an ancient, faded carpet lined one of the walls. And in the distance, the table with its precious vase.

'Partition,' Asha observed, 'has been good to this family.'

She rose, fingered the soft velvet of the carpet, and moved towards the vase. It called to her like the inspector's contraband and she slowly reached a hand out to touch it. Then she heard a noise, a rustle of a sari, and she hurried back to her seat.

A woman entered. This appeared to be Om's mother, and the girl rose. She put her hands together and muttered her greetings. The woman nodded. 'You belong to the Prakash family?'

'Yes.'

The woman shuffled slowly forward, staring hard. 'You're Shiela's daughter?'

'Yes,' said Asha. She saw the woman cast a critical eye over her clothes, and she knew the old sepoy retainer had been describing her. 'That scamp,' she thought, but she took care to appear pleasant. 'I've been travelling,' she explained. 'I've just come in from Pakistan.'

There was no response. 'My parents,' began Asha.

'They didn't make it,' said the woman simply.

'No.'

The woman nodded. She stared at her newly uphol-stered *divan* with some concern, and Asha steeled herself to say, 'Om-*ji* had been given some jewellery by my mother for safekeeping, and so I came . . .'

'Oh,' said the woman with a hard smile. 'Is that right?'

'Yes,' said Asha firmly, but as the woman continued her scrutiny, she felt herself colour.

'Of course,' the woman finally said. 'Of course.'

She shuffled off without another word, and Asha sat miserably down. There was no mention of Om. 'Horrible woman,' she fumed. There was to be no marriage, the old witch would make sure of that. She would find the milk-skinned beauty, force her on her son, just as something similar would soon be done in Suhanpur. The almond-eyed Lahori would be brought into the house overlooking the uprooted banyan tree, and another woman's children would play on her cricket pitch.

Asha set her jaw. Om's image flashed in her mind, a broad nose over an endless, smiling mouth. 'No,' she thought firmly. 'No, I don't accept.'

She heard raised voices in the next room. '*Beta*,' she heard the woman plead. 'Son, listen to me. You can have your pick now. Why settle for her?'

'Ma,' said a soft, patient voice. 'I like her. I'd even asked for her hand in Suhanpur.'

'But *Beta*,' said his mother. 'Things were different then. Her father was a respected lawyer. She would have brought a decent dowry. And you hadn't risen as much as you have over the past few months.' Om's mother began cajoling now, 'How well my son has done. You have blossomed in the midst of all this devastation.' There was silence for a moment, then she began again. 'What is she worth now? Nothing.'

Asha's heart sank. He would let her go.

Om spoke softly, and Asha strained to listen. ' . . .have enough . . .'

'And she's nothing to look at.'

'Ma . . .'

'She has nothing, *Beta*.'

She couldn't hear his reply, but knew Om's mother was thinking of the lines of eager girls who waited outside.

'Her nose isn't straight . . .'

'*Bus* . . .'

'She's short.'

'So am I,' replied an exasperated Om.

'*Chup*,' scolded Ma. 'You're my prince.'

His next words escaped Asha. She stood no chance.

'She has a nice smile, I suppose,' said Ma reluctantly.

'I like her,' said Om plainly, audibly, and Asha's heart lifted. 'I like her smile.'

'Her smile,' sniffed his mother. 'Her smile? You could have any girl in Delhi, and you choose a common orphan because of her smile?' Asha shifted in her seat. The cloth moved under her, and she heard Ma speak again, but she couldn't stop smiling. She brought her hand up to her mouth and touched the corners of her lips. He liked her smile. 'Friendship,' she thought. 'Kindness, a bit of luck.'

She heard Om rise. A chair was scraped back, she heard footsteps move deeper into the house. She didn't hear him speak again, but Ma's voice rose loud in complaint for a long while afterwards. Her drawbacks were listed again, as if Ma was evaluating a vegetable for the evening meal. 'I wouldn't mind, Mahesh,' she said, 'but she looks so common.'

Mahesh, whom Asha recognised as the retainer, provided a ready echo to all of Ma's concerns. 'Yes, Maji,' she heard. 'So common,' but Asha's hand remained by her smile.

She was in Delhi. She would be safe, and with a bit of luck, she would be happy.

7

'You know,' Om said to Asha. They were sitting on their marital bed, and each was positioned to maintain maximum respectful distance from the other. Asha stayed at the foot of the bed, while Om placed himself a little below the pillow at its head. Their bodies were inclined to each other to indicate camaraderie, but they didn't touch. Not their hands, which they kept folded on their laps, nor their feet, which chastely skimmed the floor. It was their wedding night.

They had been married in a rushed ceremony. Her bridal outfit was a damson pink *sari* borrowed from Bina. Bhaiya fawned over her now, claiming the role of cupid. His jokes had been the loudest at the end of the ceremony as they escorted the newlyweds to their room.

'*Chalo*,' he had said, as they had all laughed raucously. 'There's no need for us now.' They had all sniggered as they shut the door behind them. 'Lock up, Om,' Bhaiya had cried, 'You don't want to be disturbed tonight.'

Om had apologetically risen and locked the door. He had returned to the bed, and Asha had clamped her eyes shut. She had inhaled the smells that were to form the backdrop of her daily life; the slightly damp, old house smell of their room; the newly claustrophobic perfume of jasmine; and a nearer, newer scent – the earthy

155

combination of lavender talc and sweat that accompanied Om. Asha caressed a jasmine bud. How laughingly they had strewn them on the covers, how cheerfully they had foretold wedding night terrors. Her hand closed on a bud, felt its petals clasped as close as a desperate prayer.

'You know,' Om repeated, leaning towards her, and Asha's hand moved defensively back to her lap.

He was silent now, so she opened her eyes and smiled, repeating Nargis' *mantra* to herself. *Friendship, kindness, a bit of luck.*

'I think,' he was saying, 'that I have loved you from the very first moment I saw you. Do you remember it?'

'No,' she said softly, and as he gazed humbly at her, she shook her head.

'Really?'

'No,' she said with more bravado than she felt. 'When was it?'

'If you really don't know,' he said. He smiled again, betraying his teeth, and she looked away in confusion. 'Then I will keep the magic of that first look to myself.'

He had moved closer to her now, and she found herself squeezing the bud in her hand. All at once its aroma was unleashed, intense and threatening, as if it was in sympathy with Om's advance. Asha shut her eyes.

They were quiet for a minute, for longer. They were quiet for an eternity. She heard him breathe, she felt his night-time breath on her. She felt the jasmine bud in her hand sweat as it succumbed to her pressure.

'Asha,' he said finally. He spoke as if her name was too precious for familiarity. She saw his hand, dark, smooth, unscarred, and she moved her own under her *dupatta*. He brought her hand to his lips and kissed it. He turned it over, caressed her injured wrist, and she realised they were both uncomfortable with their intimacy. 'All this pressure on the wedding night,' he said. 'And do they think of the poor bride, lying in a strange bed for the first time?' Asha coloured, and he seemed to take heart from her reaction. 'We have a lifetime for all this.' His hands skimmed vaguely along the bed. 'And it's all happened so suddenly for you, hasn't it? Your travels, the wedding, and,' he hesitated, and for a brief instant, Asha wondered if the words were stuck in his throat. 'And,' he repeated, before losing inspiration again. *Say it*, she urged him silently. *Just say it*. 'Partition,' he said eventually, and pleased with his choice of words, he added, 'It's been a terrible time for you.' He nodded, as if to impart his words with adequate meaning. They looked at each other for a while in silence. There were no words spoken, there was no clumsy exchange of goodwill, no painful kindness conveyed, but brimming as his gaze was with good intent, it gave her hope. *This*, she thought, *is a gentle man. He's not a hero, he's not Firoze, but he will be kind.*

She heard him snore, saw the weakness of his jaw in profile. 'I have loved you from the very first moment I saw you,' he had said. There it had been, his admission of love, an act as selfless, as heedless of reciprocity as the man himself. A beam wavered in through the open windows, a brief night-time chill descended on the room and Asha shivered.

She and Nargis had been on holiday from school, and on the cusp of womanhood. One day, as the town took its afternoon rest, they had escaped to the banks of the Ravi. The monsoon was late in coming, and the river had shrunk to less than half its normal size. The two

157

had stopped by a rock, pretending to sun themselves like mermaids. *Dupattas* had slipped off their heads and shoulders, each had cast surreptitious glances at the other's budding chest.

Asha had felt full of life that afternoon, and full of a strange longing. The sun had shone hard and there had been no breeze, no sound from the town. The Ravi had been silent too, stilled as it was by the lack of rain. Asha had thought of when she had last examined her breasts in the privacy of her bedroom. How could they be at once yielding and firm? And was it possible that they conferred on her an irresistible lure? She *had* felt like a mermaid that afternoon on the banks of the Ravi, had surged with her new power.

They were silent, she and Nargis, and more than a little drowsy. Suddenly they heard footsteps, and as they rose hastily to rearrange their *dupattas* over their heads, they saw an unfamiliar boy approach. He was short and swarthy, and wore the stiff, dark blazer of a college man.

The girls looked at each other, ready to retreat, when the boy spoke. '*Namaste*,' he said, and as they stared at him, they saw him perspire under his warm clothes. He smiled; his teeth jutted out, and Asha and Nargis backed away. 'You're Prakash *sahib*'s daughter, aren't you?' he asked, and Asha blushed and turned wordlessly from him. She held her friend's hand and they ran fast to the safety of her house.

She smiled now at the memory of that distant day, and then, as her hand moved to the swell of her breast, she was struck by a thought. 'Let your *dupatta* slip,' the matron had advised her outside Om's house. 'Give a man the chance to rescue you.' She had wrinkled her nose at the thought, but now it occurred to her that the matron's advice had been well intentioned. She *had* let her *dupatta* slip, had offered up a glimpse of rising bosom. She had unwittingly let Om fall in love with her.

The next morning they were served breakfast on the back lawn in the shade of the *shamiana*. From where they sat, they heard the noise of the crowd outside.

'Nearly all of them are opportunists,' complained Mahesh. 'They've heard of *Sahib*'s kind heart and they arrive in their hundreds to try their luck.'

'Don't worry about them today,' said Ma, as she hovered around her son.

'How was your evening, *Sahib*?' Mahesh asked now. 'Did you sleep well?'

Ma tutted disapprovingly. '*Kya*, Mahesh,' she scolded. 'What a thing to say to a newlywed couple!'

She ushered the servant indoors, and the bride and groom were left alone with their paranthas and tea, with the sun and the protective shade of the *shamiana*, and with their own blushing smiles.

'There's someone I'd like you to meet,' said Om after a while. 'I've decided to set up a school for refugees. I've been on the lookout for a headmistress, and at last I believe I've found the right person. She's a refugee too, a lady called Mrs Garg.'

How little she knew about his world. She had known him to be short, to be toothy, to be unexciting. She had known him to be rich and enterprising, but this, this promise of magnanimity, was new to her.

'I'd like you to meet her,' he was saying now, 'and see if you think she'll fit into our school.' Asha looked up in surprise, and Om added, 'I'd value your opinion, Asha.'

There it was again, the tentative 'Asha', and she nodded quickly. 'Where is she from?'

'From near Suhanpur,' he said. He reached across and touched her hand. He turned it over, bending down to kiss her wrist, and she shivered. 'It's just a little down-river. There's a rock that only appears a little before the monsoon, if you remember. It's a nice spot for sunbathers.'

He went on, giving directions to Mrs Garg's town, but it was all lost on her. He was studying her closely, smiling at her, but she no longer had any claim on indifference. She coloured deeply, and as his fingers caressed the tender inside of her palm, she found she couldn't focus on his words. She had betrayed her lie. He knew now, that she knew, that she remembered that first meeting, that first look on a drowsy, sun-drenched summer's day. She saw Ma look out from a window in the house, and she leant towards him. She smiled, she returned the pressure of his hand. He *would* be kind. She *would* be happy.

8

Delhi grew slowly familiar to Asha: its rhythms, its noise, its crowds and chaos. She grew to know its narrow lanes; the dark, crowded *galis* that suddenly opened out onto wide, sweeping circuses. It was a city that somehow reconciled the intimacy of Indian life with the impassive coloniser's vision. It was a city as much of plenty as it was of gnawing want, and one where fortunes could be made, pasts reimagined, and spirits irretrievably broken. And it was all happening then, in 1947, at the crossroads of the city's destiny.

Delhi grew simultaneously unfamiliar to its natives as Muslims fled to the East, and as refugees from the West arrived in number. All through the city, ancient courtly Hindi was replaced by the immigrants' Punjabi tones. Punjabi enterprise began to fill the streets, and Queensway, that long, noble arcade, was renamed Janpath, the people's path, and portioned to hundreds of penniless, homeless arrivals from Pakistan. The smells of Punjabi cooking infiltrated the air. A neighbouring house was occupied by traders from Lahore, and one morning, as Asha opened her window, she was assaulted by the smell of pickled mango. She smelt freshly churned butter slathered on hot potato *paranthas*, and freshly set yogurt served in tiny earthenware pots. All at once

161

she was stabbed by memories: breakfast on Sundays, Mataji's famous pickles on fresh, buttered *paranthas*; and as soon as the food was finished and those around him grew sleepy, Savan vanishing to seek out Chotu on his *beedi* break.

So Delhi began to slowly belong to her, and yet there were snatches of the past that came to alienate her at the most unexpected of moments. She would be looking out at the monsoon-swollen Yamuna, or lying in bed with her husband, and out of nowhere, an illicit memory would emerge. She would see a flash of brown, smell old soap and sweat on warm skin, and she would close her eyes and throb with recalled pleasure. Her back would arch, she would sigh, she would bite colour into her lips. There was no recreating that passion, and now, in Delhi, as she looked guiltily across at her sleeping husband, there was no escaping its embrace.

Om introduced her to Mrs Garg. They were to meet at a neighbouring house that Om had acquired for the purpose of housing the school, and it was clear he was anxious for his wife to be involved in the project. He took her to the house early and gave her a tour of the rooms. 'This,' he said to her, pointing to a large reception area. 'This is where they will hold assemblies.' He turned to her eagerly, and took her by the hand. He swept open the door to a smaller, wood-panelled room, announcing, 'This will be the principal's office.' Once more he looked at her for her reaction. 'You agree, don't you?'

Asha smiled. 'I can see this is important to you.'

'You understand, then,' he replied. 'I have all the money, all the property we will ever need.' He paused placing his hands on her shoulders. 'But this is finally a way to make a difference.'

They went to the lawn to wait for Mrs Garg. From where they sat, Asha could look out onto the local park. Only a few days ago, she had run from the petitioners' queue outside Om's house, had run away to look for a haunted house and to find a way back to Firoze. The park still thronged with refugees, and if she looked hard, she could see them on the matchstick ladder that stood against the water tank. There had been reports of a fatality, but she wasn't sure if the deceased had jumped into the water or been pushed. Mahesh had come running into the house one morning, panting with excitement. 'A refugee has fallen into the tank,' he had announced. 'They're sending boys in to fetch him out.'

'*Hai Ram*,' Ma had complained. 'That's all we need. These refugees polluting our water.'

Asha closed her eyes, taking in a deep breath. Om was talking to her about his plans. 'It's important, isn't it, that their education isn't interrupted?'

'Of course.'

'And I want to focus on the girls.'

'Yes.'

'They shouldn't be left behind.'

'But,' said Asha, and as Om leaned forward, she added, 'Is that feasible?'

'Why wouldn't it be?'

'There is often such opposition to a girl's education . . .'

'No, no . . .'

'I don't mean the daughter of the educated man. I'm talking about your labourer's daughter, about your servant's daughter. These girls need help too, the daughters of lesser men, and in their case, perhaps it's more heroic to teach them skills.' He bent his head to consider her words. 'We can teach them a trade; how to embroider or to teach. Something that can give them a measure of choice.'

He was looking up now, smiling. They heard a voice call out to Om, and turned to see Mrs Garg approach. She was short, dressed in a starched *salwar kameez* that confounded the day's heat. Her hair was neatly tied into a bun, and every word, every motion was efficient. There was nothing spare about her, nothing superfluous. For a moment, Asha was struck by the certainty she had met Mrs Garg before, and then she smiled. She had the same mannerisms; the wagging finger, the narrowing eyes. She was another such one as Mrs Sodhi, the teacher who had nearly discovered her truancy in Suhanpur. She was another capable, sensible steward of vulnerable souls, and as Asha saw Om rise, she too nodded and folded her hands in welcome.

Mrs Garg spoke to them about her ideas for the school. She had been a school principal in Punjab before she had had to flee, and she rapidly sketched out plans for education, for music and physical exercise. 'We have to let their souls breathe too.' She looked around the lawn, sighing her satisfaction. 'It's a wonderful thing you're doing for the children, Om-*ji*.'

Om lifted his hands in self-deprecation. 'My wife is very interested in this project too,' he said. 'She will be getting involved.'

'Wonderful,' said Mrs Garg. She invited Asha's opinions, nodding vigorously when Asha mapped out her ideas. 'You're a pragmatist, then,' she said. 'We'll get along just fine.'

They met often now, Asha and Mrs Garg, and though

Asha was initially intimidated by the discrepancy in their ages, she found they were in sympathy with each other's opinions. Mrs Garg maintained a professional distance, and while their interaction was to carry them through several decades, she was always to call her by the honorific of Mrs Garg. The two women began to bring in children from the refugee camps, and slowly, they began to set up lessons. Asha taught them Hindi and English, Mrs Garg Mathematics and the Sciences. Bina, who turned out to be a keen historian, was roped in to tutor the children in a history that was yet to be put to paper. Om came in once a week to take charge of the children's physical education.

They were with them for six hours, from seven in the morning until just past one, but still Mrs Garg and Asha weren't satisfied. 'Their souls are breathing,' the older lady told Asha now. 'But we're not doing enough.'

'I agree,' said Asha. The children were returning to the camps after school, and she worried they weren't eating enough. Every week someone came in with a head full of lice, and the first few days of the week would be spent controlling the infestation. Then they had the children who didn't return, those they lost to the calls of labour or to disease. She thought of the old turbaned man holding his grandson out to Bhaiya on their way to Delhi. She thought of the longing in his eyes, of the hope. 'Do your best,' he'd begged them.

'I'd like to be able to give them breakfast and lunch,' Mrs Garg was saying. 'That would be such help to their families.'

'But how?' asked Asha. They already had too much work, what with the teaching and pastoral care. She returned home in the early evening, by which point

165

Ma was garrulous. 'A wife's place is at home,' she said. 'What use are you if you're not giving comfort to Om and to me?' Asha had attempted to point out that she worked at the school at Om's invitation, but Ma was not to be mollified. She began to mutter about expecting grandchildren. Bina was pregnant now, and even though her stomach was still smooth, every time she visited, Asha saw Ma looking unhappily at her friend's belly.

Strangely enough, it was the Ma-Bina combination that provided Asha with her solution.

Bhaiya and Bina had come over to the house one evening for dinner, and they sat up on the terrace to take advantage of the dying day's last sun. Mahesh brought up a tray full of lime sodas that the men spiked with gin. Ma sent up *samosas* and fried gram flour *pakoras*. She herself followed, and allowed the men to seat her. She was offered a drink: a lime soda, a cup of tea, but all this was turned down. '*Bus*,' she instructed Mahesh, 'Just fetch me a glass of water,' and the retainer went slowly on his arthritic legs back down to the kitchen.

'Ma,' Bhaiya was saying. There it was again, that bitten lip, that unctuous attention. 'What a great thing your son has done to set up this school for refugees.'

Om batted the praise away. 'It's nothing,' he said. He blushed under their friends' scrutiny. 'Besides,' he added, 'It's more Asha's than mine.'

'*Arre*, she'll be busy soon enough,' laughed Bhaiya. 'She'll have kids to think about.' He reached across to stroke his wife's growing belly, and Ma nodded.

'*Haan Beta*,' she said to her son in a beseeching voice. 'All I live for now is to see my grandchildren . . .'

'We hope for children,' agreed Om, looking straight at

his wife, but she looked away. His gaze didn't waver, and though she refused to look at him, she knew his attention remained firm on her. She grew irritated. What a way for Om to communicate his decisions, in front of Bina and Bhaiya. And Ma. *We hope for children.* Couldn't he have brought these topics up earlier, when they were alone? She flushed with anger, and her audience smiled, imagining her embarrassed.

She looked out towards the street. It was quiet now, and the hordes had cleared from outside the area's houses. A gentle breeze had picked up, and for a moment she revelled in its hypnotic rhythm. The park in the distance had been transformed into a makeshift refugee camp. There was no infrastructure here, no lines for food, no water for bathing, but it was still a place for the desperate to rest. She thought of the man they had dragged out of the tank. It had taken three men to carry him down the stairs, and any time anyone stumbled and then righted themselves, the crowds cheered. Asha rose and walked to the railing at the edge of the terrace. She held her wrist out, examining her scar. It was starting to purse together like a carelessly mended cloth, and the 'Om' tattoo underneath was beginning to reassert itself. She looked at the street below. How little everyone seemed at this remove, and how picturesque. Just like Savan had said. There was no squalor, no teeming camps, no starvation, no cholera. There was no suffering. Then, as she prepared to turn back to her party, she thought she saw something shift on the street outside the house. It was a slight figure in a dusty, torn *salwar kameez*. She leant over, peering, and saw it was a girl. She was squatting on the ground, and as the breeze picked up, she swept a lock of hair off her forehead. There was something about her that gave Asha pause. Perhaps it was her height or her manner that brought Roopa to mind, or perhaps her lack of care – she was easy prey for any predator this late in the day.

'*Arre*, Asha,' she heard Om call out. Bina was rising and walking towards her, but she was looking down at the girl she was certain was Roopa, and a moment later she was tripping downstairs and out of the house.

9

Ma had a hundred objections to the girl. 'She's too young, this Sanam,' she said. 'She's hardly fifteen. She doesn't have a tongue in her mouth. What work will she be able to do?'

Asha struggled to hide her disappointment. It hadn't been Roopa after all. It had been another lost stray, another orphan birthed by the Partition. She would never see Roopa again. Odds were she hadn't survived. 'Ma, you yourself have said there's too much work for Mahesh,' she repeated patiently. 'And we want to serve food at the school. This girl solves our problems.'

Ma looked the girl straight in the eye, and as Sanam looked away embarrassed, Ma crowed. 'See,' she said. 'She can't even look at me.'

'But Ma,' repeated Asha for the hundredth time. 'She will cook the school's food, then help Mahesh.'

Ma subjected Sanam to the same manner of scrutiny Asha had endured. Mahesh, standing by the door, and ostensibly clearing cobwebs from a wall, paid attention too. He climbed slowly and painfully up a set of creaking wooden stairs. From his height, he reached down, running a wicker broom along the wall to beat out cobwebs, but each time Sanam opened her mouth to speak, he paused in his efforts. Together, the terrible twosome took in each bedraggled detail of Sanam's outfit. They stared at her tattered *salwar kameez*, sighed at the dirt on her bare feet. 'Too common,' she saw them think. They smiled thinly at Sanam, they shut their eyes, as if in prelude to a prayer, and she saw them think, 'Another refugee, and another mess.'

Ma said out loud, '*Asha Beta*, she looks untrustworthy. Her eyes,' Ma continued, scowling at Sanam, 'are set too close together. And see how she fidgets.'

Next, Asha was taken aside and counselled, 'See how pretty she is. Look at her long, thick hair, look at her eyes. Do you feel comfortable having her around your husband?'

'She's a child,' pointed out Asha. 'And besides, you just said her eyes were close-set.'

'*Arre*,' harrumphed Ma. She bemoaned Asha's naïveté, thought of a dozen further objections, but she refused to give voice to her main cause of complaint. Sanam was Muslim, and after all the terror of the past few months, after the paranoia and rising enmity, after the ceaseless, mindless violence, a Muslim was not worthy of a Hindu's trust. She was not deserving of a Hindu's largesse. Asha thought of Ammi and the Maulvi. 'They're humans too,' he had said to an incensed Muslim, and she set her jaw. 'The girl stays,' she told her mother-in-law.

They were outside on the lawn now, and free of the hallway where Ma and Mahesh had passed their pitiless judgement on the girl. The smell of jasmine filled the air. Sanam smiled, she breathed in deeply. She looked down at her clothes. 'They burnt my house down. I have nothing else to wear.'

'It doesn't matter,' replied Asha. She thought of the

day she had seen the Muslim being burnt alive. She shut her eyes, but her senses filled with the stench of burning flesh. Her hands balled into a fist, she touched her wrist and her healing scar. She turned her wrist up, offered it up for Sanam to view. The girl flinched. 'I came here in filthy clothes too.'

Sanam was on the point of tears. 'I don't know where to go, Didi . . .'

Asha looked at her carefully. Sanam *was* pretty; her complexion light, her eyes as bright as a tiger's, but just then, as she stood there rubbing the tears from her eyes, she was barely human. She was a street child, frightened and wild. Her hair was matted, her face dirty. Her clothes were unwashed and fraying, she wore no shoes. Children like her came round daily. They asked for help, for money for their treasured trinkets, or for work. In the beginning she had helped. She had quietly distributed money, but Om scolded her out of the habit. 'What good is a few *paise* going to do? They'll buy food for the day, and they'll be in the same desperate position the next day. Save your money for the school.'

Now she asked Sanam, 'Where's your family?'

The girl looked at the ground.

That's right, thought Asha. *Somehow tragedy becomes our burden. A girl is left unprotected, and the shame falls on her.* 'Have you no one left in Delhi?' she asked.

Sanam shook her head. 'They attacked us while we slept,' she said dispassionately, as if she was reading the tragedy from a history book. *A million dead, countless more left homeless.* As if she herself hadn't been affected. She didn't look at Asha as she spoke. 'I was left for dead.'

Asha had heard the same story countless times on both sides of the border. She could almost finish the

171

girl's story off for her. Sanam spoke again in her soft, emotionless voice. 'Father dead, mother dead, brothers dead, and as for me – '

Asha grimaced. She thought back to the bus shelter in Pakistan where her family had so ruthlessly been killed. 'Father dead,' she thought, 'Mother dead, brother dead, and as for me . . .'

Mahesh came out. He stalked up to the girl, cleared his throat menacingly. 'What do you want me to do with her?' he asked.

'Clear a room for her,' said Asha.

'But she's Muslim,' said Mahesh. There it was finally, his and Ma's uncomfortable prejudice.

Asha said. 'Until last year you were from Suhanpur. If Om hadn't come here, you would have been in this girl's shoes. So, for that matter, would I.'

Sanam was looking down, embarrassed, ashamed. 'I'm taking her in,' Asha said. She put a hand around her, and as Mahesh gaped, she shepherded the girl indoors.

'Didi,' Sanam was saying. She stopped in the hall, pausing to take in her surroundings. She gazed at the chandelier, the carpets, the tusks and the vase and the screen. Asha saw her smooth down her clothes, and suddenly grow aware of her unkempt appearance. She saw her think the same thought that had struck her. 'Partition has been kind to these people.'

'Come,' said Asha gently. She lifted her hand to Sanam's arm, and guided her into the house, and as Sanam looked like protesting, she said, 'Come on. Let's wash the Partition off you.'

10

She heard a noise, and she half rose. She patted the bed groggily, but Om's side was empty. It hadn't been slept in, and for a moment Asha worried. She remembered her dreams: Firoze on a burning *tonga*, trying hard, impossibly hard to outrun the flames. Her family's cries as they were lost to the world, Roopa running, and then the stench, the stomach-turning smell as the faceless Muslim was slaughtered. She gave a cry, and found herself covered in a film of sweat. Then she remembered: she was safe, she was at home and in her bed, and Om was in Amritsar, helping stranded refugees. She sighed. All was well, she was safe. Then she felt a stab of irritation. Where was Om when she needed him? And how could he expect her to bear children when he stayed away so often?

Just this morning, Bina had come to see her. Ma had fussed over her. 'When is the baby due?' She had stared at the girl's flat belly. 'You're still not showing. Maybe our Asha could be pregnant too?' The two had stared at her appraisingly, and Ma had asked Bina how she had known she was pregnant.

'*Bus*,' Bina had replied. 'Everything felt different . . .'

'*Haan*.'

'I didn't get my period . . .'

'No,' Ma had said. 'Our Asha hasn't either,' and as Asha had stared, taken aback by Ma's knowledge, the older woman had added, 'But were there any other signs?'

'Everything felt sore.'

'Well?' Ma had asked her daughter-in-law. 'Do you feel sore?'

'Ma,' Asha protested, and Ma had sighed her dissatisfaction.

Bina had hurried to change the topic. Talk had turned to the school, to Mrs Garg's efficiency, to Sanam's preparing meals for the children. 'I'll have to slow down soon,' she had said. 'My family is against me working while I'm pregnant.'

'I wish *she* would slow down,' Ma had said. She hadn't spoken further, but they had both seen all that was encompassed in her expression: Om's continued travel, Sanam's arrival, Asha's failure to conceive. As Sanam had come out with cups of tea, she turned away. 'No,' she said petulantly. 'What do I want with all this? I'll eat next when Asha tells me she's pregnant.'

'Ma,' Asha began, but as Ma pursed her lips, she made her excuses and rushed to her room.

In front of the mirror by her dressing table, Asha lifted her tunic *kameez* to display a taut, slender stomach. She patted it, once softly, then again, then slowly cradled it with the palm of her left hand, just as she had on the day Riaz had come into her room. But this was different. She felt nothing. Her breasts weren't sore; her insides didn't churn, there was no nausea, no dizziness, nothing she could pin her hopes on. She repeated her calculations. When had she first felt Firoze's child taking root inside her? As soon as the school holidays had started? On the

174

day of the radio broadcast? She could not be sure. But it was still early, and as she patted the emptiness in her womb, as she retied her *salwar* higher on her waist, as she wrapped her *dupatta* around herself and prepared to return to her mother-in-law, she repeated this *mantra* to herself. It was still early.

She heard the noise again. It was a low, hoarse cry, a little like a winter cough. She got up and went into the corridor. She went first towards Ma's room, but there was no sound there. She remained a while in the dark, trying to decide her next steps. She knew Sanam slept in a room down the corridor, and though Ma had wanted the girl in the servants' quarters, Asha had insisted. 'She's too pretty to be safe in the quarters,' she had said, but now she hesitated. What if she had imagined the noise?

Then she heard the voice again, a groan, a cry, and she moved in its direction. She stopped outside Sanam's door and knocked. There was silence for a moment, but then she heard steps shuffling towards her, and Sanam opened the door.

'Didi?'

Asha looked at the child. She was pale, her forehead damp. She dabbed at her face with her *dupatta*. Her eyes seemed larger than normal, beautiful and desperate, her cheekbones more pronounced. 'She's lost weight,' thought Asha guiltily, and as the girl patted her brow again, Asha knew. She thought of Ma's warning; 'The girl is too pretty to be up to any good.' She knew Om loved her, knew he had married her despite Ma's opposition, but still, a demon troubled her, the spectre of Om's absence. Had Sanam been responsible for this?

'Is all well?' she asked.

'Didi.' Sanam looked down, embarrassed and alone, and Asha pushed her way inside the room. She sat the girl down on her thin mattress, and with trembling hands, fetched her a glass of water. This Sanam drank, quickly and noisily, and Asha asked again in a voice she took care to modulate, 'Is something the matter?' She looked down at Sanam's stomach, so neat still, so trim. Hers had been the same too, and she recognised the girl's haunted eyes all too well. 'You know you can talk to me.'

'Didi,' started Sanam, then looked down. *There it is again*, thought Asha, *that look of shame*. She was quiet for a long while. At length Asha extended her hand, took the maid's in her own. 'That night,' said Sanam. 'You know, when my family was . . .'

She struggled for speech, and instead, she began to take in great gulps of air. 'I know,' said Asha. She stroked the girl's hand, squeezed it hard. 'I know.'

'That night,' said Sanam again. She spoke softly now, and close though Asha was to her, she had to lean forward to hear her. 'That night there was a man.'

'Oh, Sanam.' She smoothed a lock of the girl's hair behind her ear, and Sanam started at the contact. The room was still, the sun slowly splintered into the room, and as Asha squeezed the girl's hand, she found it cold. 'I was quiet,' she said without emotion, 'and absolutely still. I kept my eyes shut, and I think he thought I was dead.'

She was quiet now, looking away. She put her hand on the bedspread, took to caressing its frayed edge. They didn't speak. Every once in a while, Sanam rocked forward in discomfort. A small cry would escape her lips, and then she would be calm again, her hand back to agitating against the bedspread. 'Child,' said Asha. 'How long have you known?'

'For a while,' replied Sanam. Her head turned downwards; she refused to look Asha in the face. 'For the past few days I haven't felt well. And this morning I was preparing breakfast for the children, and my stomach . . .' Asha felt her own stomach knot, and her hand raced to her belly. 'And Didi,' Sanam added, 'He saw me, that Mahesh saw me. He was looking strangely at me, and I'm sure he knows.'

'But are you sure you're pregnant?' asked Asha, even though she knew the answer. Just as she knew she wasn't carrying a baby for Om. Still, she repeated her question, 'Are you sure?'

Sanam didn't reply. She retched, raising a hand to her throat. She turned her face to the older girl, and again, Asha was struck by her beauty. Her face glowed, despite the discomfort, her eyes shone. 'What am I going to do?' Sanam asked.

'What?'

'Can I get rid of it?'

Asha thought of her *tonga* ride out of Suhanpur. She thought of her relief as the bleeding started. 'No,' she said.

'But I can't keep it,' said Sanam. Her face creased in distress, she pressed both hands on her belly and squeezed it hard. 'Don't,' said Asha. She reached out to stop the girl, but Sanam pushed her away. 'Don't you see, Didi?' she said. 'This child's father raped me. He killed my family.'

She got up and began to pace up and down the room. It was a tiny space, smaller even than Asha's bathroom. She covered the area in six strides, turned around, paced in the opposite direction. 'Poor girl,' thought Asha. She looked at her walking to and fro like a caged animal. 'But still, despite all her troubles, there is a child growing inside her.'

'Don't do anything sudden,' she said to Sanam. She rose, brought the girl back to the bedding. Sanam gazed at her with her desperate tiger's eyes, and Asha said, 'I'll figure something out.' Sanam shook her head and Asha repeated, 'Please don't do anything sudden.'

'I won't even be able to work, will I, with a baby?' Sanam pushed her hand down on her stomach.

'You're so young,' said Asha kindly, and the maid began to sob.

'This *harami*,' Sanam hissed. 'This bastard. It won't let me survive. I won't be able to work. I won't be able to eat. I won't be able to live.'

The sun grew warmer, darker – as dark as a mustard flower – and the noise of the household rose. She heard breakfast being prepared, she heard Ma descending the stairs. 'You won't have to bring up the child,' she promised. She looked at the girl, gauging her reaction, and as Sanam stayed silent, she went on. 'You just carry on as normal, or they'll suspect something is wrong,'

Sanam didn't speak.

'Go now,' said Asha kindly. 'Go back to your work. I'll take care of your child for you.'

11

'Sit, sit,' said Ma, 'The others will take care of the arrangements.'

It was the morning of Asha's *Goad Bharai* ceremony, her baby shower. Soon the house would be full of guests bearing treasures for the unborn child: gold coins, silver bottles, black bead *nazariyas* to ward off the evil eye. Mahesh and Sanam had spent the morning preparing food for the guests. 'Take care with your cooking,' Ma told them. 'This food will feed my grandson.'

'It's too much,' complained Asha.

'The smell, *Beta*?' asked Ma solicitously.

'Everything. The decorations, the food. Anyone would think it's a wedding.'

'*Arre*,' tutted Ma. 'I had to rush my son's wedding. Let me at least celebrate this as I want to.'

Mahesh climbed the staircase, looping marigold flowers the colour of sunshine through a wooden trellis. Sanam entered the room with a cup of tea, and Asha studied her carefully. She was now in her third month of pregnancy, but there were no signs to show for it. Her sickness had subsided, as had her fatigue. Her skin glowed now, her hair shone, and Asha thought back to the way she had looked before her bleed. 'Thank God I don't have a son,' Mrs Malik had said. 'Or else he would have spirited you away.'

179

'*Chai*, Didi,' Sanam was saying. 'With ginger.'

'Good,' smiled Ma. 'And take these cushions,' she said to Sanam. 'Put them under her back. Make her comfortable.'

Sanam followed the older woman's instructions, and Ma continued to scold her daughter-in-law. 'You really should be taking it easier. Why, I couldn't do anything when I was pregnant.' Ma sat down on the sofa next to Asha. She put down the tiny booties she was knitting for the baby, and gestured Sanam away. She leant towards Asha, speaking in a hoarse stage whisper. 'I couldn't stand the smell of flowers, I couldn't stand the taste of turmeric. I couldn't go anywhere. So I lay in my bed for nine months, ate gram flour *laddoos* and drank milk.' She smiled conspiratorially, winked. 'It was the best time of my life.'

'Yes, Ma,' said Asha dutifully. She brought a hand to the crook of her waist, pretended to find it sore. '*Oof*,' she said, and as her mother-in-law smiled benignly, she moved the cushions around to make herself more comfortable.

'And *Beta*,' said Ma. She spoke slowly, her mouth open, and Asha could see the remains of her mother-in-law's breakfast between her two front teeth. 'This son of mine,' Ma said. 'I hope he's not troubling you at night?'

Asha's lip quivered. 'Ma,' she replied.

'I've told him,' she said. 'There's time enough for all that . . .' Ma wrinkled her nose, and waved her hands outwards, as if warding off an ill breeze. 'There's time enough once the child is safely born.'

There was something in Ma's expression just then – just as she wrinkled her nose and exposed her teeth – that reminded Asha of Om. It was the image of Om in

contemplation, of Om reading the newspaper, or of him
troubling out an answer to a problem at work. She had
taken to bringing him a glass of almond *sharbat* in the
evening, just as he returned home after work. He sat out
in the garden, fresh from his evening shower, and as she
neared him, she smelt the lavender talc he applied on his
drying skin. 'Bus,' he said to her as she offered him the
drink. 'You need to rest.' He looked up at her with Ma's
worried face, foreseeing fatigue, or aversion to food, to
work, to exertion.

'No,' she replied. 'I'm fine, I really am,' and then, as
his nose wrinkled in disbelief, she lifted a hand to her
waist. She arched her back, pushing out her belly. 'Well,'
she said. 'I *am* a bit tired . . .'

He made her sit down, made her drink his *sharbat*. She
made a face at the sweetness of the drink. 'Of course,' he
said. 'You sit here. I'll call for ginger tea.' He rushed out
before she could stop him, and on his return, he said,
'Ma told me ginger tea would be good for your, your,
your . . .' He struggled for the right word, and she said:

'My morning sickness.'

'Yes,' he said gratefully. 'You're really suffering, aren't
you?'

'No,' said Asha, even as he insisted she cut down
her hours at school. He fussed about her, fetching her
cushions, then a footstool. He came to sit next to her, he
stroked her belly through her clothes, and she immediately flinched. She was tired.

'Of course,' said Om. He rose, moved away. 'You
rest,' he said to her. She smelt his lavender talc. 'These
months will pass before you know it,' he said. 'In the
meantime, my *jaan*, my life, just you rest.'

And now his mother looked at her with the same

worried expression. 'I've told him in no uncertain terms,' she repeated, 'To leave off all this romance-showmance business until the baby is born.'

'I know,' said Asha, feeling disloyal. 'But you know what men are like.'

There was a noise at the gate, and Ma looked up crossly. 'It's too early for guests,' she grumbled. 'Nothing is ready.' She rose, and as Asha moved to rise too, she sat her back down. 'No, *Beta*,' Ma said, 'No work for you,' but her care was needless as the door opened and Mahesh came wheezing in.

'Sorry,' he said, 'But there is someone asking to see you.'

'Haven't I told you,' said Ma, 'There are to be no more of those refugees.'

The retainer cleared his throat. 'No, Ma-ji,' he elaborated as he turned to Asha, 'This person is asking for *you*.'

'Me?'

'*Arre*,' said Ma. 'They'll have heard she's been married into this family, that she's doing charity work. Of course they'll come for her too now.'

'This person said she was from Suhanpur.'

Nargis. It was Nargis, with Firoze close behind. Asha knew it was impossible, this fantasy of hers, but just then, as Mahesh and Ma stood debating what to do, she grew full of the likelihood.

'There are thousands who came here from Suhanpur.'

'Should I send her away then?'

'Yes,' said Ma.

'No.' Asha rose, and despite Ma stepping forward protectively, she turned and walked towards the hall.

182

It was Roopa. Tall, gangly, and as awkwardly dressed as she remembered, but their time apart seemed to have sharpened her angularities. She was thinner, bonier, taller. She grinned as Asha rushed to her.

'Roopa!'

'It's a good thing your Mataji made us write down this address,' she said.

There she was, right in front of her. It was as if the events of the last few months hadn't taken place. As if she hadn't parted from Nargis, from Firoze, as if her family hadn't been lost forever. She felt it rise, the terror in her throat, the smell of blood on her wrist, the stench of charred flesh, and she was swooning. Then Ma came in, and stopped, staring hard at Roopa. 'Don't you know?' she exclaimed. 'Can't you take care of her in her condition?'

'Her condition?' Roopa said, puzzled, and as Ma rushed off to fetch a chair for her to sit on, Asha began to laugh.

'What is it?' asked Roopa. She held Asha close. 'What is it that woman was saying about your condition?'

But Asha was beyond words. She was beyond care, beyond worry or sadness, for now she laughed, like an infant, without control. 'You're here,' she said to her friend, and as Roopa smiled, as she raised her eyebrow in her old pantomime manner, she laughed again. 'To see you again, to actually see you, after everything that has happened . . .'

'But what's happened to you?'

'Me?' asked Asha, still hysterical. She calmed down at last, and studied her friend closely. There were lines on Roopa's face now, her hair bleached blond by the baking sun. She had lost more weight than Asha had first realised,

183

and her shoulder blades rose painfully when she swallowed. Roopa smiled, held her hand, and now Asha began to cry. It was Roopa who calmed her. It was she who stroked her back and told her everything would be all right.

'Tell me,' said Asha. 'All about your journey. I want to know how you got here.'

'No,' said Roopa. There was a new firmness in her voice, a resistance Asha hadn't known before.

'But . . .'

'Look, I walked. I walked the wrong way first, deeper into Pakistan.' There it was again, the steel in her voice. 'Then I met a convoy of people heading East. I walked with them.' She looked around, at Asha, at the hall with its antique tapestries, with its elephant tusks, with its prized, priceless vase, and she shrugged. 'And so,' she said, 'here I am.'

'Here you are,' echoed Asha. This, she knew, was all the detail she would ever get. There would be no talking of the journey, of the camps, of disease or of death. If she was lucky she would get occasional glimpses into Roopa's travel. There would be a hot summer, and Roopa would sigh her remembrance. She would look overhead at the fan, at the cool white ceiling, and she would shudder. She would see a street beggar, and though they would all advise her against handing out money, though they would all warn that her largesse would only fuel crime, she would reach into her purse and empty it out into thrilled, wary hands. This would be all the access Asha would be allowed into Roopa's summer of the year of their Independence. The rest would have to be gleaned from her silences.

'But Asha,' Roopa asked again. 'Who is that lady? And what was she saying about your condition?'

'Oh that,' said Asha dismissively. She couldn't lie, not to Roopa, not just then.

'But you are, aren't you?' Roopa was beaming. She was looking up, smiling as Ma returned, as Sanam dragged a chair in. 'You're expecting!'

'Yes,' said Asha in confusion, 'No.' She looked at her mother-in-law, at Sanam's retreating back, and now she said, 'Yes.'

'*Arre*,' Ma was scolding. 'So long you two have been talking for.' She wagged a fat finger at Asha. 'And you didn't even tell your friend the most important news?'

Asha blushed. Ma turned to Roopa now, and asked if she had family to go to.

'Yes,' nodded Roopa. 'My sister. I went to see her first, and then,' she said, looking across at Asha, 'I had to come and see if Asha had reached Delhi safely.'

'*Hai, Beta*,' Ma was saying. 'It's so good for my Asha to have a friend from her Suhanpur days . . .'

'Ma,' said Asha quickly. 'Can't Roopa stay here?'

'Here?' croaked Ma uncomfortably. 'But won't her sister want her . . .'

'Just for a few days,' pleaded Asha. 'She's all I have left of my past . . .'

'But *Beta*. . . .'

'Please, Ma,' insisted the girl. 'It'll be such great comfort to me.'

And there it was: the trump card. All had to be sacrificed for Asha's comfort while she was pregnant. Ma agreed, gracious now. 'Of course, *Beta*,' she said. 'We'll ask Roopa to stay.'

Asha turned to her friend. 'Will your sister agree to let you stay?'

185

'What a question!' grumbled Ma. 'I've said it's ok, haven't I? Leave the rest to me. I'll talk to Roopa's sister.'

Roopa's arrival suited everyone but Om. Roopa moved into their room; Om was banished to one near Ma's. He was good-humoured about the eviction. He was gentle and kind and pleasant, but he was not Firoze. He still smiled too readily and too often, he was still too toothy. A little something in Asha still shuddered at his smile, at his eagerness to please, at his worshipful enunciation of her name, and yet, she found she was beginning to get accustomed to him. She found herself regretting her secret, or at any rate, that it was one she couldn't share with him.

Night time with Roopa began to feel like feast days at Suhanpur. A little like Asha and Nargis' night time adventures on the inspector's roof terrace. They spoke late into the night. They paused whenever they heard a footstep outside.

'Tell me,' asked Roopa one night. 'Can you feel it as yet?'

'No,' said Asha. She turned on her side, pretending to sleep. More than anything else, she minded lying to Roopa. They'd shared too much, and it was Roopa now, more than anyone else, who carried a sense of what Asha had been through. She had waited at the bus shelter too, she too had been rooted to the spot as her family lay dying. It wasn't right, lying to her. Asha thought of how she could word her admission. 'Sanam was in trouble,' but then she closed her eyes. It was impossible, unthinkable. The words were beyond her.

'No kicking?' Roopa was asking.

'No,' sighed Asha. She sat up, wincing as she

remembered she had to be more measured in her movements. 'No kicking. No nausea, no tiredness. No nothing.'

'Do you think it's all right?' asked Roopa, concerned, and Asha nodded. She took care with her words.

'It's been a good pregnancy, thank God.'

They fell silent. The room grew darker and from outside, they heard the beat of the night watchman's *lathi*. 'Be vigilant,' he cried. 'Be vigilant.' Asha shut her eyes, but she was back there, she was back in the Suhanpur of her nightmares. '*Allah ho Akbar*,' she heard. A thousand fevered footsteps rushed through the streets, beating sticks against the soil, shouting as loudly as they could, 'Allah is great.'

Roopa was silent beside her, and Asha knew her friend was thinking of Suhanpur too. Often, at least once a night, one of them would wake. Asha would hear a snuffling, a whispering, a prayer ushered into the night, and her body would tense as she lay. She would think of Riaz, of a vanishing Firoze, and in the end, always of that hateful, smiling Pathan. She would think of her slaughtered family, of the silenced Savan. She would remember her inability to move, or to call for help. She would sit up in bed, drenched with fear, and turn to see Roopa sitting up beside her. She too was unable to shake her fear, she too was unable to sleep, or to forget.

'Asha,' Roopa asked softly. 'Do you think it's a boy?'

'What?'

'My mother used to say that if the nausea went away, it would be a boy.' Roopa paused, and there it was again, another ghost of the past. Another voice that would never speak again. 'My mother said she was sick all the time she was carrying me. Maybe it's a boy.'

187

'Maybe,' said Asha sadly. The dark enveloped them more fully, and she added under her breath, 'But I'm not pregnant.'

There was no reply. Asha heard a soft sound next to her, a deep breath, and was sure Roopa had gone to sleep. She sighed. It was just as well, keeping her secret to herself. It was safer. Then she realised Roopa was sitting up. 'What?' she asked, 'You're not pregnant?'

Out it all came: Asha's inability to conceive, Ma's pressure, Sanam's predicament. 'It just seemed like the easiest solution.'

Roopa shook her head, then leaned over and put her arms around her. 'What a sorry, sorry mess this Partition is.' Roopa held on to her for an eternity, and though Asha felt her shake her head again, she smiled. This was it, her burden eased. Roopa knew, and she would help Asha out. Together they would worry out an answer. Roopa asked, 'What do you plan to do as Sanam begins to show?'

'I've picked up some looser clothes for her,' said Asha. 'And I'll tell Ma that Sanam has to spend more time at the school, that she will be sleeping over there for a few months.'

'Will the girl be safe there?'

Asha shrugged unhappily. 'There's a man who is sniffing around her.' She thought of Salim, their neighbour's gardener. Sinewy, sun-hardened, with silent eyes that always caught her by surprise. She had seen him look at Sanam. He would stop his work, literally stop in his tracks as she walked past, and anything he held – pot or hoe or manure – would remain glued to his hand until she had gone out of view and he had recovered his equanimity. Flowers had spilled, pots had broken, manure

188

dirtied lawns, and still Sanam hadn't noticed. 'He spoke to me one day,' said Asha now, 'and asked if Sanam was married. He won't harm her.'

Roopa nodded, then turned a worried face to her. 'And you?' she asked. 'What will you do as the months progress and your tummy remains flat?'

'Well,' replied Asha. A slow smile. 'I'll have to use a pillow.'

Roopa was smiling too, and soon they were both shaking, both taken with the absurdity of Asha's situation. 'You poor child,' said Roopa. 'You poor silly, hopeless child.' She held her still, held Asha's head against her bony shoulder. Asha heard the watchman's *lathi* strike the ground. 'Be vigilant,' she heard. Her breathing began to slow, her head felt heavy and Asha smiled wearily. The *lathi* beat hard against the ground. She brought her hand to her womb. 'Be vigilant,' went the watchman's call, and she nodded. She sighed softly, and she began hcr slow, weightless descent into unconsciousness.

12

Then one day, she saw Firoze.

Asha had been walking in the Lodhi Gardens with Om. This was their evening routine as the weather turned cooler, and on days she claimed to be tired, he bullied her into coming out. 'The baby will be here soon,' he said. 'And then there'll be no time to go out.' It was always slightly chilly in the evenings now, but in a Delhi recovering from a hot, traumatic summer, the chill was welcome. She wore a shawl as she walked, and outside the house she lowered her *dupatta* off her head. 'It's a good idea,' encouraged her husband. 'Times are changing.'

Om spoke to her about work, about his plans for their school. 'I want us to start teaching the girls the skills you spoke of,' he said. 'They need to be able to stand on their own feet.' He smiled sheepishly. 'Look at me,' he said. 'Talking as if I know anything about these matters.'

Asha felt indulgent on these walks outside with her husband, she felt indulged. She felt young and liberal. She looked around her, at the proud *Ashoka* trees lining their path, she felt her husband steal a glance at her, and she felt herself throbbing with possibility. 'The branches will burst into flames soon,' said Om to her as she paused under a tree. She looked at him, and he

190

smiled self-consciously at his words. 'Another month or two, and the air will be full with them,' he continued. He leant towards her, his hand grazing hers. 'They'll burn yellow, bright red. They'll blaze in time for our prince's birth.' She blushed, not answering, but she smiled. *Yes*, she thought to herself, *I can be happy*.

They had just reached the end of their walk. They saw the entrance to the park in front of them. It was crowded, full of office workers seeking the last rays of the day's sun. Street vendors did a brisk trade in snacks: crisp gram beans, blackened corn on the cob. 'Another round?' asked Om, and they were about to turn back into the path when she saw a familiar glint of brown.

She looked again. It was there, the fleetest brown head leaving the park. It was Firoze she saw. It had to be. He had the same bearing, the same height, the same light colouring. She was sure she recognised his sweater; she was certain it was the one his mother had presented to him on his graduation from college. How proud he had been that day, and how thrilled to begin work for Pappaji. 'See,' he had said at the end of his first day's work, 'You will never be free of me now.'

He was walking out. She raised her arm and began to run in his direction.

'Asha!' Om was after her in a second, snatching her hand, slowing her down. 'Running in your condition!'

'No,' she said, though she stopped. 'I have to – '

'What is it?'

'I think I saw,' she faltered. She gestured towards the entrance, beginning to move again.

He hurried after her. 'Who?' he asked. 'Was it someone from home?'

He was nowhere to be seen. They were by the entrance

191

now, and she rushed out onto the road. He had vanished, and as she strained to look across the road, all she could see was passing traffic. A bus moved noisily by, and once it was gone, she looked again. It was growing dark, and the streets thronged with people on their way home from work. There was no knowing him now.

Om tugged at her sleeve. 'Who was it?' he asked. 'Someone I know?'

'No,' said Asha. 'Yes. Yes,' she repeated, 'Yes it was.'

'Who?' he asked eagerly. His face shone under the last light of the evening, and he looked at her expectantly.

'My neighbour,' she said. He continued looking at her, and she added in desperation. 'Nargis.'

'Nargis?' he asked. 'That friend of yours?' He scanned the road in front of them, shaking his head. 'No Asha, it can't be her. What would a Pakistani girl be doing so far from home? And now, when they're talking of war? No, no, it's not her.' Still he went on looking. 'No,' he repeated, 'How could it be?'

'I don't know,' said Asha in confusion. 'I was sure it was her. It looked exactly like . . .'

'Nargis!' Om was laughing. He had led her back into the park. They returned to their stroll, walked briskly under a darkening sky. 'Do you remember that time . . .' He paused. They were under a tree with low branches, a *Peepal* perhaps like they had growing in the courtyard in Suhanpur. 'Do you remember that day you kept the *Karva Chauth* fast?' She nodded silently. 'How the both of you terrified me!' He looked across at her, saw a hint of a smile on her face, and he pounced at that. 'So you do remember,' he said. 'You did know how hard it was for me!' She was laughing too now, though she tried to hide her mirth. She lifted her *dupatta* to her mouth, turned her

192

face away from her husband, but he knew she laughed.

'Do you know what I did that day?' Om asked. They started to walk again, and as the winter chill set in for the evening, he drew closer. 'I asked your father for your hand in marriage,' he said. He spoke softly, almost in a whisper, and Asha nodded.

'Did you know that?' he asked. He put his arm around her. She didn't resist, didn't answer his question, and he brought her into his embrace. 'Asha,' he said into her ear. 'Asha, I loved you when I first saw you,' and Asha thought of how she had sunned herself like a mermaid by the Ravi. His arms were around her now. His hands were hot on her. Asha was scandalised for an instant, then she saw that it was dark around them, and she allowed herself to lean into him. His hands were on her back. He was saying, 'How I've missed you,' and a hand was reaching to the front, was embracing her belly.

'No,' cried Asha in a rush, but he was touching her. He felt the soft padding of her pillow, pressed it and felt its flimsy resistance. 'Asha,' he said, pulling away. He looked at her in the dark, he looked at her swollen belly. He patted her again, but as she pushed him away, he didn't say another word.

He drove them to the United Coffee House. They were silent as they ordered their food. They were silent as they ate. He didn't smile. He didn't talk. He didn't steal quick glances at her belly. There was no darting look at her plate, no invitation to eat more, to rest, to allow him to arrange another cushion behind her. There were no toothy smiles. There were no compliments.

Om wrinkled his nose at the taste of his food, and

as Asha leaned forward solicitously, he raised his hand. 'Waiter,' he said imperiously. 'I need salt.'

This was placed courteously on the table, and Om laughed. 'And you,' he said to his wife. 'What do you need? Salt?'

She shook her head.

'No,' he agreed. 'I didn't think so. Some ginger tea, maybe?'

'Om . . .'

He was eating now, shovelling spoonfuls of rice into his mouth. He added a liberal helping of salt onto his dish, too much to suit his taste, but he didn't complain, eating instead with manic zeal.

The conversation at the tables around them was animated. Just behind them sat four earnest, moustachioed men with military bearing. 'So it's settled, then?' one asked. 'Kashmir is ours?'

'Yes,' said another. 'I received word this afternoon.'

Om looked up briefly, then returned to his dinner.

'And are they still there?' asked one of the men. 'Those Pakistani scoundrels?'

'Alas,' replied his friend. 'Yes.'

'Enough of the Mahatma's non-violence,' said another. 'We should remove those bloody Pakistanis from our land.'

'Ha!' laughed Om. He clapped a hand on his trouser leg, and the table next to them turned around at the noise. He whispered in his mother's loud hiss, 'Pakistan! Suhanpur! Today's sighting of Nargis! Was any of it true, Asha?'

'Please,' pleaded his wife. She looked down as he stared at her, unblinking, unsmiling, and he laughed again. The waiter returned and cleared their plates away

194

with officious ceremony. 'Anything else, Sir?' he asked, but Om waved him away.

Asha began to speak. She had wanted to help Sanam, and she had worried that she hadn't fallen pregnant herself. This – this solution – had seemed an answer to all their problems.

'That's why,' he said. He laughed, seemingly without reason, and Asha had to look away.

'That's why!' he repeated, clapping his hands. The waiter approached, but Om turned and gestured him away. 'All this time I've been wondering what I've done to offend you, and it wasn't me at all!'

'Om, please . . .'

'Of course not,' he said. 'You just didn't want me to touch that, that . . .' He floundered. The hopeful waiter leaned forward, then fell back into the shadows as Om turned to his wife. 'Tell me,' he asked. 'Just what is it?' She didn't reply, and he repeated, 'What is it, that, that . . .'

'A pillow.'

'A pillow! A pillow!' he laughed hysterically.

They were quiet again, and Asha prayed he would pay the bill. It was too loud in the restaurant, too bright, too cheerful. There was a snort, and she looked up. He was laughing again, clapping his hands together with zeal. 'A pillow!' he was crying, 'A pillow.' The military men at the next table turned to look at them. They smiled, charmed at the sight of a young couple enjoying a night out. 'Thank God,' said one, 'that it isn't all war.'

'Of course,' he was hooting. He was saluting them, he was turning back to his wife. 'Of course it was a pillow.'

He reached out, lifted her hands from her lap. These he fixed on the table wrist side up, her scar visible, and as she attempted to pull away, he whispered, 'No you don't, Asha. Not now.'

She looked into his face. His eyes were expressionless, but he was intent on studying her. She looked away again, but he applied pressure on her wrists. She felt a stab of remembered pain, and she looked up in surprise. He held her look for a long, unyielding time, and at the end of it, he laughed again. 'A pillow,' he said.

'Please,' said Asha. 'Om, please.'

He rose. He straightened his trousers, suddenly meticulous. 'What a mess,' he was saying to himself, and she remembered how she left clothes lying around in their room. She'd be tidier now. Roopa's sister was eager to have her live with them, to get her married, and she would finally let her go. Om could move back in. Anything, anything he asked for – she just wanted her husband back.

'What a mess,' he repeated. He brushed a crumb off his shirt.

'Please,' she said. 'Please, Om.'

He looked at her, then rose and left the room.

She didn't move. She sat waiting for him. The diners who had looked at them so smilingly left, and a new party sat down in their place. It was a family – a loud, opinionated mother, a tired father, a pretty, embarrassed daughter, a teenage son – and for a while she lost herself in their noise. The waiter approached her, 'Ma'am, is there anything else you need?' and the family turned to look her way. Their noise died down, they took in her solitude. The loud mother smiled through fleshy lips.

'Yes,' said Asha quickly to the waiter. 'I'll have another fresh lime soda,' and the waiter hurried to do her bidding.

The family stared at her for a while, then were distracted by their food. They ate, the son began to clamour for dessert, and as the order was placed, Om walked back in. His steps were uncertain, and he sat down heavily. He put his hands on the table to steady himself, and Asha's glass nearly toppled over. Her lemonade spilt. 'Om,' she started.

He held his hand up. 'Tell me,' he said. 'Why?'

They were looking her way again. She leant towards him, speaking softly. 'I wasn't getting pregnant.'

He was silent.

'I was so scared. I thought,' she said, then faltered. 'I thought I would have fallen pregnant . . . .'

'We had only just got married.'

He laughed, that senseless, hysterical trill of his. The family next to them turned towards them. She leant forward. 'Please believe me, Om.'

Dessert arrived, and the family dived into it. Loud exclamations followed, and then a delighted silence. 'And Ma . . .'

'She told me not to listen to you.'

'But Om . . .'

'She said you were only marrying me because you had no other options.'

She sat still. There was a loud scraping of spoon against plate from the next table, someone belched their satisfaction at the meal.

'No,' she murmured.

'And what were you saying about Ma, anyway?'

'She asked me every day if I was pregnant.'

'So?'

'You don't know how desperate I felt.'

'Sometimes it takes time to feel the symptoms.'

'I wasn't pregnant,' she said. 'I'm not.'

'And you didn't think of waiting?'

Asha shrugged.

'You didn't think of letting me touch you?'

She looked across the table, past her empty lime soda, past the debris of their meal. His features, so familiar to her now, were still capable of surprising her. They were quiet for a long moment, and now it was he who looked away.

'Please,' she said again. 'I'm not asking you to understand.'

The family at the next table began to rise. They looked their way, and seeing Asha was emotional, exchanged arch looks. 'Fight,' they muttered, 'Brute,' and as they swept slowly past them, Om asked her, 'And you didn't think I deserved to know the truth?'

'Om,' pleaded Asha. 'I did such a terrible thing to you . . .'

'But you could have asked me to understand . . .'

She looked up. 'Would you have understood?'

'Yes,' he said. 'No. I don't know.' Suddenly he rose and walked out of the restaurant. Asha considered getting up and following him out, but all at once he was back again. He was clapping the waiter on the back, ordering another drink, slapping her roguishly on her back. 'Come,' he said. 'Join me in a drink.'

The waiter stared. 'But Sir,' he said. 'Madam is expecting.'

'I'm so sorry,' Om said. The waiter backed away, and he laughed. 'I'm so, so sorry.'

'*Bus*,' she said miserably. 'Let's go.'

He ordered another drink. They sat together while he nursed it. The ice cubes jangled loudly against the glass.

Several times she opened her mouth to speak, but her courage gave way.

He took a sip, took an ice chip into his mouth, chewed loudly. 'You didn't think I should know?'

'Om, I'm so . . .'

'I took you in. I married you when you had nothing.'

Asha was crying again. 'Om, please . . .'

They drove back home. He was too fast, climbing onto pavements, missing turns, and she was sure they would die. They saw a light shine in their faces, they saw a car approach them, and he swerved to avoid it. He swerved too hard, too fast, and they found themselves parked into a tree stump.

'*Hey Bhagwan*,' prayed Asha.

The crash seemed to have restored some of his composure, and he said softly, 'How alone you must be.'

She looked dazed.

'I'm going to help you.'

'Om . . .'

'You probably think me a fool. Maybe I am. God knows my mother tells me I'm silly about you.' Her mouth was parched and she found she couldn't speak. 'But I'll do it. We will bring this baby up as our own. And I expect there to be no secrets between us from now onwards. Is that understood?'

Asha saw a flash of brown in a passer-by's head, closed her eyes against it and nodded. 'Of course,' she replied. Her hand raced to her padded stomach, then across the car to his hand, and she nodded. 'Of course,' she said, 'No more secrets.'

13

The days lengthened. The Pakistani incursion into Kashmir escalated into a full-blown war. They were enemies now, the two countries, and though Asha still thought of Suhanpur as home, she learnt to think of Pakistan as a hostile state. Her dearest friends were Pakistani, and she was Indian. Om was Indian, Roopa was Indian, Sanam was too. Her unborn child would be Indian.

By the middle of March, it was starting to grow warm. The flowers on Om's *Ashoka* trees took bud, and now they sprang forth a blazoning, fragrant red. By the time the festival of *Holi* came around, everyone was complaining about the weather. '*Hai Ram*,' cried Ma as her son dutifully anointed her forehead with red *gulal* powder. 'It was never this hot in Suhanpur.' She shied away as others approached her with the powder, and when people moved towards Asha, she drew herself to her full five feet. 'No,' she said.

Mrs Garg was made to step back. Sanam, who struggled to hide her shape, was instructed to fan Asha. 'It's too hot,' Ma repeated. 'It's a wonder the poor girl doesn't faint.' Roopa, now living with her sister, remonstrated, but Ma held firm. Endless anecdotes about the additives they put in the colour were recounted. 'No, no,' she

200

insisted. 'Not with the child inside you. You can play all the *Holi* you like next year.'

Bina gave birth to her child, a boy called Prem. She delivered late, and when Asha went to see her, she complained. 'It wouldn't end, the labour. Hour after hour . . . .'

Bhaiya smiled. '*Haan*, Asha,' he laughed. 'You're in for a good time.'

Om winced, and Bhaiya added, 'I was never as grateful for being a man as when my wife was going through her labour.' He smiled at Asha, and as she averted her eyes, he said, 'Don't worry so much, Asha. Every woman goes through childbirth.'

Bina saw Asha staring at her with wide eyes, she saw Om's look of horror, and she hurried to compensate for her husband's words. 'It wasn't that bad, really,' she said, and frowning at her husband, she added, 'What are you thinking of, worrying the two of them like that?'

'Bina, I was just . . .'

'But one thing is certain,' Bina spoke over Bhaiya. 'The heat was a killer.' She turned to Om. 'Take her away if you can . . .'

Asha laughed nervously, but Bina was insistent. She cradled her newborn in her arms, then passed him gently over to Asha. He was light, his skin as soft as a lotus flower. As soft, and as fragrant. She bent down to him, studied his tiny, puckered face. He shifted in his sleep, his fine, downy eyebrows lifted and then fell. He whinnied, and Asha found herself falling in love. She ached with longing. She looked up, and saw Om was smiling. 'Soon,' he said, patting her hand. 'Soon we'll have our own.'

Bina had fallen asleep. She woke now at Om's speech,

and repeated drowsily, 'Really, you two. Go somewhere you can be comfortable. Go to the mountains.'

As Sanam approached her due date, Om grew increasingly uncomfortable about the delivery. They had never taken the girl to see a doctor; they couldn't be certain of any doctor remaining discreet. The city was beginning to feel like a village, and everywhere they went, they seemed to know someone. They recognised faces from Suhanpur, or relatives of relatives. They knew fellow refugees; they knew fellow landowners. They weren't safe anywhere.

Instead, they had spoken in nebulous terms of women giving birth every day. Sanam would survive. Besides, they were there to help her, Om and Asha, they were sure to manage.

'Why,' Roopa had replied briskly when she was consulted. 'Of course you don't need a doctor. A woman in my convoy even gave birth on the journey from Pakistan.' She fell silent as she thought of that lone, lonely birth.

There it was again, the past flashing through her mind: the horror of the bus shelter, the unarticulated terror, Pappaji speechless, the blood, the filth and the rain, and then that beautiful, beautiful Pathan. They looked at each other quickly, Asha and Roopa, then both averted their eyes. There was no discussing that past, even here, even now that both were safe.

There was no erasing the imprints of Partition either. Asha still had the scar on her wrist, and no matter how she hid it, with long sleeves, with wrists turned permanently inwards, it kept her ceaseless company. She felt it burn in the heat, felt it prickle for relief in the arid

202

cold of Delhi's winter. And as for Roopa, the Partition had branded her too. She *had* put on some weight since arriving in Delhi, but there was still a fold of spare skin that hung loose at the base of her neck. She ate with the ferocity of the starving, she covered her neck with *dupattas* even as the summer advanced, but it was no good. The skin remained slack, a reminder of her journey from Pakistan. She still refused to talk about it, but it was clear; no amount of feasting, no change in luck would be able to erase the mark of what had passed. 'Oh,' Roopa shuddered as she thought about the doctorless childbirth on the road to India, 'I don't know how that poor thing managed.'

'That's it,' said Om. 'We have to think of Sanam and the baby.'

They saw Sanam suffer in the heat of the kitchen, saw her sleep on a thin mattress on the floor of the school room. She struggled to hide her pregnancy, and though Salim, the Muslim servant who worked for their neighbour, had maintained his interest, it was clear Sanam wasn't comfortable.

'He comes to see me every day,' she complained one morning to Asha. The two were alone in the school. Sanam was preparing the vegetables for the children's meal, washing the spinach, then shredding it thin. She took out daal, measured it, checked through it for impurities, and as she bent to her task, Asha saw her wince. 'He says he wants to marry me,' she added, 'But how long before he sees I'm pregnant?'

Asha nodded. She was too pretty, the girl. There was sure to be trouble if they remained. 'We've been thinking,' she told her. 'One of our friends has a cottage in the hills. It's only half a day's drive away. We'll be safe there.'

203

They stayed at Om's friend's cottage at the edge of Kasauli. A jasmine creeper, as tender as a blush, hung over the gate to the front. There was a wood fire in the living room, a library with books and an endless supply of board games. There was a rustic kitchen off the living room, built more for aesthetic pleasure than for function. They tried to prepare tea in it, and they found themselves bumping into each other. Sanam, who was tired from her travel, was sent to her ground floor bedroom.

Asha prepared tea for the others, scented it with *tulsi* leaves she found growing in the garden behind the house. She took the tea in for Sanam, then poured some into a tea service for herself and her husband. She found a tea cosy and rested it on top of the teapot. 'Just imagine,' she smiled as she brought it out into the living room. 'This is our first holiday together.' They couldn't find wood for the fire, so instead, they huddled together, their hands warm on the tea. They went upstairs to their bedroom. They had a four-poster bed, and a tiny, wrought-iron-grilled balcony beyond, much like the one outside Nargis' room. They had a view looking down at the town, and from where they sat, they saw bells ringing in the church. They saw a congregation leave, they saw a school break for the day. They saw a light go on in a shop, so they stepped out of the cottage to find a doctor.

They took the wrong turn out of the cottage and went up a steep path. The path narrowed as they climbed, and after passing a few cottages, they found they were completely alone. It had grown colder now, and Asha in particular suffered. She had wrapped a shawl around her summer *salwar kameez*, but this was insufficient cover against the cold of the hills. Her legs stung with the chill, and she found herself rooted to the spot anytime the wind blew. Om took off his blazer and put it around his wife, and though she claimed not to need it, she didn't take it off.

She grumbled they were lost. There was sure to be no doctor this far away from civilisation. They heard a noise, and she began to worry about *cheetahs*. It grew in volume, echoed through the hills. It grew otherworldly in her imagination. 'There are sure to be ghosts here,' she claimed, shivering through the blazer. Her cotton *salwar* clung to her legs, and she found herself leaning towards Om. 'I'm telling you. There will have been murders here. Listen.' She paused, pointed towards a pine tree that shivered in the breeze. 'There it is . . .'

'It's just the mist,' said Om, but Asha was backing away. She stepped on a twig and jumped at the sound. She stumbled, fell back against a tree, its icy leaves rustling against her.

'And there's no one to help us,' she whispered. They turned back, rushing downhill, with Asha half-running, half-stumbling, past the last, frontier cottages, past their own one, and back down into town. They hurried gratefully into a little guesthouse, where they ordered a plate of fried potato *pakoras* and restorative cups of steaming hot tea. There was something, both said, about a hot cup of tea on a cold day. Both were silent as they ate, and now the silence grew comfortable. Asha didn't complain about the weather, they didn't worry about the impending labour.

It grew cooler still. The guesthouse caretaker went around the room, lighting yellow beeswax candles in tall glasses. The candles cast a gloom over the room, and all at once it was darker. All at once they were closer together. Om reached out, held her hand. 'This,' he told her, 'This will be our honeymoon,' and she smiled, before remembering to frown in disapproval. Such talk, such brazenness, just a few hours away from Delhi! What would Ma say?

'*Hai Ram*,' she chided him. 'What's come over you?' but the fragrance had grown closer, and when Om next reached his hand out, she didn't push him away.

The doctor said the delivery was imminent. 'Today, tomorrow,' he said, waving his hands vaguely around the room. 'It really could be any day.'

They stood in the cramped living room. Om had managed to procure wood and had spent hours coaxing a frail fire to life. The doctor, a large, loquacious Mr Sinha, had come, examined Sanam, and asked more questions than he answered.

'You've come from Delhi, *haan*?' he wanted to know. 'But why come to Kasauli for the delivery?' He grew instantly conscious that he may have implied he wasn't capable, and spent the next several minutes defending his practice. 'But still,' he said as curiosity reasserted itself. 'Why leave Delhi at this time?'

They complained about Delhi's heat. There was no getting Sanam, who they introduced as Asha's sister, comfortable. And after her husband had died in the Partition, this was the least they could do to make her comfortable. Dr Sinha's eyes misted over. 'Poor girl,' he said. 'Poor, beautiful girl. We must do all we can to make her comfortable.'

A fresh basket of oranges was sent for, for Sanam. He brought around honey the next time he visited, and a paste of herbs that was sure to strengthen her for delivery. Sanam was nonplussed by the attention. She stood when the doctor visited as had been taught her by Mahesh. 'Stand to attention,' she had been told, and even here, when she was the object of Dr Sinha's visits, she remained servile. She smiled, she didn't complain, she acquiesced to whatever he suggested. 'What do I say to him?' she asked Asha. 'He's always smiling at me, always telling me these jokes in English. I don't understand a word he says, and when I don't laugh at his jokes, he looks pained. And then he sends another basket of fruit. What am I to do?'

'Nothing,' replied Asha.

'You know,' said Sanam in embarrassment. 'He told me he wasn't married.'

'Really?'

'Yes,' said Sanam. Asha shrugged, and the maid returned to her knitting. She was making a blue blanket for the baby, and as she applied herself to her task, Asha found herself admiring the girl's beauty. Young and heavily pregnant, and still the prettiest girl she had ever seen. It was no wonder Salim hankered after her. It was no wonder that even Dr Sinha was tempted. Sanam looked up and saw Asha studying her. 'Didi,' she asked. 'Why did he tell me he wasn't married?'

'*Arre*,' Asha scolded. 'You're growing restless, cooped up in this cottage. That's why you're focusing on every word the doctor says. He just speaks a lot, that's all.'

'Yes,' agreed a chastened Sanam, and as Asha prepared to leave, she asked. 'But Didi, will I never get married?'

Asha stopped. She looked at the girl.

'Didi,' Sanam stammered. 'You're keeping the child, so I thought . . .' She trailed off.

'Yes,' Asha said uncertainly. 'Perhaps.' She turned to go out, then paused. 'Do you have someone in mind?'

'No,' came the reply, but it was so swiftly pronounced that Asha disregarded it.

'Tell me,' she asked. 'Is it that Salim?'

'No,' repeated Sanam, but she wasn't equal to meeting Asha's eye.

'In that case,' said Asha, and as Sanam looked up quickly, she smiled. Sanam didn't want the child, but who knew how she might feel in a year's time. Already she was smiling as she knitted him his blankets and booties, already she was looking forward to when he would be able to stand. 'Yes,' she said to the girl. 'I'll sort it out.'

May arrived and no baby was born. Asha and Sanam tried to work out an estimated due date, but given that they couldn't be sure of any dates or times, they were going on guess work. 'It was around the time of Independence,' said Sanam. 'We were given tricolour *barfis* in the street. I remember thinking how lucky we were.'

Sanam's belly was swelling, her back was aching, and this was as good an augury as could be hoped for. They knitted together in the mornings as Om slept in. Asha would prepare tea and take it into Sanam's room. She would open up the back door onto the garden, onto a new, fragrant world. They would smell jasmine and suddenly their shared son would be a famous poet. An easterly breeze would send in a waft of lemon, or of rosemary, and he would become an adventurer. A mountaineer, an explorer. 'But no,' Asha would say, 'Think of the dangers. He could come across cheetahs or worse.' She thought of her own brief foray up the hill and shuddered. Sanam would think of the diseases he could encounter. 'TB, cholera,' she said, 'Pnee-monia,' and there her catalogue ended, but it was enough to ward them off travel. The door would be shut against the temptations of the outdoors, and they would return to their knitting.

They were near the middle of May. Letters arrived from Ma – there was no phone in the cottage – asking for updates, and they sent the same reply each time. 'Nothing,' they said, 'We'll let you know the moment he's born.'

Dr Sinha began to look worried. 'Can't you be sure?' he asked Sanam. 'Can't you try and remember the dates?' She looked mutely at Asha, who turned to the doctor and shook her head. 'She's been through so much,' she explained.

'Of course,' said Dr Sinha, suddenly brisk. 'But there's a danger to the baby if she goes overdue. Does she not have any idea?' and Asha could only shrug helplessly.

They waited. The end of May approached, and the weather turned. The air was still. The days were hot and humid, and the nights passed uneasily. There was a thunderstorm on the night of the 21st. Sanam complained that she couldn't sleep. She said she was scared of the thunder, said she felt her child kick with each peal, and though Asha accused her of melodrama, that night she stayed downstairs. She sat in front of the fire, and after a while, Sanam came to join her. They spoke of the boy they shared. Though it was Ma who had first identified the baby as a boy, his personality had grown through the pregnancy. His future exploits, his life and loves, had been foretold with every purl of Sanam's knitting needle. His every future cough had been worried over by Asha. She had tutted away his disappointments, had hushed his

209

fears away. Over the months of Sanam's confinement, they had raised a boy. And they had raised him well. He was loving and dutiful, handsome and magnanimous; he was intelligent and kind, rich and righteous.

And then it all began. Sanam felt her contractions intensify. Asha raced upstairs to rouse Om from his sleep. He drove the car downhill on pitch-black roads to the doctor, and now Asha worried about his safety as well as the baby's. Sanam's contractions grew stronger, her cries grew louder. The men didn't return for an age, for an hour or longer. The air crackled, and for the first time since she left her house in Suhanpur, Asha found herself praying. When Dr Sinha finally arrived, he set to caring for Sanam. Asha was pushed to one side, and she joined her husband pacing the upper rooms. They were redundant now.

Sanam's screams rose high in the air, splintering their reserve. They attempted conversation intermittently, but it was no use. They were too full of nervous energy to concentrate, and every time Sanam screamed, they jumped apart and resumed their pacing.

Finally, as the sun began to rise over the town below them, they heard a new cry. It was loud and lone and undeniable, and as they rushed downstairs, tripping over their shawls, they saw Dr Sinha turn to them. His shirt was untucked, his moustache wet with moisture. His hair was askew, but he smiled broadly as he bundled an angry, bloody infant in a blanket and said to them, 'Congratulations, it's a girl.'

SANAM

Sanam's first memory: her mother cradling her head as she sang her to sleep. There had been a scuffle; her older brother had grabbed her toy and refused to return it to her, and when she had cried, he had attempted to thrash her into silence. His plan had backfired, and now it was she who rested her weary, throbbing head on Ammi's lap, it was she who was told she was precious and loved.

'You must remember,' Ammi said to her, 'A woman is like a stream. She can be young and wilful, or,' and here, with a slow smile, Ammi pointed at herself, 'she can be older and sluggish, but she will always have to come up against stronger forces. She will have to contend with mountains, with trees and rocks, with the vagaries of the weather, and she will always have to succumb to them. Her grace lies in her giving way, or appearing to, and in her forging an imperceptible, lasting path through the earth.'

'But . . .'

'No, *Beta*,' Ammi had insisted. 'They're bigger than us, they're stronger than us.' She had looked down at her, stroking her hair with such tenderness that Sanam had all but forgotten her disquiet. 'We just have to be cleverer.'

This was her then, a mountain stream, bowing to greater forces. She had birthed the baby, had nursed her, trained her into night-time sleep and morning wakefulness. She had held that small, warm body in her arms, seen those papery lashes flutter open, had allowed herself to look into those dark infant eyes that were at once foreign and all her own, and she had told herself she didn't mind.

She handed the baby over to Asha, let Om rest his hand on her head. She watched as Ma had called in the priest, as they chose the child's name in an elaborate ceremony. Priya, they called her. *Beloved*.

She smiled, blushed even, when Asha suggested she marry Salim. 'Thank you, Didi,' she had said. 'I'll do as you see fit,' and Asha smiled at her compliance.

'But this isn't the end,' Asha promised. 'You will be part of this family for the rest of your life.' Asha had become tearful. 'You'll be there every *Diwali*, every birthday, do you understand?'

How Sanam had wanted to understand Asha. Here she was, another refugee of the Partition, another orphan, another woman grateful to marry, and the difference between the two! How ordinary Asha was, smooth-faced and unexceptional. But she had remained unattainable all those years, loving her husband a little less than he loved her, and that had been her magic. Ammi had been wrong to tell her to adapt, to flow with the seasons.

'I want you to come see us for every birthday, every festival,' and Sanam had agreed. That was the secret then. To love a little less than she was loved. It was something she was incapable of. She couldn't want Priya, couldn't want a family a little less than they wanted her.

Not that she was unhappy. Salim was kind, but he was subject to his own constraints. There were mountains of tradition he was unable to conquer. He was to work, she was to stay at home. Sanam's contact with the school came to an end. 'You're too beautiful to work,' Salim told her, even though that's just how he had met her. 'You can never tell what kind of creature is watching you.'

She was to provide him with a family, and when she failed in her task, matters were never the same. He laboured over her night after night, his efforts growing more frenzied as the years passed without issue. His caresses ended, his hotly whispered endearments, and now he simply tore off her clothes, clawed at her breasts, and she wondered what the difference was, in the end, between married husband and murderous, raping infidel. She wasn't even sure if he saw her when he emptied his seed into her, wasn't sure if the act brought him any manner of comfort.

And here too, they were united, Sanam and Asha. Both unable to conceive. Asha put up with Ma's barbs about there being no grandson, no one to inherit Om's properties, and she turned to Sanam. 'What do I say to her?' she asked. 'She doesn't even know what a miracle it is that we have Priya.' And Sanam, the facilitator of this miracle, comforted her mistress. She smiled reassuringly as month after month, Asha and Om visited doctor, visited soothsayer, visited holy site, all with the aim of birthing a boy, and all in vain. 'It doesn't matter,' she told Asha. 'There's the girl. There's Priya. At least you have her.'

That was the thing about a stream. She couldn't be sure if anyone noticed it. She bent to everyone's will, and she found she could be cast aside at will. They found a growth in Salim's chest, as big as a stone. His medicines were ruinously expensive, and when he died destitute, she was grateful to move back into the Sharma household. It was time for Priya's wedding, and her help was welcome. She saw Priya dress for her wedding, smiled a faltering, sad smile as the girl – so dark, so still-featured, so reminiscent of that dreadful night – smiled and Sanam finally caught a flash of her Ammi's face. She sat a respectful distance outside the *mandap* when the wedding *mantras* were recited, she waved a small, imperceptible goodbye as the bride and groom hugged their parents farewell.

Roopa, now married and mother to another bride-to-be, requested her assistance, and Sanam moved into her house. She helped apply a gram flour paste on the bride's body in time for the wedding night, she prepared the henna for her palms, and she helped wrap thin layers of crimson silk around the bride's trembling body in time for the ceremony.

After it was all finished, Asha took her back home. They were both older now, and more measured in their bearing. There was no pretending to be a new mountain stream any more. They were both mother to a mother. Priya had given birth to a girl they called Lana, a little thing with golden eyes and an irrepressible smile. 'We've done our bit, you and I,' Asha told her. She held her hand out, her reach encompassing the fabric of their daily lives – the raising of Priya, the scraped knees and the teenage problems with authority, the long, laborious care of Ma in her dying days, the sweets they had prepared for the festivals; for *Holi* and *Diwali*, the *henna* they had applied in time for the *Karva Chauth* fast. 'Now tell me,' she said. 'What is it that you want to do?'

'Didi,' said Sanam. 'I'd like to work in the school.

216

Teach the poorer girls the skills you always spoke of. Embroidery, cooking.'

Asha nodded. 'That's a good idea. You will sleep at home, where it's safe, but during the day, you can work at the school. You can be Mrs Garg's deputy, in charge of teaching skills. Mrs Garg has always said we need to nourish the children's souls. This will be your job.'

This was it, in the end. The school, the girls she taught and shaped. The granddaughter who grew to look like her. She bent round the mountains, gave way to chill winds, but slowly, bit by bit, she was forging a lasting path through the earth.

III

1

Asha settled herself into her seat and clamped her eyes firmly shut in prayer. 'You've flown before,' she scolded herself. 'Every year you board a flight to America.' She counted the number of times she had flown, counted the trips she had made to see her daughter Priya in New York, but she didn't acknowledge her real source of worry: for the first time in memory, she was travelling without Om. He would sit next to her, hold her hand, talk incessantly. An air hostess would spark his interest, or a young couple travelling on honeymoon. He would flip through the duty free section of the in-flight magazine, muse about the treats she would enjoy. 'Here,' he would say as he pointed to the most expensive brand, 'this perfume looks nice,' and she would scold, 'How can you tell the smell of a perfume from a photo?' He would point to a bottle of whisky, and she would swat at him in mock disgust. '*Hai Ram*,' she would scold. 'Alcohol, and at this hour?' He would turn the page, find a travel lipstick. 'Look,' he would say, 'you don't have this shade,' and she would smilingly point out to him that the shade wouldn't suit her skin colour. That she wore one shade, that she didn't like change, that she didn't need any money spent on her. He would laugh, lean back in his chair, point out that they were already

221

airborne. 'See,' he would gloat, 'distracting you works every time!'

Priya had offered to come to India to pick her up, but Asha had refused. Lana, Priya's daughter, had offered too. 'Come on, Nani,' she had cajoled in her American drawl. 'It'll be fun, just you and me together,' and though Asha had been sorely tempted by the idea of her company, she had said that she would travel alone. It was just two flights. Delhi to London, then London to New York. All the announcements would be in English. The signs would be in English. She had made the trip a dozen times before. She would manage it herself.

She closed her eyes, swallowing hard. Lana scolded her for calling herself old, but that was what she was now. That's what they all were: her, Roopa, Bina, Sanam, all the veterans of Om's school. Old and alone. Om had passed away, as had Bhaiya, Roopa's husband Nalin, Salim too. Their children lived in different glittering cities across the world; in London, Hong Kong, Singapore, New York and Bombay. They were busy with their careers, with their families, and though they kept in touch, and though they visited, there was so much that was missed from one weekly phone call to the next.

Not the details, not the bills and the doctor's reports. Nor the news from the children. Everything was shared at length: teething problems, homework, college applications. No, it was the intangibles of their lives that weren't shared, the shifts at the margins of perception. The way the sight of an unruly, unsteady toddler, smiling and offering up a chocolate-stained hand to shake, had filled them with an ache that plagued them for days. The miraculously sweet papaya the fruit vendor had delivered in the morning, the new pain felt – suppressed and ignored, but nevertheless felt – in the right knee.

Aches and pains. There had been plenty of those. Asha had studied herself in the mirror as she wrapped the folds of her *sari* around herself in the morning. There was less cloth, there were fewer wraps around her torso all of a sudden. This was the worst time to be too meagrely covered, now that her skin had grown folds of its own. Love handles, Lana had called them. She had patted her tummy when Asha had last visited, and told her to leave off thinking of portions. 'When I'm your age,' she had said, tossing her long, straight hair back, 'I will eat all I like.'

Asha smiled at her granddaughter's tyranny. How like the girl to make her feel simultaneously desirable and obsolete. 'When I'm your age' as if it was an affliction, a stage to be borne with patience. Like puberty, like the end of desire.

Asha heard a deep, full-throated throttle as the plane's engine came to life. They moved an inch, paused, moved again. The glass on her table shifted slightly, and she saw a splash of water being spilt. '*Hai Ram!*' She clasped her hands together in prayer, began to appeal to all the Gods she could think of. A little like Bhaiya on their exodus from Pakistan. 'Ram-*ji*, Krishan-*ji*, Ganesh-*ji*, keep us safe!'

Someone leant towards her and asked, 'Are you feeling well, Aunty?'

Asha opened her eyes. It was a young girl, no more than eighteen or nineteen. No older than when she had got married. She was pretty, with almond shaped eyes and a smooth, unmarked face. She frowned now, asking

223

again, 'Are you well, Aunty?' and Asha hurried to reassure her.

'Of course,' she said. 'I'm just being a baby about flying.' The girl giggled, and Asha, pleased to have elicited a positive response, added, 'Can you imagine, at my age?'

'It's my first flight,' confided the girl. 'I'm a little scared too.'

'Going to college?' asked Asha, and the girl nodded. 'It'll be fine,' Asha said. 'I've never even hit a tailwind.' The girl laughed, and she asked, 'What's your name, child?'

'Nargis.'

Asha looked hard at the girl. There was something in her that seemed familiar. The high cheekbones, the light colouring, the beautiful eyes. She wore a pale green top, the same colour as Nargis had worn for one of her marriage ceremonies, and suddenly it all returned to her. The songs, the noise, the smell of roasting meat. The flash of brown under the sun, the surge of the river, and then, as inevitably happened, another memory took over. The bus shelter in the rain, and the hack of steel against beloved bone. An air steward passed by, tall and fair with chiselled cheekbones, and handsome as the Pathan had been, and Asha instinctively flinched. She closed her eyes, breathed in deeply. She felt the plane move again.

'Are you sure you're well?' the girl asked again, and Asha nodded. She looked at the child, took in the features that were so familiar to her, and asked the first senseless question that occurred to her, 'Are you Pakistani, child?'

'No,' laughed the girl unselfconsciously. 'My mother chose the name. There was an old film heroine she loved . . .'

224

Asha nodded. It was impossible, of course, a child from Pakistan boarding a flight from India. And all of the rest of that, the memories, the music, the sounds, the flashes of colour, they were just that. Memories. The ghosts that still haunted her. 'That old film heroine,' she said with a smile, 'was my age.'

They spoke all journey long. Nargis was going to enrol in a college with an unpronounceable name. 'Massa,' tried Asha when Nargis proudly announced it, 'Massa-what?'

'Boston,' said Nargis finally, and this satisfied Asha.

'Yes,' she nodded approvingly. 'There are lots of good colleges in Boston. My Lana studied there, you know. Now of course, she is finishing her Masters in International Relations from New York University.' She heard herself, an old, crowing grandmother. She looked down at her hands, mottled with the sun. The scar on her wrist was the worst. Dry, and so sensitive to any variation in temperature. It burnt in the summer, and in the winter, she felt it shrivel into her skin. She bathed her skin liberally with almond oil and with the extravagant creams the girls sent her, but it remained stubbornly puckered. Like a mango skin left to dry under the summer sun. 'Face it,' she said to herself. 'You're growing old.'

They took their time going home. Lana herded Asha's bags together, and as they neared the exit, she stalled. 'Come, Nani,' she said. 'Let's have a coffee.'

'Lana,' asked Asha. 'Where is your mother?'

'Mama . . .' said Lana half-heartedly. 'She's stuck at work. She'll be back by the time we return,' and Asha knew the two had fallen out. The girl looked around to check they had all her luggage. She didn't complain about

225

her mother, didn't sigh or push out her lower lip as she had during childhood tantrums, but Asha understood. This was more than a disagreement about an outfit or a holiday.

'Nani,' Lana was saying. 'I have something to say to you.'

Here, thought Asha, was finally a link with her mother. How sheepish both girls looked at the point of confession. 'Yes, darling?' she asked.

'Nani, there's a boy.'

Asha smiled. For all her years in America, for all her accent and her clothes, the girl still grew shy when talking of love. Priya had been the same, blushing and blustering. She had met Sunil, the New York based surgeon she would marry, through friends. They hadn't heard anything about it, Om and Asha, and as they searched their network for a suitable groom for their daughter, Priya hadn't objected. She carried on with her pharmacist's studies, sat her exams, sat through endless teas with prospective husbands. Then, one evening, as the year drew to a close, she had said, 'Ma, there's a boy.'

Asha had risen, she had sat back down. She had attempted a smile before lapsing into a frown. Love marriages, girls meeting boys, it was still considered unorthodox. Then, as Priya had wrapped her shawl around herself defiantly, Asha had asked, 'Aren't you going to tell me anything about him?'

Priya had smiled. 'Ok,' she had said. 'I'll let you meet him.'

Lana changed the topic now, moving onto her studies. '*Arre*,' complained Asha. 'Aren't you going to tell me anything about him?'

226

Lana smiled. 'Ok,' she said. 'I'll let you meet him. Now come on,' she urged, 'Let's get that coffee.'

Lana settled her at a table, then went to the front of the café to order them the caramel-laced coffee Asha pretended to dislike. How quiet it was here, in New York, after the noise of Delhi. She saw a couple push past Lana in the queue, she saw her granddaughter frown at their rudeness, and she smiled. This was nothing, this was paradise. She saw the woman turn to Lana with an apologetic shrug. They waited here, by and large, stood in long, patient lines for their food. They said sorry and please and excuse me. And yet, there was something about Delhi, a oneness, an enveloping sense of belonging. In many ways, it remained the shambolic village it had become in the aftermath of the Partition, filled as it was equally with expectation and a fatalistic understanding of the failings of man.

As Lana walked back to their table, her mouth still turned down from her encounter in the queue, Asha found herself forgetting to breathe. Her granddaughter was pretty, no, more, with chiselled features, a high forehead and a proud, straight-backed bearing. *Just like Sanam all those years ago*, she thought. *Just like Sanam when she first came to me*. Lana was taller, of course, and glossier. She was more expensively dressed, and her hair wasn't the matted mess Sanam's had been, but in all the essentials, they were the same. Both had the same oval face, the same tear-shaped tiger's eyes, the same pale colouring – a shade identical to freshly churned cream – both had the same errant wave skimming the bottom of their hair. Asha smiled at her granddaughter, then frowned at her cup of coffee before sipping from it. '*Oof*,' she pretended to complain, 'It's too sweet. *Oof*,'

227

she added as she took another large sip, 'It's too heavy.'

She smiled wryly; all these years, and she was still surprised by Lana's looks. More surprising perhaps was that no one else seemed to have noticed. Of course, Sanam was older now, a grey, spent trace of her former self, and if any photos had been taken of her in her youth, no one thought to look for them. But still, Lana was so different in appearance from her parents. Ma *had* hesitated before holding Lana. She had made Asha carry her to the window, had made her hold the infant up to the light. She had been nearly blind by this point, but she had peered hard at the baby. 'I don't know,' she had said to her daughter-in-law. 'I can't make out who she looks like.'

2

The air was still when they reached home. Asha turned towards their building, but Lana held her back. 'Isn't it beautiful?' she said to her grandmother, buying time, and Asha smiled her agreement. It *was* beautiful. The sky had turned a blinding white; the purest, palest, glimmering silver. The peace wouldn't last long. Offices would begin to turn their workers out for the day soon, and in a matter of minutes, the streets would be full of noise. She'd see lovers reuniting, or friends meeting for a meal. She'd see families heading homewards, and life – New York life, as frenetic and frantic and publicly lived as it was – would resound loudly around her. This was not real, this quiet. It was only a blink, an ephemeral yawn. But now, for the moment, it was all hers. New York, its brilliant sky, this empty, tree-canopied street corner.

'Come,' she said to Lana. She looped her arm round her granddaughter's and led her inside. 'Priya will be waiting.'

Priya *was* waiting. She stood at the entrance to their apartment as they exited the lift. Her hands were on her hips, her mouth was turned down, but as Asha moved towards her, she broke into a smile.

'You took so long,' she complained. She didn't wait

for her mother to reply, adding, 'And how was the flight? I worried about the transfer. Next time I'll come to Delhi to pick you up.'

'You're just like your father,' Asha scolded. 'He would never let me get a word in either.' Priya had her father's generous heart too; she was guilty – as much as he had been – of impetuousness as much as she was of heart-stopping benevolence.

It was Priya who checked in on Asha daily. It was she who called up the widowed Bina and Roopa too, even though they had children of their own. 'They helped bring me up,' she would tell her mother. 'Can't I do this much for them?' It was Priya who took care of the medical expenses when Mrs Garg finally succumbed to her diabetes.

And it was Priya who now sat on the board of the school Asha and Om had set up. Once a year, she held a benefit to raise money for its operations. She sent friends, journalists – anyone she could find – to India to visit the facility. She offered work placements in her New York pharmacy to a graduate every year, and it seemed her efforts were inspiring an entire generation. In village after village on the outskirts of Delhi, pharmacies bearing the name 'Priya Chemists' were springing up.

'But seriously, Ma,' Priya was saying. Her hands remained firmly on her hips. 'Do you know how long I've been waiting?'

'Sorry, *Beta* . . .'

'It's not your fault,' her daughter was saying. 'It's that granddaughter of yours.' She pointed towards Lana, who raised her eyebrows to the heavens. 'And don't you try that innocent act,' her mother scolded. 'Have you told your grandmother what you've been up to?'

230

'Ma!' Lana exclaimed, and as Asha turned towards her, she grew flustered. 'Nani knows,' she said defensively. A pause, a deep flush, a careful choosing of her words, and she spoke again, 'I told her I've found the man I'm going to marry.'

'That's great, *Beta*,' said Asha.

'But Ma,' said Priya. 'Has she told you who it is?'

'Mama, come on . . .'

'Priya,' echoed Asha. 'You have to let the girl make her own choice.'

Priya turned a worried face towards her. 'Even if it's a mistake?'

'*Arre*.' Asha looked at Lana, smiling, waiting for approbation, expecting to be understood. She had always been precocious, Lana, and precious. She had grown up with an only child's certainty of her value. Still, she was sensible. Asha turned to her daughter and said, 'She's a clever girl, our Lana. She won't make any mistakes.'

'If you say so,' shrugged Priya. She turned to her daughter. 'Tell her . . .'

'Later, Mama. Nani will be tired from her travels . . .'

'I wish you'd been so considerate when you were falling in love with this boy. After all she went through during the Partition. She lost her family, you know . . .'

'Mama, please . . .'

'No,' insisted Priya. She held up a fist, counted out each lost loved one on a finger. 'Her mother,' she said. 'Her father, her younger brother. She lost everything.'

'Mama,' said Lana. 'It wasn't Hussain's doing . . .'

Hussain, so that was it. A Muslim boy. 'Priya,' said Asha in a conciliatory tone. 'So he's a Muslim. So what?'

'But Ma,' began Priya, but Asha held up her hand.

'And they both live in America. Who cares if they're Hindu or Muslim?'

'But,' said Priya slowly. 'What if he's Pakistani?' She spoke slowly, enunciating each syllable with force. Pa-kiss-tan-ee.

Asha looked at her daughter. There it was, the wrinkled nose, that family herald of concern. Priya began to speak again. 'Ma, I've told her a million times. It's easy to fall in love, it's easy to think of yourself as a liberal. But what happens if he doesn't let you pray to your God? What happens if he doesn't let your children go to India, or to celebrate Diwali? What happens then?'

It had been the same all those years ago. 'It's fine for me,' Firoze had explained to her. 'My children will be brought up as Muslims.' Priya was looking at her with concern, and Asha started. She knew she had missed the thrust of her daughter's argument.

'Don't you agree?' Priya said, and Asha nodded wordlessly. She looked at her granddaughter, and as the girl looked away with a mixture of remorse and resolve, she moved into the apartment. 'It's late,' she said, 'and I'm tired. I'd like to lie down for a bit.' Priya followed her mother into the apartment and offered her refreshments, but she shook her head.

'Nani,' she heard Lana say. 'I meant to tell you.'

'I know.'

'Really I did.'

She heard the emotion in the girl's voice. 'I know,' she repeated kindly. It had been impossible for Asha to tell anyone about Firoze. Firoze, she thought, and it was as if a hot wind had blown across the desert. Raking, seething, but such a welcome, blessed relief. 'I know, my darling.'

'Nani, I want you to meet him.'

'Yes, *Beta*. But now I'm going to go to my room,' and as they both nodded, mother and worried daughter, Asha added kindly. 'I'll rest, unpack, check on things at home. We'll talk in the morning.'

There was no trying to unpack. There was no attempting to rest, to lie down, to look out onto New York's dusk. Instead, Asha's hand hovered over the phone.

She thought of what she would say to Bina, or to Roopa. 'Lana is in love with a Pakistani.' It sounded so reasonable in her voice, so plausible, but a transformation would take place over the line. A raw note would enter her voice, a shrill, desperate edge. Her friend would echo breathlessly, 'Pakistani?'

'Yes,' she would have to reply. 'Pakistani,' but again her voice would catch, and her friend would hear, 'Yes. Murderer of family, ravager of dearest friends, looter of childhood memories.'

In the end she called Sanam. There was no one else who would understand. '*Kaise ho*,' she asked. 'Is all well?'

'*Bus,* Didi,' came the reply. 'Nuclear weapons are all people are talking about at the moment. Did you know that those Pakistanis have tested theirs now?'

There it was, the start of trouble. Poor Lana. Poor, poor Lana, repeating her grandmother's youth and too brave to step back. There was a pause, and Sanam asked, 'How are the children?'

There was never a direct question, never a direct claim. No reference to her daughter, or to the granddaughter who so resembled her. It was almost as if Sanam didn't want to know. Even when they met in Delhi, Sanam

233

folded her hands in polite, distant greeting, and it would be the girls who would go up to Sanam and hug her. 'Sanam *Maasi, kaise ho*?'

'Sanam,' said Asha now. 'There's some news.'

'*Achcha*?'

'Lana wants to get married.'

'But Didi,' said Sanam. 'That's wonderful!'

'Yes,' was all Asha said, but Sanam instantly picked up on her concern.

'*Kya hua*, Didi?' she asked. 'Is all well?'

'The boy is Pakistani.'

There it was, the admission. Like a body being flung into still water. 'Muslim?' Sanam asked.

'Yes.'

All she could hear was Sanam's breathing. Then silence. Asha checked her receiver, called out, 'Sanam, are you there?'

'Yes, Didi,' Sanam replied, and then, 'What does Priya say?'

'She's against the match,' said Asha simply. She shut her eyes, refused to let in thoughts of Firoze. To think of him was to think of all she had lost. 'Of course she is,' she added robustly. 'Marriage with a Pakistani complicates things.'

'*Haan*, Didi.' There was no sign that Sanam was surprised or pleased.

'And honestly, I don't know what Lana was thinking.'

'Do you think she could know?' asked Sanam in a tremulous whisper. As if the idea itself was too fearful to commit to sound. 'Could she know she has Muslim blood?'

'No,' replied Asha sharply. 'We've never told the girls.'

'Of course.' Lana was marrying a Pakistani, but she

was still theirs, still Om's, still Asha's. Still Hindu, still a Sharma. They said their farewells and hung up. There it was, the thud. The body finally settling into the water. All was tranquil again.

3

For all the years she had learned to live without him, and for all the years she hadn't permitted herself the indulgence of his memory, Asha had never thought of him as a Pakistani.

'But Ma,' she heard Lana reason, 'Try and get to know him. He is the same colour as us. He likes the same music as we do. He eats the same food.'

Firoze had been Muslim, he'd been a boy, he'd been her dearest friend's brother. He'd been a lawyer, he'd been her father's protégé. He'd been all those things, but never a Pakistani. Never a boy from an enemy country.

She thought of all the headlines she had read in the papers on the flight over. The euphoria over fifty years of Independence had died down. They had held the march-pasts in front of Rashtrapati Bhavan – the old Viceroy's Palace. They had seen all the programmes that had been prepared for the occasion; documentaries on Independence and the Partition, telefilms on lovers parted as the country was cleaved in two. They had feted themselves, they had shed tears, they had looked ahead to the next fifty years, but now, as the fiftieth anniversary of Independence drew to a close, the two countries stood on the brink of a nuclear race. Both planned to test weapons, both were counselled by the existing nuclear powers to step back. As she had boarded the plane, she had heard someone in the seat behind her. 'We've launched,' she heard, 'we've launched,' and the row behind her had burst into applause, as if it had been a great achievement. 'They'll behave better now, those Pakistanis,' she heard, 'We'll finally have our seat on the Security Council.'

Nargis, the child sitting next to her, had beamed proudly. 'Wow,' she had said. The news had spread through the plane, like forest fire, a little like the frenzy surrounding the Partition, and as the aisles had crowded with revellers – distributing sweets, breaking into a celebratory *Bhangra* – Nargis had laughed out loud. 'Aunty,' she had said. 'What a great day this is!'

All the regret they'd shown over the Partition a few months ago, all the grandstanding, all the hyperbolic gyrating of politics, and now this. Nuclear tests carried out by India, and by Pakistan too. And then what? War, peace, more hand-wringing in the future? And her poor Lana, in love with a Pakistani boy.

4

They got out of the cab by Grand Central Station. Lana was nervous, that much was clear. It was a warm spring day, she wore a short, flared skirt, and kept smoothing it self-consciously down as she walked, as if anticipating a rogue breeze. She wore more make-up than normal, had spent an age in the bathroom blending eyeshadows and dipping her makeup brush in pots of powder. 'This,' she said to her grandmother, 'is my foundation. This is my blotting powder, this my concealer, and this . . .' She had pointed to a pot of pink powder, and Asha had waved her hands in despair. 'In my day,' she had said, and as her grand-daughter giggled, she had continued in mock serious-ness, 'It was considered daring when I went out with my head uncovered.'

'Oh Nani,' Lana had protested, and Asha had pretended to be offended. 'Why child,' she had said. 'We bit our lips for colour.'

'Really, Nani, you are too much.' Asha was still not certain if Lana believed her. She had rolled her eyes at her grandmother, as if it was a joke, an uncovered head, a bare mouth. As if she had spoken of life without fire. Now she smoothed down her skirt, wet her lips. Now she shivered in her lightweight jacket, in spite of the sun,

238

and though Asha considered offering the girl her shawl, she knew it would be refused.

She hadn't said a word to Asha about the purpose of their outing, but Asha had guessed. Lana had waited until her parents had left the apartment for the day before telling her grandmother to get ready. She had chosen Asha's clothes for her, had forbidden her from wearing her reading glasses. 'We're going out,' she said. 'You won't need them. And besides,' as Asha frowned. 'I want you to look nice.' She had been nervous as she dressed, and any time she heard a noise – a neighbour's door opening, the wind gathering pace – she had looked up. Whenever Asha asked a question, she had lifted a finger to her lips. Patience, she had urged. Patience and speed.

They turned a corner and entered a park. Asha paused to admire a neoclassical façade in front of her, but Lana rushed her on. 'It's the library,' she said, and as Asha turned back to look at it, Lana hurried her again. 'Please, Nani,' she said. 'We'll come here again.'

'It's Hussain, isn't it?' asked Asha, and though Lana didn't reply, she burnt scarlet beneath her powder.

They had stopped in front of a sunlit table. Lana was nodding to a boy with quiet eyes and a dark, new suit; she was gesturing Asha forward, and the boy was standing, he was nodding and folding his palms in greeting, and he was saying to her, 'It's so nice to finally meet you, Nani.'

He was polite; she noticed that from the very start. He had risen at her approach, he had pulled out her chair for her, and had seated her and then Lana before sitting down himself. Hussain had called her Nani, or grandmother, without her invitation. He had asked after her health, had asked after her flight. She had told him it was a long journey, and he had nodded. He had family in Pakistan, and the journey over to New York took the best part of the day. His Nanu had just arrived from Pakistan, actually. He consulted his watch anxiously. He should have landed a couple of hours ago. He would be dropping by to pick up keys to Hussain's apartment. He looked at the two women, said he hoped they wouldn't mind.

'Of course not,' said Asha. 'Where in Pakistan is he travelling from?'

'Islamabad,' Hussain replied. 'He's a Minister in the Government.' Asha nodded politely, and family pride asserted itself in the boy, who added, 'He's here for meetings at the UN.'

He was involved with the nuclear tests then. She knew they had all started scrambling, Indian and Pakistani diplomats, to the centres of power. To put forward their case, to forge alliances. Hussain's Nanu, then, was one of the advocates of Pakistan's nuclear tests. He would go to the UN, tell them about the threat to Pakistan. India had tested first, after all, and they were not to be trusted. Pakistan required a credible deterrent in case their larger neighbour to the East turned aggressive.

Hussain looked around. He half rose in his seat, then turned to Asha apologetically. 'I'm sorry, Nani,' he said. 'But do you think he'll be able to find us?'

She looked around, took in the rows of tables. It was approaching the hours of lunch – that void of time straddling the hours between eleven and three – and the park was starting to fill up. 'It *is* a rather large space,' she said.

He got up, walked as far as the library before turning back. 'No,' he said as he sat back down. 'No sign of him.'

They were silent for a moment. All sensed the obstacle to the match – his being Pakistani, her being Indian – even though they were in America, even though they were New Yorkers, living, breathing, working under a different sun. How different their life was to that back home; how little they were concerned by nuclear tests, by power strikes, by the building of dams over the subcontinent's rivers.

Asha studied him as he sipped his coffee. He smoothed his hair, cleared his throat. He had high cheekbones, a full mouth, and if she looked carefully, a slight slant to his eyes. He was tall, taller than Lana in her heels, and had soft, silky brown hair that looked a touch overlong. But his suit looked new, and perhaps he had just begun work, and maybe he was new to the regulation that professional life demanded. A daily shave, a weekly shoe polish, a monthly haircut, all these were rituals to grow into.

'I work around the corner,' he said. 'I'm sorry you had to travel so far to see me.'

'*Arre, Beta*,' scolded Asha. 'What a thing to say.'

He began talking about his work. He had just joined a think tank. He named it with pride, then paused to observe her reaction, and she obliged by smiling. 'Oh yes,' she said, 'How wonderful,' and he smiled too, pleased at her recognition. He turned in his seat, trying to attract a waitress's attention. He ordered drinks for the table, smiling at Lana.

'Do you know, *Beta*?' said Asha. 'I was born and raised in Pakistan.'

'I know,' smiled Hussain. It really was a nice smile, slow and shy. *Like a purdah curtain over a desired object.* He looked towards Lana. 'Lana told me. Where was it you lived?'

'Suhanpur,' said Asha. 'Of course, they call it by another name now.'

'Mianbad,' he said. 'I have family there. My mother's mother,' he added. 'My Nani.'

'Have you been there?' she asked.

'Not for years.'

'I still remember every corner of it,' said Asha. 'The market, the square that led off all the main streets . . .'

'That's still there,' he said, and she smiled. 'Then there's a fountain in the square, and the great mosque at one end of it . . .'

'That,' she said wonderingly, 'is all new. It must have been built after the Partition.'

He looked chastened, and she added, 'All things change. And what I really remember is the people. How different things were back then. We lived as one, Hindus and Muslims.' She saw Lana look at her, and felt she was speaking too much, but she saw Hussain lean forward in his chair, and she added, 'My best friend was Muslim . . .'

He nodded. 'My Nani said the same thing. She said she had a friend who was Hindu. She said they were like sisters. I told her about Lana in the month before she died, and she understood. She understood completely.' He paused. 'But Nani, have I said something to upset you?' He rose, came to her side of the table, and knelt to look in her face. She waved away his concerns, but there was no hiding her distress. She was crying now, openly, and as Lana hurried to her side, and as a few curious passers-by paused in their walk, she whispered, 'Nargis.' The two young people were looking at her with rising concern. Lana was bending down, she had her arms in a shield around Asha. She was wiping away her tears, but it was no use. She tried to clamp her eyes shut, she tried

242

to will herself calm, but it was no use. 'Please, Nani,' said Lana, and as Asha continued to cry, she attempted a joke. 'Please stop, Nani, or Hussain will think you hate him.'

Asha's hand crept out from under her shawl. She gripped the boy's hand with her own, then turned towards her granddaughter and attempted a smile. 'I'm sorry,' she stammered, 'It's been so long since . . .', but she was off again, crying and sniffing and turning away from curious stares.

The sun grew stronger. The breeze that had worried Lana as they walked had died down, and instead, they turned their faces towards the light. They had finished their drinks, but the waitress didn't move to clear their cups. 'Another tea?' offered Hussain, but Asha waved his offer away.

A couple walked past them, arms entwined. They stopped at the next table and took out the remains of a sandwich lunch. The girl bent down and began to scatter bread on the ground. Soon the air was filled with birds, with pigeons, with magpies, with others they couldn't identify. 'Who knew,' said Lana, 'that there were so many in Manhattan?' They hustled each other, the birds, they pecked, they pushed, they scrapped over the bread. The couple brushed crumbs off their hands. The girl rose, and they began to walk away. The birds carried on eating, then realising they had been abandoned, rose in a black cloud to follow the couple out of the park.

Hussain and Lana held hands. The sun shone on the girl's hair. Asha saw her turn at his touch, she saw her incline her body towards him. She saw her smile at him, a secret smile – joyous and hopeful – and she knew the

243

two would be married. They were healthy and young and full of promise. As they sat together, facing the sun, they were in perfect harmony with each other, and she knew they would be happy.

They heard steps approach them. 'Hussain,' they heard a voice call out.

'It's Nanu,' said Hussain to the women, and they turned as one to the newcomer.

A tall man walked their way. There was something familiar about him, something in his stride, something in the cut of his hair, and Asha was sure she knew him. She wished she had insisted on carrying her glasses. It was no use though, and try as she might, she couldn't make out any feature. Still, a certainty grew inside her. She drew her shawl tightly around her, and she knew her body recognised him before she did.

She waited for him to draw nearer, and then she gasped. No one heard her, focused as they were on Hussain's Nanu, but it *was* him.

It was Firoze.

She saw him approach, saw him lift a hand to his hair as he had in their youth. She saw him smile at Hussain. '*Beta*,' she heard him say, and she felt a stab. Hussain was his. Firoze had lived a life beyond her. She saw him look at Lana, saw his smile broaden, and her misery grew. How happy he had been without her. Over the years, she had imagined meeting him again. He was young in her mind, as young as when they were last together, and as full of her love. She was never invisible to him. He was never full of excitement at the sight of another. He was never addressed by another as Nanu. Firoze had never, not in all the years he had existed in her memory, had a life independent of her. She felt goosebumps on her arms, and she grew furious with herself. Such betrayal by her senses, such longing after all this time.

She saw him more clearly now, and could count his frailties. He was thinner than he had been. He seemed shorter than she remembered, and darker too. He walked with purpose, but with a slower, measured tread. His eyes had sunk in their sockets, his hair was grey. But it was no good, he was unmistakably the same man. Warm and vital, full of confidence. And as for her? She had lost her fleetness. She had studied herself in the mirror in the morning, counted her wrinkles. She had aged. Her face had set in shape, and any time she frowned or smiled or cried, her face crumpled and she looked the same. Dumpy and plain. Old. Not like him, still young, still vibrant.

Firoze was embracing Hussain. He was clapping him on the back, he was stepping forward to embrace Lana. There it was, the same crease-edged smile. The creases were a little deeper now, the lines around his face firmer. Asha turned to look at Hussain. She had readied herself to love him like a son, but the details she had missed! How had she not noticed his hair, as brown, as ablaze under the sun as Firoze's had been? How had she not noticed his lean, long frame, or his full mouth? How had she not noticed the high contours of his face?

Lana was gesturing to Asha now, introducing her to Firoze. He was nodding, smiling. It was a suave, polite smile; it sat well on him, a lawyer, a prosperous elder. He was folding his palms together, speaking in her Hindi, speaking in his Urdu. He was bending down, looking at her, looking back at Hussain, then dropping down to a chair. He was smiling, nodding as the children around them spoke, nodding, smiling, nodding again. He was looking at her, and as she thought, despite herself, of their last, fateful meeting on the banks of the Ravi, she knew he thought of it too. She saw him colour, saw his hands rise to his hair. Her own hand rose in reply, once more her scar burnt in the chill. She saw him smile at the bantering lovers in front of them, saw him pronounce Lana beautiful, but she knew his mind was consumed with her.

'So tell me,' Firoze was saying. He looked up at Asha, then smiled at the young couple. 'How did the two of you meet?'

'Nanu,' said Lana, then paused shyly. 'I can call you Nanu, can't I?'

'Of course, *Beta*.'

'Nanu, what can I tell you?' Lana complained. 'This Hussain of yours never left me alone. He kept following me.' She looked up at her grandmother, remembering the song she had taught her. *You follow me, you follow me.* 'He just didn't take no for an answer.'

'Well done, my boy,' said Firoze. He clapped his hands together, sneaking a look at Asha. Both thought of his wavering shadow on the banks of the Ravi. The sun shone strongly on them. *Dham*, she thought. *Dharak dham.*

'*Arre*, Nanu,' Hussain was saying stoutly. 'They're all lies. She looks so innocent, this girl, but she knew I liked her.' Lana shook her head furiously. She smacked Hussain's wrist, she swore never to talk to him, and he said to her, 'My *jaan*, my life, listen to reason.' There it was again, another stolen look, another crease-edged smile. 'And the truth is,' Hussain said. 'You liked me liking you.'

Lana rose in protest, and Firoze held his hand up. 'I don't know what the truth is,' he said. 'But one thing is certain. You have excellent taste, my boy.'

Lana blushed, and sat down again. This had always been Firoze's magic; his ability to make another feel cherished. She saw her granddaughter sitting on her chair as if it was a throne, she saw her laughing at Firoze's words.

She looked at him, saw the crease around his eyes deepen as he grew aware of her attention. Whatever had he seen in her? He who could have had his pick of beauties? There had been the milk-skinned wonder Nargis had been so in awe of. Maybe that was who he had married. She felt jealousy rise in her again. She had only married to avoid becoming a refugee. What possible impetus could he have had? She became conscious that the others were looking at her. Firoze was speaking.

'Really?' he was saying with polite interest.

'Yes,' said Hussain, 'Lana's Nani is from Mianbad too.'

Firoze looked across at Asha, smiled uncertainly, and she told herself to hold firm. He was the one who had rushed to marry the next available woman. 'Perhaps,' Hussain was saying, 'your families knew each other?'

His Nanu turned to Asha, watching her for a cue. She held his look, saw Lana and Hussain look at them with their innocent interest, and she turned away in confusion. Firoze appeared to be studying her, as if trying to remember an acquaintance in her features. There was a tiny smile at the corner of his lips, an infinitesimal lift at the edge of his eyes. 'Perhaps,' he said in the end, 'perhaps we did.'

'What was the name of her friend?' Hussain asked.

Firoze didn't reply for a moment, and his grandson prompted him. 'You know, the girl she said was like a sister to her?'

'Asha,' said Firoze softly. He was scratching his head, as if he had had to struggle to remember her name, and as Lana exclaimed, he looked up in surprise.

'But Nani's name is Asha!' she said.

'Asha!' he said. He clapped his hands. 'You're Asha?'

They were clapping too now, the two children, excited. This discovery was like a prize to them, a legitimising of their relationship. Asha and Firoze looked at each other, and both were struck by their deception. They didn't exchange a word, and Lana had begun to recount an anecdote, but both smiled.

A man approached, another bird feeder. Once more they observed the swarm of black wings, as swift and as sudden as a monsoon shower. As undeniable as the beat of the Ravi all those years back. Asha asked him, 'How's Nargis?'

'She passed away last month. It was her heart.'

She nodded. These ailments, the arthritis, the diabetes, the heart problems, what did they have to do with them? It was another Nargis who had died, an elderly woman. The girl she had left behind had been on the cusp of life. 'How I wish I had seen her get married!'

'She was a beautiful bride.'

'How excited she had been! How she had been looking forward to putting on her bridal wear! I still remember the embroidery on her *salwar kameez*.' Asha sighed. She saw her granddaughter look at her with interest. She closed her eyes. She shook her head. '*Oof*,' she said. 'How I wish I had been there.'

'She missed you,' he said. 'I know that.'

Hussain stood up. 'I have to get back to work,' he said apologetically. 'I'll see you back at home, Nanu.' He hugged Lana, then reached forward and embraced Asha. He was almost the same as his grandfather. The same hair, the same eyes. The same warmth. 'And,' he added, 'I want you to tell me all about Nani.'

'Nani?' asked Asha. 'You called Nargis Nani?'

'Of course,' he said. He moved forward to hug Firoze, then began to walk in the direction of the Library.

'I'll just walk him to the exit,' said Lana. 'You don't mind, do you, Nani?' She didn't wait for Asha's response, running quickly to catch up with Hussain.

Asha turned to Firoze. 'Hussain is Nargis' grandson?'

Firoze nodded. He was looking at her, smiling. 'It's so good to see you, Asha.'

She brought her hand to her scar, felt the stiffness in her joints. Firoze was looking at her with surprise. She felt herself tear up again, but now she held her eyes firmly shut. This wasn't the time. 'I thought,' she said, then found she had to pause. She took in a deep breath, felt the cool, spring air flow through her, then tried again. 'I thought,' but she trailed off again. Firoze was leaning forward now, resting his hand on the table, a moment away from her. 'But Hussain,' she asked. 'He called you Nanu.'

'I never married,' he said simply. He was staring at her, and though she looked away, watching for a returning Lana, his eyes never moved from her face. 'Nargis' grandchildren call me Nanu.'

She didn't dare look at him, but she asked her trembling question, 'You never married?'

'No,' he replied. He leaned forward. His hands moved towards hers, and she quickly took hers off the table.

She saw him study every inch of her, as if matching her to his memory of half a century ago, and he added, 'I can't claim to have been a saint. But there was no one I wanted to marry.'

Yes. She could believe him. Firoze in Suhanpur, and then in Islamabad, growing into a prominent lawyer. He was a man who liked to talk, he was a man who needed company. And yet he hadn't married. There had been no fresh-faced, milk-skinned bride. She trembled at the thought, then saw him looking at her. 'I came to look for you,' he said. 'I came to Delhi, I searched through all the camps. I saw no sign of you, nor of your family.'

So it had been him. That evening in the Lodhi Gardens, as she took her evening walk with Om. 'No,' she said. She looked steadily at him, told herself she wasn't going to cry. 'After you left me in your *tonga*, there was an ambush.' He winced, shaking his head as if to ward off her words. 'And when I got to Delhi, there was nowhere I could go. A friend from our Suhanpur days took me in. He was kind to me. He married me.'

Firoze nodded. 'Did I know him?'

'I don't know,' she replied. 'His name was Om Sharma.'

He frowned, trying to remember, and she had to remind herself to stop studying the lines on his forehead. She had once reached out and smoothed them out. It may have been one secret morning in Pappaji's library, or it might have been when he walked her to school. He had smiled at her touch, and the lines had disappeared. 'See,' she had crowed, 'I've cured you of your lines,' and he had frowned at her words. His lines had promptly reappeared. 'Touch me again,' he had said. 'And cure me again.'

'I don't know,' he was saying. 'Was he a lawyer? Would I have met him at court?'

250

Asha shook her head, but there was no time for more. Lana was running back, her hair whipping around her. The breeze she had been so mindful of earlier was picking up, and she was smoothing down her skirt as she reached them. 'It's so nice to finally meet you,' she said to Firoze.

They rose and walked to the park's exit. Firoze hailed a cab for them and waited as they were seated. His hand brushed past the end of her *sari*, she felt it linger as he gathered her shawl around her. Then the cab was pulling away, and Lana was turning and waving at him. Asha didn't permit herself to turn at once, but as Lana sat down, and as the cab stopped impatiently in front of traffic, she allowed herself to look back. He was still there, she was sure, a dot in a grey raincoat. She couldn't see if he was looking her way, couldn't see if he saw her. The cab driver pressed firmly down on his horn, and quickly cleared the path for them to proceed homewards.

5

Once everyone was safely occupied with their day – Sunil with the hospital, Priya with her pharmacy, and Lana with college – she turned to the phone. She had a great desire to unburden herself, to share the events she hadn't yet dared to acknowledge.

She called Roopa. 'I don't know,' she said now, 'I'm not sure if you remember Nargis, my friend from Suhanpur . . .'

'Of course I do,' replied Roopa. Her voice was excited, and Asha could just picture her, eyebrow raised, hand on hip, milky tea beside her. 'Asha,' Roopa was saying, 'Is Nargis in New York?'

'No.' *Not her.* 'But Roopa, Lana is in love. She's in love with Nargis' grandson.'

'With Nargis' boy?'

'Yes.'

'Not a Muslim?'

There it was again, the truth unthinkingly spoken. 'Yes, a Muslim.'

There was a sharp intake of breath. 'What does Priya think of it?'

'She's worried, clearly . . .'

'But Asha,' broke in Roopa breathily, and now Asha knew she felt it too; the wonder, the rising delight. She knew Roopa sensed the breathing, heaving presence of Suhanpur – the warmth of its summers, the rush of the river, the noise of the market, the *barfi* crumbled into their morning *lassi*. 'Is it really Nargis' boy?'

And Firoze's. All she had to do was whisper it onto the line, as she had done in bed all those years ago. *I'm not pregnant.* Roopa had heard the words then. She had to offer something up to the ether, another admission, and if Roopa caught the words, then so be it. She said the words to herself in preparation, but they were too scandalous, even for her. 'Firoze and I,' she thought, and shivered against the phone. She grew suddenly conscious of it, of the clinical black of the receiver, of the sacred secrets it would rob her of. There was more now to think of than their summer romance. There was the horror of the bus shelter, there were the scars they carried. There were the wars they had fought, the suspicions that had festered over the years. There were the nuclear tests, and Firoze arriving, actually flying to New York to argue on Pakistan's side. 'No,' she thought. This she couldn't share.

'Don't I know what she meant to you?' Roopa was saying. 'Anytime you taste *rasmalai*, you remember those you ate at Nargis' house. And anytime we took our children swimming.' Yes. Here it was, despite her best intentions, the rush, the river, here it came. 'You never could stop talking about your morning dips in the Ravi.' Yes, the Ravi. *Dham, dharak dham.* It washed over her, the pleasure, the memory, his crease-edged smile.

'How do you feel about the match?'

'Me?' asked Asha. She paused, felt the rush of the river again, the irresistible lure of that smile. 'He makes her happy, Roopa.' She smiled, and said with certainty. 'I just want her to be happy.'

Asha walked towards the tiny playground she had been in the habit of taking Lana to. It grew boisterous in the hours after school, but now, during the early hours of the work day, it was deserted. She took a thermos filled with tea and a magazine, planning to spend a couple of unhurried hours in the sun.

She thought she saw Firoze the moment she left the apartment block. She saw a flash of brown, perhaps, or a wide-mouthed smile, and then it was gone. 'Stop it!' she said sternly to herself. 'His hair isn't even brown anymore.' She turned the corner. The sun was bright, and as she blinked to adjust her eyes to the light, she was sure she felt something. His shadow, his arm brushing against her. She walked down to the playground, and she was certain she saw a familiar shadow waver by her. How she had loved him! She shook her head. It was impossible. He had his work at the UN, he was sure to be occupied with that. Still, she paused. There he was, standing a foot away from her, smiling sheepishly, flushing dark. He stammered uncomfortably, 'What a surprise, seeing you here.' The old wedding tune came into her mind. *You follow me, you follow me,* and she was smiling too, flushing and extending her hand in a formal handshake.

They walked to the playground. 'There,' pointed Asha as they sat at her usual bench. 'Just across the street is Priya's pharmacy. She can see me if she pops her head out of the window.'

'Oh,' said Firoze. 'How wonderful,' but he was

standing up, he was pointing to another bench at the opposite end of the playground. 'It's a sunnier spot,' and he was leading her there.

They spoke about the children. He spoke slowly and thoughtfully. How precise he had become. She wondered if they would have been happy together, if he would have found her too chaotic and disorganised. But then, she had been happy with Om. She smiled sadly. All those years with Om and she'd thought of Firoze, and now that she was finally sitting next to Firoze, her thoughts kept returning to her husband. 'Lana is beautiful,' Firoze was saying now, but it was Asha he was looking at. 'Asha,' he said suddenly, 'It's so good to see you.' He reached his hand out, but her own retreated under her *dupatta*.

'Nargis,' she said quickly. 'Do you know, I never saw her husband. We didn't even know what he looked like.'

Firoze smiled.

'Was he handsome? Were they happy?' and as he paused, she blurted out, 'Did he have a moustache?'

'Yes,' he said solemnly. There was no sign he found her question unreasonable. 'He had a moustache. He was kind, and they were happy.' He leant back on the bench, patting his stomach. 'He ran to fat in his last years. That's what got him in the end, his diabetes.'

'Oh,' said Asha, but she was thinking of Om, of the thickness around his neck. He hadn't been able to button his shirt collar by the end. 'What's the use,' he had said. 'It's not like I wear ties anymore.'

'He was a good man,' Firoze said, and Asha gave a start. He looked at his hands, laid one neatly on top of the other. He spotted some smudge on a trouser leg, and took to rubbing at it. He looked up at her. 'And how have you been, Asha?'

'Well,' she said, too quickly, and she saw he expected more. She thought of Om, of the toothiness that had so repulsed her in the beginning. She thought of the Delhi house, of its gargoyles, Ma and Mahesh. She thought of her work at the school. She thought of Sanam and Priya, she thought of the children she and Om had been unable to bear. She thought of the child, their child, that she had lost. Her hand covered her belly, and his eye fell on her scar.

'Asha,' he asked. He took her hand in his own, turned it up. 'Wasn't this your tattoo?'

She nodded. He was running his fingers along the jagged line of the scar, bringing her hand up to his forehead. He was touching it to his head, as if in prayer, and Asha said, 'It was after the ambush, after Mataji and Pappaji . . .' She felt his breath on her skin, and she tailed off.

'Yes,' he said. 'Yes,' and he was bringing her hand down to his mouth. He was kissing it. She felt the smooth skin of his cheek, she felt the curl in his lip, and she quickly took back her hand, as if she had been stabbed once more.

The next morning he was waiting for her at the playground. He didn't make any excuses, didn't act surprised to see her, and as she sat down next to him, she thought she could hear a strain of the wedding song, *You follow me, you follow me* . . .

He was there the morning after too. And the morning after that. He had been scheduled to leave New York after a week, but he quietly extended his trip. Hussain was pleased by the change in Firoze's plans. 'You never normally stay long enough . . .'

256

'I have a great desire,' replied his Nanu, 'to spend a little more time with you.'

'If only you'd arrived before I started work,' Hussain said. 'I'm going to be stuck in the office most of the day.'

'It doesn't matter,' lied Firoze without any sense of shame. 'We'll make the most of our time together.'

In the park Asha shared her tea with Firoze. She handed him sandwiches. 'Cheese and chutney,' she said quietly. 'You must be hungry.'

'Thank you,' he said. His phone rang. 'It's work,' he said. 'Sorry.' He rose, walked as he spoke, and every once in a while, she heard snatches of conversation.

'Our sovereignty . . .' she heard. 'But those Indians,' and then, after a pause, 'We must be allowed to defend ourselves,' and she knew he was discussing the nuclear test. She thought of Priya's complaint. 'What was Lana thinking, Ma?' she had said. 'Didn't she pause to think he was Pakistani before she fell in love?'

Firoze looked at Asha apologetically. *Hadn't she paused to think he was Pakistani before she fell in love?* Firoze lifted his index finger, and mouthed, 'One minute,' and she nodded. He came back to sit next to her. 'How nice it is,' he said. 'To sit next to you after all these years.'

'Yes.'

'How I've longed to see you over the years.' He leaned forward in the bench. His face was inches away from her, and Priya just had to walk out of her pharmacy, she just had to cross the road, and she would catch them. Asha told herself to back away. She told herself the distances between them were too insurmountable, and she made to move, but she smelt his morning soap, still the same

257

after all those years, and it was as if she was rooted to the spot.

'How I've wondered what life has done to you. I've imagined you fat and old and bitter and unhappy.'

'So have I.'

He moved closer. 'I've imagined myself happy, Asha,' he said. 'I've imagined myself happy without you.'

'And have you been unhappy?'

He considered his next words. 'No,' he said finally. 'No, I haven't been unhappy.'

She was disappointed by the answer, by his measured rationale. But she nodded too, she too agreed with his assessment. 'I know,' she said. 'I haven't been unhappy either.'

He was up now. He was pacing the playground, he was returning. 'I think we would have been happy together.'

She didn't look at him.

'Asha,' he said, and she closed her eyes. It was too much to hope for.

'Please Asha, just listen to me.' She was shaking her head. She was crying, squeezing her eyes firmly shut. 'No,' she was whispering, but he spoke over her. 'I'm not asking for much,' he was saying. 'We will never have our youth back. We will never have children together.'

She saw him looking at her, with such love, such trust, and now he repeated his words. 'I know we won't have children,' and she doubled over at his words, her hands lifted to her mouth. 'Our children,' she said bitterly, 'our child.' Tears streamed down her face.

'Our child?'

She couldn't speak. She went on hugging herself, and a sob escaped her for the loss she had never before acknowledged.

'Our child, Asha?'

Her lips were parched. 'Our . . .' she began, before she was beset by tears again. She spoke in ragged, tearful bursts, telling him about her changing body, and about her bleed on the *tonga* ride away from Suhanpur. She knew she was barely making sense, but his face changed.

He turned away from her. 'You never told me.'

'How could I have?' she cried, 'You stopped talking to me right after we . . .' He still looked away, and her voice trailed off, 'After we . . .'

He came back to sit next to her. 'I'm sorry,' he was saying. 'I'd made a promise to your Pappaji, and I thought it was for the best. What a fool I was. What a fool I was to let you go away.' His hand was on her back now, caressing her. It wasn't the fevered touch of their courtship. And yet she felt herself burn. She felt herself arch in yearning. 'Please,' he said. 'Can't we be happy now?'

Asha laid her head against his chest. She felt him breathe, she smelt the morning soap on his skin. She held his hand and stroked it with her own. She saw the age spots on his skin, saw how slack it was in the webbing between his fingers.

'We can grow old together.' There was a husky knot in his throat.

She lifted her hand to his neck, saw him shiver. She put aside thoughts of Priya and her objections to Lana's marriage. 'Yes,' she smiled. 'We can be happy.'

'Asha,' he said. He lowered his face to kiss her eyelids, her nose. She thought of the crow's feet lining her eyes, thought of the rough skin by her cheeks, but he was kissing her softly, gently, as if she was fragile, as if she was precious.

As if she was the desired object behind the purdah curtain.

His fingers were on her mouth, and now he lowered his mouth to her lips. Passers-by smiled as they passed the elderly couple still in love with each other. He was taking her into his arms. She thought of pulling back, conscious of the folds of flesh around her back, but here it was again, the wonder in his touch, and she was closing her eyes. Her mind was filling with thunder, *Dham dharak dham*. She was answering the pressure of his mouth, and she found that she was forgetting to register any complaint at all.

6

She rose while it was still dark in New York. The lights were switched off down the hallway, and Asha walked gingerly towards the dim outline of the kitchen door. Her knees were beginning to cause her some discomfort, and Om had fretted it was the start of arthritis. She had refused to see the doctor. 'I'm growing old,' she had laughed when he turned angry. 'That's all.' She felt them lock up most in the chill of New York's early mornings, and as she held on to the wall for support, she remembered his words. 'I'll come with you, Asha. You needn't be afraid of the doctor.'

'Come on,' she told herself. 'It's only a few more steps.'

She sat alone in the kitchen for an hour or more each morning. She refused to turn on the lights, afraid of waking the rest of the household. Instead she prepared tea the Indian way, in a saucepan. She added tea leaves to boiling water, left it until it roiled a dark, intense brown. Then she poured in milk, added a liberal spoonful of sugar, then the flavourings she varied according to her mood; fragrant cardamom when she felt nostalgic, allspice when it rained, or long, thin slivers of restorative ginger.

She took her time with her tea, pouring out two servings into her cup. This was her quiet time. There was no rush for the hospital, for the pharmacy or for college. There was no shopping to be done, no calls to be answered. There was no Firoze to see, no Hussain to worry about. She was alone with her thoughts, and at this time of the day, they were placid. Her memories were happy, her mind uncluttered with the burden of chores. For the hour or so she was alone in the mornings, she was on holiday. By the time her tea was drunk, the sky would begin to grow light. This, she felt, was her cue to rouse the rest of her family. She would switch on the kitchen light, begin to cook breakfast. She refused to prepare the pancakes Lana favoured, cooking instead semolina pudding fat with raisins or buttery potato *paranthas* she served with thick yogurt from the Greek deli down the road.

'Rest,' Lana told her as she came in. 'Lie in. You're on holiday.'

'I am,' she smiled. She saw her granddaughter pause in front of the saucepan with its last cup of tea. She saw her inhale and smile. As Lana poured herself a cup, she said, '*Beta*, I was thinking of inviting Hussain's uncle over for tea.'

'Nani?' the girl asked, and she knew Lana and Hussain had discussed them. She knew they had spoken of his grandmother, knew they had spoken of Firoze never having married. The girl was looking at her curiously now.

'Tell me about Firoze Nanu,' Lana said. She brought her cup of tea up to her nose. 'Mmm,' she said. 'Nani, your tea is the best.' It was all so casual, her voice, her words, as if her request had been a throw-away comment. Then as Asha returned to stirring the pot on the stove, she asked, 'How well did you know him?'

262

'*Arre*,' said Asha. She waved her hand in the air. 'We were neighbours, you know. His sister – Hussain's grandmother – was my best friend.' Lana settled herself to listen, and Asha knew she expected details. 'It's hard to think about it today, isn't it? An Indian and a Pakistani. But we really were like sisters. We ate from the same plate. I fasted for *Ramzan*, she for *Karva Chauth*. We kept each other's secrets, we knew each other's dreams. *Arre*,' and here she smiled an impish, delighted smile, 'We even stole her father's *beedi* cigarettes. How terrified we were when we first smoked them out on her terrace. And how we coughed when we took that first drag.'

Lana smiled. 'Just imagine,' she said. 'My Nani and Hussain's Nani.'

'Those were good days.'

'Nani,' interrupted Lana. 'Hussain says there was a girl Firoze Nanu loved . . .'

Asha's voice was deliberately nonchalant. '*Achcha*?'

'Yes,' and though Asha took care to stir her tea, to add another spoon of sugar and let it dissolve, she knew Lana was studying her closely. 'She was Hindu.'

A nod, a shake of the head. 'I see.'

'Maybe you knew her?'

'No, *Beta*,' and as Lana remained silent, she added, 'These things would have been hidden. It wasn't done, in those days, a Hindu-Muslim marriage.'

'Ok.'

As the silence continued, Asha began to ramble. 'It was a different time. We stayed within our boundaries. We married the people our families chose. We covered our heads; we didn't wear any make up. And as for those short skirts of yours . . .' And there it was finally, Lana's smile, so feline, utterly impossible to resist. It lulled Asha into a sense of security and emboldened her to ask, 'What happened to her, the girl your Firoze Nanu loved?'

'No one knows,' said Lana. She rose to pour herself a fresh cup of tea. 'The country was partitioned,' she said, her tiger's eyes narrowed. 'She headed East . . .'

There was another expectant pause 'Partition was a terrible time, *Beta*,' Asha said finally. She looked straight at Lana, challenging her to ask another question, challenging her to delve into that painful period of her life.

'I'm sorry, Nani,' Lana said. She hugged her grandmother. 'I shouldn't have asked you all those stilly questions.'

'Seeing you, seeing Hussain,' Asha said hesitantly. 'Even his Nanu. It brought back good memories.' *We can be happy*, she thought. *We can be spend our last years together*. She brought her hands up to her face, breathed deeply. She felt her heart rush. She was burning, she was shaking. She was sure she would collapse. *Breathe*, she told herself. She closed her eyes, willed herself still. 'I haven't allowed myself to remember for more than fifty years,' she said at length. Her voice shook, and as Lana approached her, she forced herself to slow down. 'For a lifetime I've told myself I was lucky to escape,' she said. 'That everything I had left behind was horrible. They were all murderers in the West. They were all rapists, all religious fanatics.'

'I'm so sorry,' said Lana. She knelt down by Asha. She didn't touch her, didn't speak. Her hair was loose on her shoulders, and in the sunny kitchen it grew a brilliant brown. *Lana*, Asha thought, my beautiful, clever, sensitive child. She caressed the girl's head.

'I needed to remember those times.' She brought her hand down to Lana's, and gripped it tightly. 'I needed to remember those I loved in Suhanpur.'

Lana's smile was semi-serious, the smile of a child playing at being grown-up. 'You do think I'm doing the right thing, don't you, Nani?'

Asha nodded. 'I want your mother to meet Hussain's family,' she said. 'I want to invite his Nanu over for tea.'

There was another fleet look in her direction, and as Asha held her gaze, Lana turned away guiltily. 'I can . . .'

'No,' said Asha quickly. 'I don't want you there. I don't want Hussain there. That'll be too much for your mother to take in.'

'But Nani . . .'

Asha nodded encouragingly. 'Let her get to know Firoze,' she said. 'Let her see that he's educated, that he's civilised. She's scared of you going into a hostile environment. Let her see that she's wrong, and then we can let her meet Hussain.'

Asha spoke to Priya and Sunil the same day. 'We have to discuss the Lana situation.'

Priya agreed readily. 'I worry so much about the girl.'

Sunil looked half-heartedly up from his newspaper, and as his wife crossed her arms, he straightened his paper out, and began to fold it. He took his time, folding it over once, lovingly reassembling the different sections. He didn't complain about his weekend paper ritual being interrupted, but his reluctance was evident. 'I don't understand why it's such a big deal.'

'You don't understand?' asked Priya shrilly.

265

'Well,' Sunil was saying. 'What does it matter?' His wife sniffed, and he added, 'Both children live in America. So they support different teams when it comes to a cricket match. So what?'

'Don't be so complacent,' scolded his wife. There was a proxy war going on at the moment, and how secure would Lana feel as a daughter-in-law in a Pakistani household?

'They'll live on their own,' pointed out Sunil. 'The rest of his family is in Pakistan.'

Priya held her hands up. Would Lana even be welcomed into her in-laws' home? These things mattered in a marriage. They married into families in their culture. A son-in-law was exactly that, a son. A daughter-in-law was a daughter. Would a Pakistani family accept Lana? Asha thought of Firoze's arguments half a century ago. It was all right for him, he said, but the girl's family would always oppose a Hindu-Muslim match.

Priya's protest carried on. Would Lana have to convert? Would their children have to be brought up as Muslims? All those years since Partition, and people were still worried about the same thing. Pappaji had voiced the same fears. Asha could almost laugh. They were all a little Muslim now. His biological grandchild – the baby who bled away on the *tonga* ride that took them towards India – had been Muslim. His granddaughter Priya was born to a Muslim mother. And Lana, who was outwardly all Hindu, even she was about to marry a Muslim boy. All those years, all that opposition, all that death in the name of religion, and they had all become a little Muslim.

Sunil stood up now. He held his hands out in surrender. 'What do you want me to say, Priya?' he asked.

266

'I want you to be involved. I want to know that you're worried too.'

'I'm worried,' Sunil admitted. 'It's not ideal she's marrying a Pakistani boy. But really,' he added, 'Isn't it better than marrying someone who won't understand her? She's funny, a little irreverent, and she's as sharp a girl as I've ever met. Isn't it better she's marrying a man who can love her? Isn't it better for her to marry a Pakistani than for her to marry an alcoholic or a gambler or a drug addict?'

'Yes,' sniffed Priya. 'These are the only options open to my beautiful, bright daughter. A Pakistani or a drug addict.'

'Priya,' said Sunil. 'I want her to be happy.'

'So do I . . .'

'I know,' he said reasonably. 'I know you do. But really, you need to think of what's best for her. She's a good girl, a clever girl. And if she's decided that Hussain will make her happy, then I will support her decision . . .'

'But Sunil . . .'

'Enough,' said Asha. The two duellers turned to her in surprise, as if registering her presence for the first time. 'You'll give this a try,' she said. 'Hussain's uncle is in town. We'll invite him for tea.'

'But..'

'No but,' insisted Asha. 'I knew his family from my time in Suhanpur. They're decent people . . .'

'But . . .'

'I mean it,' said Asha sternly. 'We'll invite him over for a quiet cup of tea. Surely there's no harm in that.'

Priya wrung her hands in agitation.

'Hussain is a nice boy,' Asha said gently. 'I knew their

family in Suhanpur; his grandmother was like a sister to me.' Priya snorted, and Asha didn't bother rebuking her. 'Really,' she said to her daughter. 'It'll just be a cup of tea. And you never know, maybe you'll even change your mind about this boy.'

7

They spent the entire weekend readying the flat. Firoze was to visit on Monday morning, and the preparations began early on Saturday. Lana was dispatched to buy flowers. Rooms were aired, curtains washed and ironed. Asha hung rugs out over the balcony, beating them with the back of a wooden broom.

On Sunday, they cooked. They prepared two dozen samosas, little pastry triangles they stuffed with a spicy potato mixture. 'We'll fry them on Monday,' said Asha. She created a spice mix for the tea she planned to prepare, with crushed cardamom seeds, cinnamon bark and fennel. She roasted cumin to add to old Chotu's treasured lemonade recipe.

'All this effort,' grumbled Priya, but Sunil pointed out, 'The boy's side is coming to the house. We can't do enough.' Asha smiled and bent to her work.

Firoze was late. The hallway clock chimed the hour, and Priya looked at her watch. 'I'm not sure,' she told her mother, 'that it's such a good idea to meet this man.'

Asha hurried to calm her. 'It's his first time here, *Beta*,' she said, blushing at her lie. 'Maybe he's lost.'

Priya returned to her bedroom to refresh her lipstick. Asha put her hands up to her hair, certain her bun was coming loose. It was all there, the pins neatly stuck in as they always were, and she resisted the urge to rise and check her appearance. Priya was sure to be back in a moment, and what would she think of her mother's vanity?

The bell rang. Priya was still in her bedroom. Asha rose. She saw Firoze's full, silver head over the entry-phone. 'It's Firoze Khan,' he said. 'I've come to see Lana's family.'

'Of course,' she was saying. 'Come in, Firoze-*ji*.'

Asha heard the elevator stop at their floor. She heard his footsteps approach. He rang the doorbell, and she walked back to the entrance. She opened the door, smiling in welcome. If he was surprised to see her alone, he didn't show it. 'It's so nice to see you again,' he began, then smiled his secret smile at her. Tenderly, she smoothed the familiar crease at the edge of his eye. Then she took the bunch of flowers he handed to her.

'Thank you for coming,' she said out loud. 'I hope you didn't have a problem finding the place.' He tilted his head in bemusement. She smiled, and indicated towards Priya's closed door. 'Sorry,' she whispered, and led him into the living room.

She offered him fruit, which he refused. She offered him almonds, peanuts, walnuts, cashew nuts, each of which she pointed out. 'These are smoked,' she said, with pride. 'Priya got them yesterday. And the peanuts are roasted with salt and a pinch of chilli.' She felt herself rambling. *Stop it*, she scolded herself. *You're acting like an old woman.*

It felt different here, in Priya's apartment. They were hemmed in, they were reverting to type. She was Lana's grandmother, ageing and arthritic, and he was the refined, worldly politician. She smoothed down her *kameez*, suddenly conscious. She hid her hands behind her *dupatta*. She should have gone to check her hair, after all. She itched to lift her hand to her bun, but she dared not. He was looking at her. 'Oh,' she said. 'We have lemonade too.'

He was smiling his suave, polite smile, and she hated herself for her lack of composure. She rose, stumbled, righted herself, and rushed towards the kitchen. She poured out two glasses of Chotu's lemonade, placed them on a tray, and hurried back.

Priya was sitting with him. They were smiling politely at each other, but she knew they hadn't spoken.

'Sorry, *Beta*,' Asha said. 'I'll get you a glass.'

Priya stopped her. 'Sit, Ma,' she said. 'I'll go get myself a glass.'

So Asha sat opposite Firoze. They sipped their drinks, looked at each other, smiled. Suddenly, his smile widened. 'Asha,' he said. 'I haven't tasted this for years.'

'No.'

'No,' he repeated simply, but she knew he remembered. The library, its echoes, their fear of the creaking servant discovering them. 'Not for years.'

Priya came in and seated herself on the sofa next to Asha. 'Ma,' she said, looking suspiciously at her glass. 'What have you put in the lemonade?'

'*Jeera*,' said Asha. 'Ground cumin.'

'It's lovely,' said Firoze. 'We used to drink it as children.' Priya looked unconvinced, and he added. 'It was very kind of your mother to remember.'

'Ma tells me,' Priya said politely, 'that your families knew each other before Independence.'

'Yes.'

'Did you know my father too?'

Firoze shook his head. 'We were neighbours, you see,' he said, gesturing towards Asha. 'Your mother was friends with my sister. I was training with your grandfather to become a lawyer.'

Priya turned to her mother for confirmation. 'With Pappaji?' she asked.

'Yes, *Beta.*'

'But what happened after Partition? I mean, with Pappaji gone, what happened to your training?'

'He was already practising by then.'

'Your grandfather left me his practice,' said Firoze.

'Oh,' said Priya. 'Oh.' Asha saw a change come over her daughter. 'So you did well out of the Partition.'

'*Beta*, what a thing to say. '

'Lana tells me your father was Police Commissioner for all of Punjab.'

'Yes,' said Firoze.

'Really?' asked Asha. 'Khan Uncle was made Police Commissioner?'

'Yes.'

'When was this?' asked Priya sweetly. She smiled innocently at their guest, and Asha knew her daughter was up to something.

'Come,' she said to Firoze. 'You haven't had a thing to eat,' but Firoze turned towards Priya.

'You're right,' he said. 'You're absolutely right in your inference. The Police Commissioner had been a Hindu gentleman. A Mr Bhatia. He had to leave after the troubles started.' He was silent for a moment. He wove his hands together, studying his knuckles. 'I had been active in politics before everything turned violent. I had been in

272

favour of the creation of Pakistan.' He glanced at Asha, but she looked away. She thought of the pamphlets she'd found in Nargis' room. She thought of how he'd started to avoid her. 'The authorities rewarded me for my loyalty after Partition,' he said. 'I was given some prestigious cases. Abba was made Commissioner of Police.'

'So,' said Priya. Her voice was soft and courteous; a respectful child talking to an elder. 'You did well out of the Partition.'

'Priya!'

'We didn't,' she said. She pointed towards her mother, and added, 'Pappaji, your mentor, well, he wasn't so lucky. He was hacked to death by a Muslim mob. His wife was killed, as was his teenage son . . .'

Firoze shut his eyes. 'When I learnt . . .'

'Ma was attacked.' Priya raised her mother's hand, held her scar up to view. 'See what they did to her . . .'

'I was rescued by Muslims,' said Asha steadily.

'And if she hadn't been rescued,' Priya spoke over her mother. Her voice never rose, never betrayed any emotion, but her audience didn't dare interrupt her. 'If she hadn't been rescued,' she repeated, 'I don't even know if she would be alive today. I know I certainly wouldn't be here. Neither would Lana.'

'But,' repeated Asha. 'I was rescued. I was rescued by a Muslim family.'

'And then,' said Priya. 'She was a refugee in Delhi. She had nothing, no money, no property, no clothes even. If my father hadn't taken her in . . .'

She paused. The room filled with the smell of the flowers Lana had bought. The sun shone on a lily and it burst instantly into colour. Suddenly, its heady, sweet scent permeated the room. No one spoke.

Firoze, suave, poised, but now unsure, looked down at the floor, the wooden floor they had just vacuumed. He removed an imaginary speck of dust from his trousers, then he wove his hands together and studied his knuckles again.

Asha offered snacks to Firoze, but he didn't respond. 'Some tea, perhaps?' she asked.

'No, Ma,' said Priya, 'Please, let's not pretend nothing's happened.'

'It was a terrible time,' Firoze said. 'You say I've done well out of the Partition, and I'm not saying you're wrong. I didn't have to leave my home. My services were in demand. My views were in sympathy with the eventual victors in my land. I have done well in life, and the partition of our land was a factor in my success.' The sun moved, a tree cast its filigree shadow on the room. Firoze stretched his hands out, holding them to the light, and for a long while he was quiet. Several times he began to speak before changing his mind. 'I felt,' he said, 'I sincerely felt the need for a land for Muslims. I felt there was no space for us in India. I still feel that today, and I can't regret the creation of our country. I don't. That was the right thing to have done.'

Priya turned to her mother. 'See,' she began, but Firoze held his hand up.

'Please,' he said, 'Let me finish. I'm not sorry Pakistan was created. But I am sorry about the violence it led to. I regret that there were – that there still are – constituents in Pakistan who believe that the country should only be home to Muslims.'

'Come,' said Asha. 'India isn't perfect either.'

Priya began to clap slowly. 'Spoken,' she said, 'Like a true politician.'

274

'*Beta*!' said Firoze. He got up. 'I know I can never undo the pain your family suffered,' he said. 'I know that. But believe me. *Beta*, believe me when I say I regret what happened with every fibre of my being. I don't, I can't regret Pakistan's creation, but I regret all the extremism, all the violence that followed.'

'*Arre*,' smiled Asha. Priya hadn't responded to Firoze's speech, and now she tried to lighten the mood. 'All this is in the past . . .'

'You're right,' Priya said. 'We should be focusing on the children. But when I think of what Ma went through – ' She smiled at Firoze. 'I know you understand,' she said. She offered refreshments to Firoze, but he refused. 'Please,' she insisted with a new earnestness. 'We bought these strawberries from the farmer's market yesterday.' He sat down and took a couple onto his plate, praising the fruit.

'You should try it someday yourself,' Priya said. She gave him directions to the market, told him which stalls she liked best.

Firoze put another strawberry on his plate and bit into it with his clean, even teeth. 'Perhaps we can all go one Sunday,' he said, smiling at Priya. 'Take the children too.'

Priya pressed the roasted peanuts on him. 'Lana roasted them herself,' she said. 'The girl never cooks,' she confided, smiling, 'But she couldn't do enough yesterday. Please,' she insisted as he patted his stomach, 'Please, just a little.'

He picked his plate up obligingly. 'And,' said Priya, 'You must tell us how you're enjoying your time in New York.'

It was wonderful, he said. He loved spending time

with Hussain, and meeting Lana was a delight.

'Did you have some business here too?'

'Yes,' he said. He set his plate neatly down on the table, placing his fork precisely where he'd found it.

'Lana said it was something at the United Nations?'

'Yes.' He still smiled, but he was on his guard. Priya spoke as politely as ever, but a new chill entered her voice.

'Something to do with the nuclear tests, I believe.'

'Yes.'

Priya looked at her mother. 'See Ma,' she said. 'All this camaraderie, all this regret he professes, and it's all a lie.'

'Of course not, *Beta* . . .'

'Don't call me *Beta*,' she said viciously.

'Priya!'

'I mean it, Ma. He's here to lobby the UN against us. He's here to defend Pakistan's nuclear tests . . .'

Firoze rose, and Asha got up too. 'What is it you want, Priya? Mr Khan is a proud Pakistani. Do you want him not to love his country?'

'Aren't you a proud Indian?' asked her daughter.

'What a thing to say.'

'So then how can we have our child marry into this family? Do we have her subsume her pride in India?'

Asha shook her head. 'The girl is American.'

'It's impossible, I tell you,' Priya said. 'There is no being friends between our two countries, and you want the two to marry?' Angry tears sprang into her eyes. Asha moved to her daughter, but she held her hands out. 'I know you think I'm overreacting. You joke about cricket matches, you say we speak the same language. But here we are, all Punjabis, all from Suhanpur, but

276

this man,' she said, pointing at Firoze, 'this man would legitimise a weapon that could vaporise all of Delhi in a minute.' Asha lifted her hand to her daughter's shoulder. She squeezed it, urging calm, but Priya grew increasingly agitated.

'Do you still think I'm overreacting, Ma?' She threw off Asha's hand. At the door, as she went out, she turned back, 'Will I still be overreacting when the two countries are at war?'

'*Beta*, please listen,' pleaded Asha, but it was no use. Priya was in the hallway. She was opening the front door, and as Asha and Firoze looked at each other, shocked, she left, banging the door hard behind her.

'She's always been passionate,' said Asha, but Firoze shook his head.

'No,' he said. 'She has a point. People were upset by marriages like this even when we were one country.' She saw him looking at her, saw him wait for a reaction, but she refused to so much as blink. She refused to breathe, she refused to turn in his direction, she refused to incline her head. 'You know,' he went on, 'Hussain keeps asking me how I know you. I think Nargis might have said something to him about you, or maybe he saw me looking at you.'

'Lana has her suspicions too . . .'

They were at the opposite ends of the room. She didn't look at him, didn't move towards him. 'Can't we be happy now?' he had asked. How simple it had all seemed, in the open, under the sun.

She knew he was watching her, but she refused to meet his eye. Instead, she looked down at the fruit bowl in front of her. She counted out the strawberries in the bowl. She imagined them turning darker, growing

277

mottled. She inhaled the scent of the lilies Lana had arranged. Then she remembered the flowers Firoze had brought. 'Something small,' he had said as he had thrust them into her hands. How they had smiled at each other. Her heart had thrilled with delight. In their youth he had promised her flowers, he had promised her estates in the hills. He had promised to still the thunder of the Ravi. He had promised to ban all *dupattas*. All those early hopes, and now they were denied the ability to spend their final years together.

'Asha,' Firoze said. 'Won't you look at me?'

'No,' she said softly.

He didn't reply. She knew he waited for her to betray her interest, to smile in spite of the severity of the situation. She knew he waited for her to give him hope. Another lily burst into bloom. 'Lana loves lilies,' she said finally. 'She says they're the most generous flowers.'

Firoze smiled sadly. 'She's a good child.'

She longed to reach out. She just had to touch him, to stroke him, and all would be well again. Instead she turned to the lilies. 'Priya is making it hard for the children.'

He nodded.

A breeze blew into the room, a curtain moved to slap a table near her, and Asha started. The shadows were beginning to lengthen, and she expected someone – Priya, Lana, Sunil – to arrive imminently. 'She'll never understand about us, will she?' she asked.

Firoze didn't speak.

'I mean, she doesn't even want the children to marry.'

'I've always thought,' he said, 'that parents can be rigid. They can have unreasonable expectations of their children, have unrealistic notions of what will make them happy. I wonder now how right I was. I wonder now if it isn't the children who are the rigid ones. They are so desperate to see their past preserved. Pakistan was once unkind to you; it must remain an enemy forever.'

Asha nodded.

'She won't like us being together.' He spoke the words without question, as if he expected no reply, and yet he looked at her, watching for her reaction. Waiting for her to give him hope.

Asha gazed at the lilies. She thought of her daughter's Muslim mother. 'It's too much for her to take in,' she said. 'The children together, us together.'

'So,' he said, 'we just forget about ourselves.' Asha looked at him at last, meeting his smile with her own. There were to be no tears, not now, not in front of him, or all would be lost.

'It's about the children now. Let them be happy,' she said, but her voice wavered. 'Our chance has passed, Firoze. We've lived our lives.'

They walked to the hallway. 'It was so nice of you to come.' She lifted the bouquet of flowers Firoze had brought, inhaling deeply. 'These really are lovely,' she said. 'Thank you so much for bringing them to us.'

'I liked the colours,' he replied formally. 'They felt like spring.' He put on his raincoat, then embraced her. She allowed herself to lean into him. She smelt him for the last time, his soap, his musk, she raised her hand to feel the wave behind his ear. 'Thank you,' she said. 'It was so nice to see you again.'

'Are you sure about this, Asha?'

'Yes,' she replied, though she refused to let go of him.

'I gave you up once,' he whispered into her ear. 'I've spent my life regretting it.'

'Firoze,' she said unhappily, 'We have to think of the children.'

She felt him nod slowly against her. His breath lingered on her skin. 'Good bye,' he said. 'Good bye, Asha.'

'Good bye,' she answered.

He smiled a sad, crooked mouthed smile before turning to leave. Asha shut the door, but found she couldn't hold firm. She rushed out towards the lift, but it was too late. He was gone.

8

Firoze left for Pakistan the next day. For days Asha didn't know, and though they had agreed to part, she kept expecting to see him. Around the block, in the street, at their favourite bench in the playground. Humming an ancient song, waiting for her eyes to meet his. Refusing to give up. She would walk out of the apartment block, walk slowly to the playground, but there was never any Firoze. There was never his smile, his smell of soap, never any appeal to memory. At the playground too she would remain undisturbed. Her sandwiches would remain uneaten, her tea untouched. It was always quiet in the mornings, and she sat alone, watching the light shift, waiting for the time she could return home and think about preparing dinner.

She considered going to Hussain's apartment. She knew it was near the park they had all met at, and she was certain she remembered how to get there. She could take the subway if she felt brave enough, or else she could just hail a taxi. She could just sneak into Lana's room one morning while she was out and look for her diary. Hussain's details would be in there: his phone number, his address, all printed out in her granddaughter's neat capitals. But it was beyond her, this unsanctioned search. She told herself she would hail a taxi instead and visit the park where they had met. She reminded herself she had admired the library, and all at once, she had a sudden urge to visit it again.

At reception, she returned the concierge's greeting, agreeing politely that it was, in fact, a lovely day. Out she walked, feeling full of possibility. It was simple. She just had to lift her hand, and one of the thousands of New York taxis would pull up next to her. She'd announce her destination, wait carefully for the driver to switch the meter on, and then she would seat herself. They were all Punjabis anyway: turbaned Sikhs or homesick Pakistani boys; and she would pass a pleasant twenty minutes as they travelled down to Bryant Park. She would count out her change, add a dollar or two as tip, then walk into the sunshine. She would find the table they had all sat at, and there, as if by sheer coincidence, she would find Firoze. Then it would be her turn to look sheepish, her turn to exclaim her surprise.

She stood at the sidewalk a good while, fifteen minutes or longer, and though she was certain she had raised her hand, no taxi stopped. The door of the apartment block opened and the concierge stepped out. 'Is everything alright, Mrs Sharma?' he asked, and she nodded.

'Just forgot my purse,' she smiled, and hurried straight back into the building.

Then one day, Lana said, 'You know Hussain's Nanu has returned to Pakistan, don't you?'

Asha smiled, miming polite interest. 'Oh?'

'Yes,' said Lana. 'He left the day after he came here for tea.'

Asha nodded. They still hadn't talked about things, not really. Lana hadn't asked her how the visit had gone, but she heard them fight, mother and daughter. She heard the emotional blackmail, she heard the call to filial regard. She heard the doors slam shut. But it was no use, not while they refused to listen to each other.

Of course Priya considered herself vindicated. Hussain was a Pakistani, his Nanu an enemy agent. This wasn't a fit match for her daughter. They sat together in the morning, Asha, Priya and Sunil, drinking their tea, reading their newspapers, and Priya always clucked when she saw news items on the nuclear tests. 'See,' she would cry as she waved headlines around. '*Indo-Pak tensions rise.* And you would have Lana go through that hell?' Another article would attract her attention, a report of cross-border talks cancelled, or of veiled insults being exchanged between the neighbours, and her smile would widen. 'Look here,' she would call out. 'They can't stay civil, these elderly men, the leaders of India and Pakistan. How can you expect children from our two countries to maintain perfect amity in a marriage?'

'They don't love each other, those elderly men,' Sunil would point out, but Priya would talk over him.

'No, no,' she would insist. 'There's no trying to live with those heathens. Haven't they fought wars with us thrice already? Haven't they rewritten the history of Punjab and Kashmir with our own blood? No, no, there's no being friends with those savages.'

Sunil would lift his newspaper again, Asha would pour out fresh cups of tea, and there the matter would rest. With Priya's voice ringing victorious in their ears.

Lana moved out at the end of the month. There had been more fights, more raised voices, and at the end of it all, the girl burst into Asha's room.

'You understand, don't you?' she asked Asha. Her eyes were large and molten. Just like Sanam's had been that long, lonely night a lifetime ago. Tiger's eyes, a spirit set ablaze. That had been another room invaded, another life claimed.

'Of course I understand, *Beta*.'

'*She* never will.'

'But *Beta*,' Asha begged. 'Try and see it from your mother's perspective. She's worried about you.'

'She won't even meet Hussain.'

'She'll come around . . . .'

'No,' said Lana firmly. 'Not her.'

'Come on,' Asha cajoled. She put a hand on her back, but Lana's body remained rigid. 'It's a lot for Priya to take in,' Asha continued. 'Hussain's religion, his nationality.'

'You took it all in. Papa did too.'

'Be fair,' said Asha. 'Sunil isn't from Punjab. His family wasn't destroyed by the Partition. Priya has been brought up on the stories of all we've lost. Asha paused. She thought of all the teas she had interrupted, all the cosy confidences Ma shared with Priya. *Those Muslims*, Ma kept on repeating to Priya. *Those butchers*, and somehow it had all become synonymous to the girl: *Muslim, butcher, rapist. Pakistani.*

And though Sanam was there, in the background, Muslim and unacknowledged mother, and though she had suffered Hindu brutality, somehow her story was easy for Priya and her grandmother to ignore. Sanam suffered under a Muslim husband too, didn't she? *Those Muslims*, Asha heard the two say. *Muslim, butcher, rapist. Pakistani.*

'Ma,' she said now to Lana, 'She never stopped telling

284

your mother about how much we Hindus lost in the Partition.'

'But Nani,' said Lana. There it was again, that fire in those eyes. 'You suffered the most. You lost the most.'

'I know,' she said. Her hand went automatically to the scar. She rubbed at it, tracing the long, thin jagged line. There it was, her Partition, her wound. 'I know, my darling,' she said. 'But don't forget, I have good memories too. I remember Suhanpur. I remember my childhood and I remember Nargis.' There was a pause here, 'Your Hussain's Nani. You see,' she added, 'I had a whole happy life in Pakistan. What happened in 1947, that was a frenzy, a hysteria. That was a shattering of the earth.' Her hand touched the line of her scar again. 'I know that there is no going back, no reuniting us. And even pre-Partition, we had our differences, we Hindus and Muslims. But still, what we had before was a sort of oneness, and that's what I remember.'

'But Nani,' Lana said, and something about the girl's stillness had given Asha pause. This wasn't a child to be coddled into complicity. 'Where does that leave me and Hussain?'

'*Beta*,' said Asha. 'Just wait a little.'

'No. She won't change her mind.' There was no further entreaty. 'I have to live my life,' Lana told Asha. 'I've found an apartment near the University. I'm moving out.'

And that was it.

There was no discussing matters. Priya refused to meet Hussain, refused to ask Lana to move back in.

Asha asked Sunil to intervene, and when he asked his wife what she had achieved, Priya replied phlegmatically, 'I won't have her be unhappy in life.'

285

'Of course not,' he had assented. 'She's moved out of her home, she's not talking to you, and is on strained terms with me and her grandmother. If that doesn't make her happy, what will?'

'Come on, Sunil.'

'And is it making you happy, causing her all this stress?'

Priya set her face. 'I just want what's best for my daughter.'

Sunil shrugged his shoulders. 'So do I,' he said simply. 'Just let her be happy.'

9

Lana waited impatiently for the henna on her hands to dry. 'This hunger,' she complained to Asha. 'It's the worst, it really is . . .'

'Patience,' advised a smiling Asha. 'This is only your first *Karva Chauth*. Think how much harder it will be in your sixties.'

Lana had called up the night before. '*Karva Chauth*,' she had said. 'What do I need to do to prepare for the fast?' and Asha had stepped out of the building the next morning, had finally raised her hand and brought a canary yellow taxi to a screeching halt.

She went to Lana's apartment downtown. It was a tiny flat near her university, with the cramped living room doubling up as bedroom, and Lana smilingly described it as a studio. She threw a cheery cover over a worn sofa, drew a beaded curtain to show Asha into the tiny galley kitchen. 'It's all I could get at such short notice,' she said. 'I'll move somewhere nicer once my job at the newspaper starts.'

'Of course, darling,' Asha said. 'And this flat,' she added, looking uncertainly around at the futon bed before them, 'this studio has everything you need within reach.'

She applied *henna* on the girl's impatient palms, and as

287

the mix dried, Asha began preparations for the evening. She found a red *salwar kameez* in Lana's wardrobe, then she stepped into the kitchen and began to cook the delicacies for the night's dinner. Lana followed her around, restless and hungry.

'*Bus*,' said Asha eventually. 'All this drama. I'm fasting too, and do you see me complain?'

'You, Nani?' asked Lana in surprise. 'Why are you still keeping the fast? Nanu is no longer . . .'

'*Arre, Beta*,' said Asha. 'I've kept the fast for as long as I can remember. It's a habit now.'

It was no more than the truth, but still, any time she closed her eyes, it was her first *Karva Chauth* that returned to her. She remembered the heat of Suhanpur, the clumsy words she had learnt from Firoze: *It's like a purdah curtain over a desired object*. She remembered the teasing, she and Nargis kneeling outside Pappaji's office. She remembered Om's proposal, and her friend's delight as she learnt that it was her brother, and not that ordinary trader whom Asha loved. She remembered Firoze waiting on the balcony for her to break her fast. It was those memories of the past that carried her through the longing of the *Karva Chauth* day.

And for all the peace she had felt with Om, that and love too, and for all they had shared, this is what she inevitably returned to each *Karva Chauth*. That same thrill, that same hidden emotion.

Hussain came to see them in the evening.

'*Arre*,' he complained as they waited for the moon to rise. They took turns looking out of the single dormer window in Lana's studio, and he said, 'You Hindu women. Fasting all day without water. And what if the

288

moon is hidden behind a cloud? What do you do then? Carry on fasting?'

'You pretend to mind,' said Asha. 'But did you know, your Nani kept this fast with me?'

'She never said . . .'

'And I fasted too,' she pointed out. 'All through Ramzan. And without complaint, if you please . . .'

The moon finally rose, and as Lana and Asha ate their first morsels of food, Hussain said, 'And now it's my turn to eat.'

'How selfish!' said Lana. 'You've been eating all day while we've been dying of hunger.'

'But so, my darling,' he answered, 'have I.'

It emerged that Hussain had kept the *Karva Chauth* fast too. He pretended to swoon, to be overcome with thirst and with love, and when Lana did feed him that first, sacred bite, he pretended to become delirious. '*Hai*!' he cried now, '*Hai*, you Hindu women!'

She studied the two children in the cramped space – her tiger-eyed Lana, and the boy, that brown-haired incarnation of her Firoze – so happy, so complete in their love. It really was possible, their future. Lana was not one to wait for permission, and Hussain, well, he wasn't one to let her slip away.

Asha returned to Priya's apartment late in the evening. Her daughter was up and sitting in the living room. She pretended to be unconcerned, but her worry was evident in every feature, in the high pitch of her voice. 'Sunil was right,' she said. 'You really have been painting the town red.'

'It was *Karva Chauth*,' replied Asha evenly, 'And *Beta*, Lana was keen to fast.'

'Ma,' said Priya wearily. 'I wish you wouldn't encourage the girl.'

'*Nahi, Beta,*' replied her mother. Priya frowned, and she quickly added, 'Hussain is perfect for Lana.'

'Ma, not that again.'

'Just meet the boy.'

Priya stared at Asha. She lifted her hand to her temples, massaging them. 'What's wrong with you people?' she asked. 'Don't you see that the boy is Muslim?'

'So what?'

'Ma, this isn't a political correctness contest. This is life. It matters that he's Muslim.'

'It doesn't, *Beta.* Not really.' Asha leant forward in her chair. 'He's a good boy. He understands our child. What else matters?'

'What about when he wants her to convert? What about when he wants his children raised as Muslims?'

'Have you asked Lana what her views are?' asked Asha. 'Do you even know if Hussain wants her to convert?'

'Of course he will.'

'But you haven't even met him, *Beta.* He's a good boy. He'll let her work, he'll let her see her family. He'll let her be herself.'

'Come on, Ma,' Priya huffed.

'He kept the *Karva Chauth* fast today. Would he have done that if he didn't care for her?'

'One little fast,' said Priya disparagingly. 'It's just a gimmick.' Her voice rose, a sure sign of her agitation. 'And what about the fact that he's Pakistani?'

'So are we,' said Asha evenly. 'Our family is from Suhanpur.'

'Don't be facile,' said Priya. 'We're not Muslim, Ma. And we'll never be. We're not the same as them.'

'I'm not sure,' said Asha, and as Priya stared, as she rolled her eyes at her mother, Asha added, 'I was brought up in Pakistan. So was your father.'

'Pah!'

'You have Muslim blood in your veins,' said Asha softly.

'Yes, Ma,' scoffed Priya, rolling her eyes. 'I have Suhanpur in my blood.'

Asha considered her next words. She could laugh, and the danger would pass. For years she had shied away from telling Priya the truth. She was theirs – hers and Om's – and there had never been any need to tell Priya otherwise. She could just smile now, just change the topic, and things would go back to normal. 'You're not ours,' she said softly, so softly that even she couldn't hear the words.

'Ma?' asked Priya, but Asha shook her head. She couldn't rewrite this history. Priya couldn't be made a stranger; Sanam couldn't be given a new family. She didn't have the courage. She'd survived the Partition. She'd survived without her loved ones, but this sacrifice, this confession of her daughter's illegitimacy, this was beyond her. She saw Priya looking expectantly at her, and she said in a rush, '*Beta*, I was going to marry a Muslim boy.'

'Rubbish!'

'I'm serious,' said Asha. 'I was in love with a Muslim.'

She knew Priya was thinking of her grandmother's words. *Those Muslims. Muslim, butcher, rapist. Pakistani.* 'What about Papa?'

'I met your father after the Partition. But before all that violence started, I was in love with a Muslim boy from Suhanpur. We were to be married. He'd even spoken to Pappaji . . .'

Asha looked up. Priya's eyes were on her. 'When our house was destroyed in the violence, it was he who drove us to safety.' Asha held her hand out. 'I've had a wonderful life, *Beta*. I've been so happy with your father. But the Partition changed my life.'

Priya looked at the coat and scarf Asha had left lying on the sofa, then began silently to fold them. How like her father she was, meticulous, fastidious. 'There's no day,' Asha said, conscious of her disloyalty to Om. 'Not one day when I don't think of him.'

Priya clenched her jaw and left the room.

Asha waited for her daughter to return, and when she didn't, she went to her room. She knocked on the door, and when she didn't receive a response, she pushed the door open. Priya was sitting on her bed, her eyes moist. '*Beta*,' said Asha, 'don't let Lana live with such regrets.'

'You were happy, Ma,' Priya said. 'Papa . . .'

'I came to respect your father,' she said. 'And yes, I came to love him. But what if Lana isn't so lucky?'

'Ma . . .'

'What if she doesn't fall in love again?'

Priya still didn't speak, and Asha saw her forehead – Om's broad, generous forehead – crease with worry. She saw her rearrange the realities of her happy childhood – loving parents, secure home. 'We *were* happy,' said Asha, 'And we loved you.'

'Yes,' said Priya.

'And I did grow to love your father. Did you ever think us unhappy?' Priya was silent, and Asha continued, 'You saw me after your father passed away.' After all the months that had passed, her voice still seized up, she still paused for composure. 'You saw how much I cared for him.' Priya finally looked at her mother with something

292

akin to recognition. 'But *Beta*,' Asha added. The Partition took place half a century ago. It brought great pain; it changed the course of my life. Don't let it change our Lana's life too.'

Her daughter still frowned, wrinkling her nose, as her father so often had. Asha saw her race through her arguments against Muslims and Pakistanis, against Lana marrying against her wishes. 'Please,' she said. 'Hussain loves your daughter. Let her be happy.'

Priya's face crumpled like a spent flower. 'Please,' Asha said to her daughter. 'Please let's forget about all that horror.'

Priya didn't speak, didn't argue or rebut any of her mother's arguments. They heard a door open down the hall, heard a neighbour enter a flat and shut a door. They saw the sky dim with the night, then the city's lights blaze out again. Like a million tigers' eyes, like her brave, determined darling girl enduring against her mother's opposition.

Later, after fresh arguments were reprised and abandoned, after Hussain was finally invited home, hugged and pronounced acceptable, after the long, stuttering call had been placed to his family in Islamabad and after dates had been set, Priya came into her mother's room.

'I never asked you,' she said. She didn't sit down, didn't smile, didn't make herself comfortable. 'Ma, what happened to that boy?'

Asha attempted ignorance. 'Which boy?'

'You know, the one you liked in Suhanpur.'

'Him?' she hedged. They were talking now, Priya and Lana, and she couldn't be sure how much they had shared. She considered telling the truth. Perhaps she and

Firoze could be together after all. Priya had accepted Hussain, and she had a big heart. Over time she would get used to the idea.

She looked across at her daughter. Priya stood still. She didn't move, didn't breathe. She smiled encouragingly at her mother, but Asha saw the effort the friendly gesture took. It wasn't possible. There was no being together for her and Firoze. 'Him,' she said slowly, 'he died in the Partition.'

'Oh.'

'Yes, in the violence following Independence.'

Priya put an awkward arm around Asha. How angular her daughter felt all of a sudden. How distant. 'But Ma,' she said, 'How did you find out what happened to him?'

Asha hedged, and in a moment of panic, she used the words she had looked to shield Priya from. 'Firoze,' and as her daughter stared, 'Hussain's Nanu, Firoze.' Her daughter's gaze stayed fixed on her, and she found she was speaking too fast, stumbling over her words. 'He knew him. He knew the boy, you know, the boy I liked, and he told me what had happened to him.'

Priya looked at her for a long instant, and then said simply, 'I'm sorry.' She took her mother into her embrace again. 'You've been so sad and I've known nothing about it.'

'It doesn't matter.' Asha felt her daughter warm against her, and smelt the lavender the girl still wore. 'It was all a long time ago, and I have been so very happy since.'

10

The bride was beautiful, the groom dashing.

They laughed at the smutty jokes the older members of the party insisted on recounting.

They danced to old Punjabi wedding songs. An elderly female relative of Hussain's managed to procure a *dholak* drum from somewhere. 'There's a shop,' she lisped. 'In Jackie-son Heights.'

They sat cross-legged on the ground, despite advancing years, despite arthritic knees. They were all full of the occasion, of the mania that envelops the normally inhibited on family celebrations. 'Father,' they sang, 'We must fly,' and as Priya tutted, as she told the singers to switch to a cheerier number, they laughed louder. They sang louder.

The elderly woman with the *dholak* turned to Asha. 'They tell me you're from India.'

'Yes,' nodded Asha. 'But I'm originally from Suhanpur. The place you now call Mianbad.'

'Yes, yes,' said the woman impatiently. 'But I want you to tell me all about India. I want you to tell me what changed in Delhi after I left.'

Asha looked at the relative. Her hair was stained with henna, her lobes sagged under the weight of her earrings. Her *dupatta* slipped, revealing the sapped bosom of another spent sub-continental mother, and Asha smiled. 'It's changed. There are new shops, new roads, new names.' She saw the woman's face fall, and she leaned forward, taking her hands in her own. 'But in spirit, it remains the same. It's still a village at heart; noisy and intrusive. There are still the narrow lanes that cross the magnificent boulevards, still the shanties beyond the grand circuses. It's still impossible to keep things secret.'

The woman closed her eyes, considered Asha's words, and a slow smile spread on her face. 'In that case,' she said, 'all *is* well.'

She lifted her knee, resting it against her drum. Her hands beat against the leather of the instrument. 'Come now,' she called out to the gathering, and all - Hindu, Sikh and Muslim, Indian and Pakistani – turned to her. She began to hum out that most eternal of their songs, '*Mera laung gawacha*,' and a score of rusty, new, and practised voices answered her, 'You follow me, you follow me.'

At the engagement ceremony, Lana was gifted jewellery by the groom's family.

Among the gifts was a set Asha recognised as that most subtle of Nargis' treasures, a gold necklace heavy with uncut diamonds. She looked at her granddaughter: high-featured, jewel-eyed, and now weighed down with a necklace that had once graced the neck of a Hindu princess. 'Kindness, friendship,' she thought. 'A bit of luck.' But there would be more, for her Lana. She would have a lifetime of love too.

Asha reached forward. She wiped some *kohl* powder from under her eyes and applied it behind Lana's ears. 'To protect you from the evil eye,' she said to the girl.

'My precious, beautiful, brave child, may you always be happy.'

Asha was introduced to Seher, Hussain's mother and Nargis' daughter.

'Are you really the same Asha?' she asked with a warmth that was all her mother's, 'Are you really the Asha my mother spoke of?'

Asha brought Seher into her embrace. The girl resembled her Nargis. She had the same curl to her lips, she had the same brown hair and the proud forehead, but there were also features she didn't recognise. There was a dimple to her chin, there was a bow to her lips that was new to Asha. This was Nargis' husband then, her brother-in-law, that unseen, moustachioed arbiter of Nargis' fortunes. 'Yes, *Beta*,' she said. She held Seher's face in her hands, and though Asha knew she was staring, she didn't flinch from her survey. 'And,' she said at length, 'I expect you to call me Maasi.'

'*Maasi*,' Seher assented readily. *Like a mother.*

They played their parts as was expected of them, Asha and Firoze. Firoze was the elder representative of his family, the only surviving member from Nargis' generation. And Asha was Lana's only remaining grandparent. They nodded at each other solemnly, folded hands, mouthed respectful *Namastes*. They exchanged presents, laughed politely when the wedding songs started up. *You follow me*, they both heard without visible emotion. They averted their gazes, they avoided being in close proximity.

They smiled as the children were married according to both customs, Hindu and Muslim. As Lana excitedly blurted out her '*Qubool Hai*' the very first time the Imam asked her if she accepted the match. It was only when both slowly circled the wedding flames in accordance with Hindu rites that they slipped. Perhaps it had something to do with the heat of the fire. It was late in the evening, past bed time for both, and the wedding party had thinned down to those in the family. Perhaps it was the intimacy of the moment, but Asha looked up, glanced across the fire, and caught Firoze's eye. She saw him look at her with such unblinking attention that for a moment she forgot where she was. She forgot she was at Lana's wedding, that it was another's marriage that was being consecrated.

The priest recited the sacred *mantras*, and the couple were instructed to lower an offering down to the flames. '*Swaha*,' she heard them invoke as more *ghee* was poured onto the fire. The flames shot up, and once more he was searching for her across the fire, once more he was watching her closely as another couple was married.

When it was all over – the preparation, the ceremonies, the farewells – after they had nodded to each other and said their final, softly articulated goodbyes; they returned to their lives. Firoze flew to Pakistan, to Islamabad and his ministership; Asha returned to Delhi, to her creaking home and her ghosts, to her school, and to the other Partition survivors she shared her life with.

IV

Long after they had all left her – Ma, Om, Sanam – Asha rattled around in the Delhi house she had come to as a refugee and bride. It was too big for her, and she was certainly not equal to its upkeep. Rooms, entire wings, were kept shuttered against the daily incursion of Delhi's dust, and if Asha knew what liberal use the new servants made of the house and its stores, she didn't let on.

Priya visited twice a year, and each time she tried to bully her mother into returning to New York with her. Asha always refused. She had a life's worth of memories in the house. It was here that she had learnt to love her husband. It was here that Priya had learnt to walk, it was here that she had become engaged. It was here that Lana had been born.

Priya said it wasn't healthy, living amongst the shadows. 'You can't talk to your memories,' she scolded, but Asha disagreed. They told a story too, the property's crevices, they betrayed the secrets of a past happiness. She led her daughter by the hand to the hallway. They walked slowly in deference to Asha's arthritis. Here, she pointed, and as Priya stared, seeing only an indistinct smudge, Asha led her closer. This was the imprint on the wall from the inlaid screen that never seemed to fade, even though the screen itself had been shipped off to Priya's

New York apartment a decade or more ago. There was the sofa – reupholstered many times – where she had sat gingerly on a kitchen towel and listened to Ma's litany of complaints against her. This was the colour of her life, these stains, these imperfections; this would be her legacy to the future inhabitants of the house.

'We'll pack up your memories, Ma,' offered Priya. 'We'll take photos,' and again Asha shook her head. She would live out her last years in Delhi. There was a sweetness in the air here; despite the smog, despite the noise and traffic, despite the crime. Tea tasted more fragrant, the milk fuller. There was a pleasure in peeling oranges in the garden under a mild winter sun; would she be able to match that joy in New York?

Of course, Priya said, and more. There were clementines and satsumas and mandarins and blood oranges so sharp you could almost taste the Italian sun. There was Central Park, there was the roof terrace. But Asha smiled and shook her head. There wasn't another such joy. Not for her.

Lana visited too, but as her life grew more crowded with work and with Hussain, she came over less. She had last come with her mother for Sanam's funeral. The girls had insisted on holding a memorial at the school. Afterwards, they had wanted to bury her with a memento, but had been uncertain what to choose.

They had gone through her room, still cool, still spare, and found the ragged blue blanket the doctor had wrapped the newborn Priya in. It was still there, at the top of her small trunk, despite the years, and Asha had picked it up with surprise. She hadn't known Sanam thought of Priya. She had asked only one question when Lana had decided to marry Hussain. *Does she know she has Muslim blood?*

At all other times she had been polite reserve, hands folded in distant greeting. She had never seemed to regret giving Priya away, and still, at the point of her death, this old, threadbare blanket was first among her treasures. This was perfect, Asha said, and though the other two wrinkled their noses at a woollen item being chosen in the middle of summer, Asha had stood firm, and Sanam had been interred with the only reminder she had permitted herself of the baby she had given up.

Then Lana became a mother – to two smiling, dimpled daughters Asha only knew from photographs – and her visits grew more infrequent still. When she called one winter morning to announce her next visit, both were surprised to note it had been four years since they'd last met. She blew in on a cold, wet January morning, laughing as Asha complained about the weather.

'It's snowing right now in New York,' she said. 'I was scared the plane wouldn't take off.'

'Where is Hussain?' asked Asha. 'And the girls?'

'The girls are with Mama,' said Lana. 'And Hussain is in Pakistan.'

Asha waited, and though she knew what must follow, she feigned curiosity. 'It's Firoze Nanu, Nani,' Lana was explaining. 'You remember him, don't you?'

She felt her knee throb, and she lowered herself slowly into a wicker chair. When it flared, her knee, when it locked, there was no trying to move. There were days now when she remained in bed. Lazy old woman, she saw the servants think. Lying in bed all day. 'Yes,' she replied, as Lana tried to make her comfortable, plumping up a cushion behind her, arranging a shawl over her knees, clucking that she wasn't taking care of herself. 'Yes, I remember him.'

The French doors were opened out to let the sun in. The wicker chairs were too old really; they were greying, the wood fading, and now it seemed the neat little wicker plaits were splintering. She ran her finger along the arm of the chair, biting her lip at the stab from the wood. If Om had been here, he would have had them replaced. And she would have to replace them too, in time for Lana's babies to come, or there would be accidents. There would be tears.

'He left something for you,' Lana was saying. Asha found she had missed all the details: how he had gone, where he'd been, who had cared for him. Lana was looking at her strangely, worriedly, with a grown daughter's care. 'Really?' Asha asked. She knew her response was insufficient, so she repeated it.

Lana left the room. She was gone for a while, and Asha leant back in her seat. She observed the shadows lengthen across her lap, she saw a crow swoop down to sip from the birdbath they had built at Priya's request. All the time they had spent building the birdbath, all the birds they had imagined it sustaining – magpies, sparrows, nightingales, peacocks even – and it was only ever the common crow who graced them with its presence. This had been her life, Om and Priya, and strangely enough, Sanam too. And she had been happy. These were her memories as her life faded, not Suhanpur, not the rush of the Ravi, not the golden, most brilliant gleam of brown, nor a young man's chest heaving hard against her. That had been glorious, that brief, brief moment in her life, like the winter sun's last, late salvo, but it hadn't been real. This was real – the dark on the wall, the splinters in her chair. This was real.

Lana was back. She held a large, cloth-wrapped bundle

in her hand. 'From Firoze Nanu,' she said, and though she didn't ask any questions, she remained holding the package in her hand. She set it unwillingly down on her grandmother's lap, but hovered around her, as if asking for an explanation. Asha nodded. 'We'd spoken of our Subanpur days,' she said. 'It was kind of him to think of sending me something.'

Lana smiled, still only half convinced. Asha shut her eyes, began to hum an old song. Cool as it was on her lap, a burst of sunshine fell across Asha's face. She leant further back in her chair, felt it resist her. Her voice grew thick, a little raspy, and she felt her eyes grow heavy. 'I'll go unpack,' she heard Lana say. The girl rearranged her shawl, and through her half-shut eyes, Asha saw her pause before Firoze's cloth package. 'You just rest,' Lana added, but she didn't respond. Lana remained standing for a minute, studying her grandmother, studying the package, and then she went out.

Asha didn't dare open her eyes for a long while. She was afraid Lana would return too soon. Mostly, she was afraid of what she would discover. This was more delicious, this not knowing, this secret gift from Firoze that lived and breathed as long as it remained unseen. She told herself it didn't matter, that Firoze's gift was unimportant. She told herself she had been happy, that she was content. She lifted her hands to her face, felt the sun's heat on her skin, then turned towards the package.

It was a light package, and as she turned it around, she heard a little sound. It was the softest chime, like a tiny bell, like the call to evening prayer. The fabric was thick cotton, white and tightly knotted. She spent an age undoing it, fretting she would be interrupted, then as she continued alone, she turned it over. Inside it was another fabric, a pretty double-toned satin, and lovely though the cloth was, she lost patience with it. She turned it over, once then repeatedly, trying to find its ends, trying to find a reason for the gift. She grew clumsy with it, shook the cloth roughly, and something fell onto the ground, a thin coil of gold. Her movements grew more frantic, and soon, another small, thin, precious disk joined the first on the floor. She bent down to retrieve them, and though her knees resisted her attempts at movement, she persisted. She found a piece of paper, slid it under the bands, and as the sun shone on them and a memory stirred in her, she pulled them swiftly to where she sat.

They were in her hands now, after more than sixty years. Her *bali* earrings, her present from Nargis on the day before the Partition. The last, precious reminder of her childhood. She'd forgotten about them, thought them lost on the *tonga* journey from Suhanpur to the bus shelter. They were just as she remembered, delicate, fragile loops of gold, with a tiny, jangly bell at the end. A flimsy, pretty, fanciful piece of jewellery. A girl's dream. She held one earring up to the light, brought it to rest against a sagging lobe. She remembered how they had caught the light, the bells, remembered how their reflection had danced on her skin as she tried them on, on the trim of her *dupatta* as she prepared for travel, and on her knees as she sat on the *tonga*.

She picked up the satin cloth. She tried to remember it, but it was new to her. It was pretty, pink and red, a girl's fancy again, and try as she might, she couldn't remember ever having seen it before. Then she thought of the Ravi, of Firoze lowering himself down to her a lifetime ago. She thought of him threatening to ban all *dupattas*. She told herself that it was all another life, that day off from school, that passion, that promised eternity, and then she smiled. She put her hand around her earrings, wrapped the *dupatta* around her hand, and as the sun slowly made way for the shadows, she closed her eyes and leant further into the fraying wicker chair.